Beyond the Bay

REBECCA BURNS

ODYSSEY
B O O K S

Copyright © Rebecca Burns 2018

Publishing in 2018 by Odyssey Books
www.odysseybooks.com.au

NATIONAL
LIBRARY
OF AUSTRALIA

A catalogue record for this
book is available from the
National Library of Australia

ISBN: 978-1-925652-48-2 (pbk)
ISBN: 978-1-925652-51-2 (ebook)

Cover design by Belinda Crawford

Also by Rebecca Burns

Catching the Barramundi

The Settling Earth

The Bishop's Girl

Artefacts and Other Stories

For Charlotte, Kate and Ruth

Part One

Isobel

The night before Esther's ship was due to dock, her sister dreamed of her. Isobel lay on the thin mattress, irons of the bed frame piercing her sleep and, on the inside of her eyelids, she saw Esther, younger by seven years, in the plaid dress their mother sewed and saved the fabric for, running carelessly through meadows toward the brook. Scabby-kneed and ripe like an apple, the girl shrugged off Isobel's hand—Isobel already matronly at fourteen—and thundered through grass and flowers, trampling down cowslips and daisies. Esther's strong brown legs shouted fire and heat and, in her dream, Isobel knew her sister had been arguing with their mother again. Then Esther was in the brook, squealing as water squelched through her toes, not caring that the stream was cold enough to leave ice on her skin. She even lay down in it; Isobel saw her, seeming to look down from above on the girl with red hair who spread her arms wide in the shallow water. Esther tugged at her dress and Isobel saw that the plaid was heavy and soaked and threatened to weigh her down. And then Isobel woke, just as Esther pulled at her shoulders, baring skin, making ready to shake the garment off.

It was dark outside as Isobel woke, her mind struggling to right itself from sleep. The eiderdown had been kicked away, over her husband's side. The air in the room moved and was cool, and her exposed skin felt numb. Her nightdress had risen—she had rolled in her dream. She pushed it down quickly, though Brendan snored and showed no sign of rousing. The memory of her sister, Esther, lingered in the dampness of the bedroom. There was a musty smell,

a scent of dirt. Isobel heard the grind of the Kauri Timber Mill down
on the foreshore and a distant, rhythmic thrust of a saw on wood,
from somewhere on Customs Street. Auckland woke up to itself, this
year of 1893; her sister's ship was due to make land today and Isobel
had to move.

∽

Brendan grumbled over tea and left early. The leaves were old and
stale and he was angry there would be no fresh tea until the end of
the week, when his pay seeped in. Sleep stuck to his face and hair as
he drank, tufts of thick brown that refused to lie flat despite smooth-
ing with water and oil. Timidly, Isobel offered to cut it again—she
used to cut her father's regularly enough, before it thinned and disappeared—but Brendan tutted her away. He held his body taut and
firm at the tiny table, seeming to crouch beside it like a bear. His
voice was guttural with fatigue and the curds of anger. He left with
the morning paper, knowing she wanted to read it.

Isobel cleared away the breakfast dishes and washed them at the
tap outside, muttering to Mrs Hilda Riley, as she usually did most
mornings. The women talked in the soft rain, Mrs Riley wiping
smears of bacon fat from the plates into her palm—precious morsels
for cooking and not to be wasted. Mrs Riley had read the morning paper; there was talk of a regatta in the harbour. She wouldn't
go, Mrs Riley—such extravagance was irritating, especially when
most of Auckland had no access to adequate drainage. There were
much better things to spend money on, much better ways to mark
another year in Auckland's pock-marked life. Isobel said little; she
was on safer ground when the conversation switched to the stone
houses on the right side of Queen Street—the ones furthest away
from Freeman's Bay—which might have mending to send out. As
always, such valuable information was shared easily between the
women, for Mrs Riley had seen Isobel in her nightdress, nights when
Brendan was in the drink and locked her out. They had both helped

with an unexpected birth from one of the women boarding on Sale Street, where prostitutes gathered. Isobel never spoke of that night, and floundered on the occasions Mrs Riley took a brutal satisfaction in recalling how she slapped sense into mother and babe, before it was too late. Mrs Riley did not tolerate buckling or weakness.

There was a little time before Esther was due to land. Isobel swept the one-roomed cottage, pushing back the bed she and Brendan shared, and shook out the one decent rug. She scrubbed the floor beside the iron box that served as the colonial oven, and pounded the cushions of the arm chair. The wind was up, shouting through the street, urging women to leave their washing and head back inside their little timber houses. Salted air from the docks curled back the newspaper from the walls again, undoing the stickiness of flour and water paste fixing strips of grey and black text to the inside of the room. Isobel had been nonplussed when she first saw newspaper used in such a way. In the early days, soon after landing, she'd step inside a house down on the wharf to ask after mending and the rooms would be crowded with sideboards and heavy furniture from home. She'd see torn newspaper stuck to the walls, a rudimentary, colonial way to keep out the wind. Mrs Riley showed her how to mix up a paste with a tiny amount of flour, and she lined their room as best she could. It was a constant battle to keep the paper on the walls. Now, after putting away her brush and cloth, she mixed sawdust and water together and stuck the paper down again.

The abattoir had been alive for hours. Occasionally the bray of a horse carried in the air and, further into Freeman's Bay, a man on a ladder shouted down to his mate about a broken gaslight. He must have produced a hammer, for Isobel heard a banging. She wondered if Brendan had sent him along to fix it, if that was one of the things he did in his new job at the gas company. She imagined him coming back that night, proudly strutting, chest swollen as though full of fluid. He'd sit down for his dinner and ask casually if his wife had noticed the lamp lightening the street outside. A lamp to which he had sent a man to repair.

Isobel turned her attention back to making the room ready. She found an old sheet and tacked it to the ceiling, so that it fell like a veil around a corner of the room, the furthest corner away from the bed. This would be where Esther would sleep. The sheet would give her a pretence of privacy. Isobel had sewn up potato sacks, bought for a few pence from Elliott's Grocers on Hobson Street, and stuffed them with hay. The makeshift mattress lay on top of packing boxes, the ones she and Brendan filled all those years ago with their life, ready for the voyage out. A last clean sheet covered the lumpy bed, and Isobel had mended a patchwork blanket as a coverlet. She stood back now, hands on hips, looking at her creation and wondered how her sister would sleep.

A church clock chimed that it was time to leave, and Isobel pulled on her coat. Her mouth felt like she had swallowed a spoonful of lemon juice. It was a thought that made her snort softly; she could not remember the last time she had money to buy a lemon. She thought of her sister, and the long years that separated them.

A cast about the room and a sigh that little could be done to improve it, and Isobel made for the off. Forcing on a pair of gloves that were several winters too thin, Isobel hurried out into the street and the wet pelt of the morning.

⁓

Another building was being thrown up down near the quay, great hunks of quarried stone hauled up on ropes above the heads of passengers belching out of ships. Isobel stepped over horse manure as buses lined up. Hoteliers and vendors crowded the harbour side, shouting out wares and prices, tittering among themselves as white-lipped, blinking new chums stepped off their boats with jelly legs. Queen Street wharf stretched far out into the dirty water of the harbour, and crowds jostled and pushed. Someone was slapped, a child found his ears boxed. Isobel stood back as two boys, no older than ten, rolled on the ground, hissing at each other like stray cats. She kicked out at one when he snagged the hem of her dress mid-fight, aiming deliberately for his white, wasted arse, hoping that nobody saw.

Their mother had telegrammed with details of Esther's ship. A boy had run round from the post office and Isobel had paid him, nauseous at the cost of sending words from London to Auckland. She'd opened the paper and read, imagining each letter unfurling on the sheet. Letters made out of shillings.

Esther was on a steamer called the *Lady Jasmine*. She had been booked into first-class quarters, for which Isobel was grateful. She'd seen steerage passengers when she crossed with Brendan ten years ago; men, women, babes forced below deck by bad weather and drunkenness. Cabins like sweat-boxes or ponds.

She could see the *Lady Jasmine* now as she stood on Queen Street wharf. It had docked at the far end of the quay, funnels belching black smoke into the grey air. Emigrants stumbled onto the wharf, gingerly finding their land feet after weeks at sea. Most wrinkled up their noses, the smell of sewage and drain water unmistakable. First-class passengers disembarked before the others. Hurrying over, Isobel straightened her dress and coat, noticing for the first time and cursing a small hole in the collar. Her tongue moved sourly in her mouth, though her stomach and bowels felt wet and loose. Ten years of distance lay awkwardly in her body; she felt the lines of it in her face. A thousand emotions jostled for prominence, her flesh falling in upon itself, her mouth working silently. She longed to see something familiar so she could anchor herself to it. She wondered if Esther still wore her hair long and flowing down her back, if the tiny scar between her sister's nose and eye from a maddened dog had faded.

A horn from a ship somewhere, and Isobel jumped, jolting loose unexpected tears. Rain fell, she passed a hand over her face, and suddenly Esther was in front of her. At least, Isobel *thought* it was Esther; the woman had the shocking red hair of her sister and her features were arranged in the same fashion. But Esther had been a girl of eleven when they'd parted—she'd worn a pinafore and a scowl back then. The woman on the dockside seemed to have stepped into the child's skin and thickened her blood. But the way Esther held her fingers to her lips, pinning her mouth closed—she was the Esther that Isobel remembered. She looked, transfixed, as the woman on the quayside pinched her face, and Isobel was back— back in the parlour, in the house on the border between Derbyshire and Nottinghamshire, and Esther was holding herself in, holding back insults for their mother. On the Auckland quayside, Isobel needed to see Esther's mouth. The urge was sudden and frightening. She reached out and touched the woman she had not touched in ten years, folding her sister's rigid bones into her own cupped hand, seeing Esther's mouth, the gnawed lips, and then the women were crying freely, not caring who on Queen Street saw them.

❧

'It's not far, we can manage without a bus or dray.' Isobel took hold of Esther's trunk. A few moments had passed. The sisters glanced at each other sheepishly, tears wiped away. Esther had produced a handkerchief and passed it over. Isobel had paused before blowing her nose, touching the lace trim carefully, thinking back to the last time she had seen such delicacy. Nothing Isobel owned was so pretty.

In their embrace, she noticed Esther had a smell about her. Weeks of sea and salt had dulled—but not removed—a smell Isobel seemed to remember in her gut. Earthy, dense, like the smell of clothes hanging on a line for too long. Of wet undergrowth and tilled soil. Her face buried in her sister's neck, Isobel closed her eyes and thought of the house, on the border of two northern English counties, a childhood marked out by wood and hill. Esther carried their home in her clothes and skin.

They walked, pushing on through the crowds. Esther paused every now and then, as if curious at the bodies around her. At one point she stopped completely, observing a noisy reunion between a man and a younger, rawer version of himself. Isobel had seen too many of such meetings to be startled; families came and went in the new colony, and her mind was already racing ahead to the moment she showed Esther into her home.

They walked down Queen Street, away from the harbour, turning right when the road forked into Wellesley Road. Instinctively, Isobel kept them on the main routes. Rain had turned the less busy, unpaved roads into squelching, treacherous strips of mud. Boots could be sucked from feet. Isobel had seen a woman stumble and flail just that morning as she walked to the harbour, potatoes spilling from the woman's basket as she waved her arms, trying not to fall over. It seemed very important to Isobel—though she hadn't thought of it before—to make the walk from harbour to cottage as uneventful as possible. Roads branching off from the main routes threatened clutter and running sewers. The smaller roads had men shouting from windows as sliced pigs were dragged from cart to butchers' shops.

Isobel led her sister along Wellesley Road, onto College Road where the grand post office loomed and then, when it was unavoidable, off the main stretch and onto a side street. A line of timber cottages edged onto the pitted road. A fellow further along had set up a makeshift shed against the side of his cottage and was repairing furniture under a wet bedsheet. He whacked wood with a hammer, cursed and spat. Someone else threw open a window and tossed out a handful of peelings and breadcrumbs onto the mud.

Then, unbelievably, they were outside the wooden house on George Street where Isobel and Brendan roomed. Isobel slowed as they approached, pretending Esther's packing trunk was heavy; in actuality, she felt weighed down by a growing sense of mortification. The letters home, the letters she wrote to their mother every two months—they did not speak of a room at the end of a shabby, dirt-streaked road. Isobel paused at the front gate, gazing down at the ferns dying in the small garden. Dish water and cat urine had done for the plants months ago. A bitter stench rose now, even in the falling rain.

'Is this the place?' Esther asked. She stood in front of the house, mouth folded over as she bit the inside of her cheek. 'Number 17, George Street?'

'This is it. It sounds different on paper, doesn't it?'

Esther wore her hair up in a bun now and, as Isobel finally pushed back the gate and opened the front door, Esther's fingers trailed a loose hair, winding it tightly so that the flesh whitened. She said nothing but continued to spiral the strand of hair as Isobel led her inside.

'Please, don't say anything yet,' Isobel said in a low voice, edging the trunk inside. 'I couldn't bear it. Brendan is away at the office. Take off your coat and sit down.'

A door banged and Sally, the neighbour, appeared around the doorframe. Her face was smeared with sleep and she sighed a welcome. 'Need milk, Bella? Am going to the diary. They have yesterday's supply going cheap. Ah, hello.'

Isobel waved a hand, hoping to repel Sally and urge Esther inside in one movement. She forced brightness into her voice. 'I have some, thank you, Sal. This is my sister, Esther. We're going to take tea. Are you … are you up for the day now?'

'Unlikely. The old bag at the bakery wants us back at six tonight and I plan on sleeping until then. I might have a scrap of bread with me when I get home in the morning, if you're interested. I'll leave you now. There's much to catch up on, I dare say.'

Sally made an odd, dreamy sort of bow and shuffled off. Esther, finally stepping fully into the room, watched the small girl head off along the street, picking her way through the dirt. Esther removed her gloves, shiny and delicately stitched, and placed them on the table.

'Bella?' she said. 'No longer Isobel, then.'

Isobel blinked slowly. There was so much to say; words tumbled down with such force that it bent her neck. And there was that smell again, close against her now they were inside and not out on the wind-buffeted dock. She breathed in and pulled out a chair.

'Sit down, Esther. Please. I'll make us tea and we can talk.'

ᴄⱷᴏ

They waited for the kettle to boil on the stove and Isobel busied herself cutting one of Sally's loaves brought home from her work at the bakery. A burnt but cheap husk. There was no butter but she found marmalade. Esther lowered herself onto a chair, looking around with pointed, bird-like glances. Both sisters studiously avoided looking at each other. An argument broke out on the street outside, and Isobel shook her head emphatically, relieved at the distraction.

She poured tea. 'Mother's rosebud set.' Isobel nodded down at the cup and saucer. 'I don't know how I've kept them safe, but they're all intact still. Not one broken piece.'

'Clever of you,' Esther said wanly, and sipped her tea. Her eyes closed momentarily, and Isobel wondered if there had been tea on the ship.

'Do you need to rest?' she asked. 'It must have been an exhausting journey.'

'That's not necessary, thank you.' A note of formality had crept into Esther's voice. She looked at the sheet hanging from the ceiling. 'Where …'

'There's a bed behind the sheet,' Isobel said. And then it all came in a rush. 'I know the place isn't how I described it to Mother, but it will be, you'll see! Bren is working now, so we can save again. It hasn't been easy, you must understand that. Land is more expensive now and there isn't so much to go around. Brendan never was much of a farmer, you remember that. He works better with paper.'

'You said you had a townhouse. Away from the city.' Esther was smooth lines and control. Her chin seemed impossibly sharp and high, exposing the shape of her long, swan neck. Isobel thought of her dream, of her sister running through the meadows to water, how the child had thrown off the chiding hand of her older sister.

Isobel leaned over and gripped Esther's hand tightly, urgently. 'My dear, I'm so happy to see you. So happy. Isn't the most important thing that we're together again?'

They talked, a little, as they drank tea. Isobel felt delirious with longing—she wanted Esther to spill all the news in one vomiting burst, so she could claw through it for morsels. 'Look!' she wanted to say, 'here's a piece of my mother! And here's a memory of my father—do you think he loved me?'

But Esther held her stories back and let them slide across to her sister in coy, slithering words. She wanted to break out with the news from home, Isobel could tell, but it was as though a glass vase had come down upon her and she could only push out a small bud at a time.

'Mother's cousin, Verity, do you remember her? She died two years ago. Her share of the mining stock passed to Mother.'

Isobel thought of the letters from her mother. 'I didn't know.'

Esther shrugged. 'An uncle died, too. Not sure on which side, you know how many there are. But Mother became wealthy. We no longer need to sell land. She's started building an extra wing, near where our bedrooms used to be.'

Isobel resisted the urge to look around her, at the wasted room. The bed frame had been bought with the last of the family silver, gifted by their grandmother. Even Brendan had sold trinkets to pay rent. The blue heat of embarrassment, felt so viscerally since Esther docked, became fluid and boiled in her chest; how could her mother not have told her about her fortune? Why did she not send something out to her eldest daughter?

'Mother must be doing well, if she's adding rooms to the house.' It was impossible to keep the bite from her voice and Esther looked at her over the top of her cup.

'We thought you were doing well, also,' she said. 'Your letters— you told us Brendan had been taken on as a clerk at the Customs House, and that you lived in a little house somewhere in the hills.' Esther stood up and walked to the dirty windowpane. 'Can you even see the hills from here?'

Isobel stared at the teapot, faded pink flowers strung around the base. The handle was chipped—it was true that she hadn't broken a piece from the set but she'd poured tea carefully, afraid the pot would crack and spill scalding water over them both.

'Are you sure you wouldn't like to rest, Esther? What a long journey you've had. Was the crossing rough?'

'Not especially.' Esther hung by the window, looking up at the grey sky. 'An old man died, that was the only thing of note. Steerage passenger, I believe.' She spoke oddly, a rueful tone. 'His family wanted him buried at sea—didn't want the trouble of finding him a grave when they landed, I suppose. What a thing that would be! Imagine, a first task upon reaching the other side of the world— arranging a burial!'

Isobel heard the waver to her sister's voice. 'Is everything all right, Esther?'

'Why wouldn't it be?' Esther did not turn round. 'One of the sailors also fell overboard near the Cape, but the water was like a millpond that day. Almost milky. He was pulled out easily and the captain said he'd had a baptism. He'd been baptised on a new journey. Quite poetic, don't you think? I almost wished I could do the same. But to die en route and be buried in a land you have no connection with … Some of the first-class crowd thought the old man's family were taking the cheap option by letting the captain put him in a shroud and push him over the side, but I think I'd want to be left in the water, just like him.'

Isobel stood up. 'I think you need to lie down, Esther, I really do. It's the shock of being on land, I expect. Come, rest a while.'

She cupped her sister's elbow and turned her around, almost expecting Esther to resist, just as she did when they were children. But Esther turned to face her. Her smile was lopsided.

'Always the mother, weren't you, Isobel? Well, where have you been for the last ten years? No, no, I'm not angry. You're probably right, I must be tired. Now, show me this bed of mine. Aren't you clever, to use packing boxes in such a way?'

She wondered if Esther would sleep, but her sister did, soon after lying down on the lumpy mattress. She had allowed Isobel to help her remove her boots, leaning back on her hands and reading the newspaper strips lining the walls as Isobel untied the lacings and eased the leather away. Isobel had handled the boots enviously—what she wouldn't give for a pair like that, with thick leather and steel toes! Her own boots had been re-heeled so many times it was impossible to remember their original colour, and they still let in water, offering no protection against the rivers of rain that poured down the streets on some days. Auckland's rain had shocked Isobel in the first years, with its warmth and ferocity.

Esther was wearing a pair of woollen stockings, smooth-heeled, and Isobel offered to help her undress, but Esther curled herself under the coverlet instead, weariness seeming to press down on her with a flat, unforgiving palm. Her breath was steady and low as Isobel pulled back the sheet to give her sister privacy. By the time Isobel had cleared away the tea and breadcrumbs, Esther was fully asleep.

Esther's trunk, a heavy mahogany item bound in brass, stood where Isobel had left it, beside the bed she shared with Brendan. She wiped her hands on a dishcloth, frowning at it. She hadn't thought of giving Esther a set of drawers or a little cabinet in which she could store her things. She would have to keep them in the trunk for now.

Isobel wanted to open the trunk. She wanted to plunge her hands into her sister's clothes—clothes that had been touched by their mother, maybe even mended on their mother's knee. And maybe there would be more of that smell again, the smell of home.

The trunk was locked, but Esther had left a small bag on the table; the key would be in there and Isobel could find it if she wanted.

The bag was surprisingly empty—a small book of poems by someone Isobel hadn't heard of, and two keys, attached together with a piece of string. Isobel bounced them gently in her hand, considering. The larger key would be to open the trunk, she was sure, but she could see nothing the smaller key would open. She felt the cool metal on her skin. Smooth, firm, determinedly present, the keys seemed to chide her. To open her sister's trunk and look through her possessions, what would that make her? Isobel looked over at the box again, unsure.

The key turned easily. It clicked satisfyingly, like dentures on wood, the lock springing open. Isobel smoothed her hands over the frame, noting the newness of the trunk and its sturdiness and strength. It must have been an expensive purchase, and Isobel felt a pang of anger again toward her mother.

A small gap appeared between the lid and the base and Isobel, sliding her fingers into the space, listened again for Esther's breathing, and pushed the lid back.

A pair of soft leather slippers. A cotton nightdress. Four pairs of woollen stockings, two pairs of thick socks. A long grey skirt that surprised Isobel with its weight when she lifted it up. Three blouses, another skirt. A velvet dress—when did Esther expect to wear that? Isobel smiled sadly. Bloomers, cotton vests. A packet of white material and several spools of cotton. A precious packet of needles. Something of Isobel's advice, then, sent in letters to her mother, had seeped through. Needles were expensive in Auckland.

Isobel looked at the clothes, laid out over her bed. They were new. She could see nothing of home, of the Esther she remembered, in the threads and folds of shop-bought fabric. She touched the leather slippers, thinking how much they would cost in Auckland. Esther would find them robbed from her feet if she tried to walk in them among the houses here, Isobel thought. Perhaps she was being unkind.

Esther's coat, the one she wore to step off the ship, looked as though it cost more than six months' rent on the room on George Street, and the clothes in the trunk must surely have cost more. Isobel's hands strayed to her own worn dress, patched around the hem and shiny with age. She had not replaced the coat she emigrated with. Fear stung her—fear that Esther would, somehow, remember and judge her for it.

She moved the clothes, seeking something. Plaid. Esther had loved plaid as a child, checks of any colour as long as there was a clash of blocks and shapes on her clothes. Their mother, in the steely, hunger-soaked days before money, scrimped and sewed a little dress for Esther, taking offcuts from the draper's shop whenever plaid material was left over. Surprisingly the girl loved it. She loved the boldness of it. But there was nothing plaid in the garments laid out on Isobel's bed. Not one thing—not even the edging on a cuff or collar.

Esther rose and sighed, and settled again. Isobel held herself rigidly, waiting for the curtain to be pulled back and for Esther to cry out. Just what exactly was she doing, looking through the trunk, anyway? Isobel turned the smaller key over in her palm, the unused key that seemed to have no home.

Other things lay in the trunk. A brown shawl. Isobel drew it out, rough wool scratching her fingers, and then the smell was unmistakable. She smelled her mother. A dry, fervent smell, like burnt dust. Isobel wadded it under her nose and breathed in. She saw a tall woman, a wearer of sharp boots. Yellow frizzed hair springing angrily from whatever bonnet or hat it was forced under. Quick and sharp with her hands, ridges instead of folds. An index finger permanently hooked and poked. That was her mother.

There were more clothes, washcloths and towels, caps, soap, and two books. Isobel drew them from the trunk, fingers catching on the frayed bindings. Jules Verne. Emily Bronte. The lettering on the spines had worn away but Isobel felt a rush of remembrance as she flicked through the pages. Illustrations she knew, sketchings in the margins. These were books from home, from their father's library. She could not believe their mother had given them to Esther; she'd not allowed Isobel to take a thing of her father's when she'd left, save for a glass snow dome that smashed in the crossing.

She remembered the afternoon she departed, the last hour before taking the coach down to Gravesend. Brendan waited in the kitchen—Mother would not allow him further into the house. He'd sat in front of the fire with Esther, the girl filling a box with straw. Isobel talked to her mother in her father's old study.

'This is the last time I'll see you,' Isobel had said, her mother's back a flinty strip of bark, rigid against the desk. The desk upon which Isobel's father had signed promissory notes and dropped the family into poverty.

Her mother had clicked her tongue. 'You always were dramatic, Isobel. You'll be back. I give you a year before he makes a mess of things and you come sailing home.'

'It wasn't Bren's fault about the job.' Isobel struggled to keep her face together. Her mouth felt as twisted as the ceiling beams above them. She wondered if her mother's heart was as tough and splintery as her body, a body that invited no caress or embrace. She found herself imagining her father, hoisting his soft, unruly form on top of the wooden woman. What must it have felt like to lie with someone who could send darts into your eyes?

'I can't give you anything,' Mother said. 'There's no money, you know that. I might have to sell land now Brendan can't help us.'

'I don't want anything. Only, well, your blessing, if you'll give it.'

Mother laughed then and spoke in a voice so arid Isobel imagined she could see smoke on her tongue. 'You have my blessing, Isobel, to follow that foolish husband of yours to the bottom of the world. And you have my blessing to stay there, if you can make life work for you.'

Isobel had stumbled out, unable to speak. She passed by Brendan in the kitchen, who rose immediately. He stood with her in the passageway, waiting.

'She'll never change,' Isobel had said, meaning her mother. Then she looked back at her sister. The girl was still intent on the box and the curious task of packing it with straw. 'What is she doing?'

'It's for Misty. Her cat.' Brendan's eyebrows were high on his head. 'It's a coffin.'

'What happened to Misty?'

'Nothing. Yet.'

☙

It really hadn't been Brendan's fault that he'd lost his employment before they struck out for New Zealand—not that time, anyway. Mr

Briggs, the bank manager, had been apologetic, Brendan said, but there was little he could do. Simply not enough for his wages, and Brendan had shrugged in that nonchalant way of his that, at that early point in their marriage, did not make Isobel want to lift his dinner and throw it in his face. But his cousin had written about opportunities overseas in New Zealand—quite a break, quite a stretch over the water, but he wanted to talk it through with Isobel. Would she be willing?

They'd been in Auckland for ten years. Isobel sat on the bed in their little room, glaring round at the newspaper wall, that feeling of being caught between two worlds sliding over her again. Sometimes, when she read and reread letters from home—from cousins or friends who still remembered her—she felt like she was back in England. She was walking through the village, the smell of the hedgerows bright and spicy in her nose, the soft fall of the river nearby. And yet, when she lifted her eyes from the paper, she was back in New Zealand. She was back among the shout and crackle of young Auckland, blinking against the glare of rough settler life.

New Zealand was nothing like Brendan had said. There was no gang of employers waiting on the quayside, hollering out for educated, numerate men like him. No pick of cheap, comfortable lodgings and platefuls of mutton. Instead, a grey sky weighed down on the emigrants' shoulders as they stepped off the boat, and the air seemed close and suffocating. Isobel remembered panting as she disembarked; not, this time, because of the ever-present eternal sea sickness, but because of the heat. Even with rain, Auckland seemed a closed bubble and, stepping onto new soil, she thought of the kiln her father took her to as a child, in the Derbyshire Dales. He'd wanted her to see how men with rough, callused fingers made beautiful pottery. The heat in the studios and near the kiln had sent six-year-old Isobel into a scratching, twitching frenzy, and she'd screamed to be let out.

No screaming would get her out of this one, she saw immediately, watching Brendan wrestle their luggage down onto the dockside. Instead, eight weeks went by before he found employment, weeks during which they lived on their tiny savings. Isobel sold every trinket from home she had.

She wondered, again, what Brendan's cousin had written, what he had said to convince Brendan to give up everything they knew and jump into the deep. Brendan had never told her and, when Isobel pushed, said he had lost the letters.

Isobel smoothed her hand over her mother's shawl, stretching the wool. It made an odd crackle. She paused, rolled her hand over the shawl again, and heard the same sound. She opened up the shawl—a letter fell out. A white envelope, folded inside the shawl.

Isobel picked it up, realising when she turned it over in her palm that she'd been holding her breath. She recognised the handwriting; a pile of letters addressed to her, written in the same hand, were in a little box under the bed. It was her mother's writing. The envelope was sealed. On the front was written: 'Esther—open in September.'

That was just over four months from now. Somehow Isobel knew her mother's letter would not be a greeting to her daughter, or a bundle of good wishes for her daughter's new life. Their mother would never write such things.

She wondered if Esther even knew about the letter. When Isobel left with Brendan, she found a letter of her own, from her mother, tucked inside her trunk. She'd discovered it when unpacking clothes in their married quarters on board the emigrant ship—a piece of paper, folded up into a small packet and sealed together. She had wept a little upon finding it as the boat lurched from side to side, hoping her mother's bold writing spoke of forgiveness and, maybe, a little love. The letter only contained the address of a family friend who had emigrated some years earlier and whom Isobel's mother wanted her to meet. Isobel had torn the paper to pieces.

A moan came from the other side of the curtain, and Isobel almost put the letter back in the trunk. Then a sigh from her sister, full of such weariness that Isobel felt her mouth fill with tears. She could not see her sister's form through the curtain, but imagined her as small and thin, red hair spilling over a plaid nightdress.

Carefully, taking time so that Esther would not be woken by the sound of unfolding paper, Isobel opened the envelope, took out the single sheet, and began to read.

Esther

Eyes open. Sunshine on an oddly decorated wall, covered completely with print, tiny print—could that be? Esther's eyes felt sticky and she blinked, wondering if sleep had muddled her vision. It happened occasionally, on the boat; the ever-present swing and sway of water sometimes turned her mind into a warm puddle and she could not read on her narrow bunk.

But the bed upon which she now lay was solid and still. Lumpy, true, but the coverlet was warm. She felt as though she had slept properly for the first time in months and awoke, wonderfully, without the first sensation being a need to dry retch into a porcelain bowl.

And yet, and yet … Esther curled up in the bed and pulled her knees to her chest, as far as they would go. She had barely slept on the boat the night before. Landfall was tantalisingly close, too close for rest. Now, on her makeshift bed, tears slipped into the corner of her eyes, leaking down her face onto the scratchy pillowcase. It had really happened. She had made the crossing, after everything. She was in New Zealand and he was thousands of miles away. She wondered if he'd forgotten her already.

Maybe she'd slept some more for, when Esther opened her eyes again, the yellow square of light streaming through the window had moved. Immediately, sitting up, she knew she was alone. She remembered exactly where she was.

She pulled back the curtain and swung her legs round, gritting her teeth as her feet touched the floor and blood surged under her skin. Cramp, again. Esther spent a moment wriggling her toes, working it out. Sometimes the cramp would disappear for a few days, but it would always come back, a knife under her toenails.

She got up and stepped further into the room. The teacups and plates from earlier were stacked neatly on a sideboard—she could see nowhere to wash them. What do they do for water? Esther thought, confused. Surely they had heard of taps and sinks in the colonies?

As if in answer there was a splash of water outside and a woman's high-pitched, giggling hoot. A child laughed. Esther moved to the window and saw a pump at the centre of a small courtyard. Women stood around, bowls of dishes in hand, some with a rag, waiting for their turn to rinse out. Esther craned her neck, trying to spot her sister.

She didn't like this cottage. The aversion was sudden but sure. She didn't like the way Isobel and Brendan's bed was pushed against the far wall, leaving only a thin strip of space between bed and window. She didn't like the lack of corner tables, or photographs, or vases. The room was stripped back and pared.

But most of all, Esther did not like the bizarre wallpaper—if it could even be called that. Slices of newspaper could hardly be considered wallpaper. There were layers of them, stuck to the walls. Some were peeling away, others were torn. Esther started to read a piece, only for the story—about export prices—to be broken up by a piece about a tea party at a provincial house, somewhere south. The wallpaper produced a jangling, fragmentary effect; political news jostled for space with fashion pieces. Passenger lists were interspersed with tales of Maori skirmishes, dating from several years before. The wallpaper seemed to press down on Esther, a sedimentary layering of New Zealand that she did not like.

She suddenly marched across the room—it only took a few steps—to her bed where she sat down and pulled on her boots. She was going to go outside and find Isobel, and sort out with her (accepting no protestations on her sister's part) how, exactly, they were going to live.

Yet when Esther reached the courtyard, her determination left her. It evaporated in the damp of the day, and in the baleful stare of women who waited to wash their crockery and who now turned to look at this handsomely dressed newcomer in their midst.

Esther stood very still as children whooped and shrieked about her, curiosity and mistrust of the women crackling the air. One woman, a robust creature with a high waistband and a solid bosom, turned to a companion and spoke leisurely, in a loud voice that was English but had an oddly clipped accent.

'Reckon this one got lost on the way to Queen Street?'

Somebody shrieked with laughter. Two women to Esther's left were crouched over an upturned table, hammer in hand, nails in their mouths. They looked at Esther and she at them; she had never seen women work in such a way, not even when her mother had no money. Back home, the mending of furniture had been men's business, or work for the carpenter. Esther looked at the hammer, transfixed. She suddenly, very desperately, wanted to see the women work. She wanted to see how they set about repairing things, how they used their hands to make and build.

The women fixing the table seemed perfectly at ease. One had a pencil stub stuck in her hair. She stood up. 'You lost?'

'I'm looking for my sister.'

At Esther's voice, a knowing look rippled between the women in the courtyard. A child, a boy of four playing with a wooden train in the dirt, looked up at Esther, mouth agape.

'New chum!' the boy yelped. He pointed at Esther and immediately a cacophony of children's voices pealed out. 'New chum! New chum!' It was a game they obviously knew well.

Esther smiled, the boy's shout seeming to smooth out the tension in the courtyard. She thought of how children were so often overlooked, but who had a way of speaking to the heart of things. The boy was only shouting what all the women were thinking.

Esther bent down, looking into the child's open face. 'Oh, I'm a new chum, all right. A special kind of new chum you've not seen before.'

'What sort?' the boy said breathlessly. His eyes were wide—this was not part of the game.

Esther pulled her hands into the shape of a claw and waved them in front of the child. 'I'm a new chum who likes to eat children! I've been on that boat for weeks, and I'm hungry!'

The boy gasped, shoulders up, and for a second Esther thought she'd misjudged. But then, in that intuitive way of children, with the natural ability to make a game from anything, the boy squealed and jumped up.

'Catch me!' he said, laughing. He sprinted away, checking over his shoulder that Esther was chasing him.

She did not, bashful again, wondering what the women would make of her. Some were nodding, all were smiling. The woman with the large bust patted her dress, the flat sound punctuating the moment. She pointed to an unoccupied wooden crate among a group of sitting women.

'Take a seat. Who's your sister?'

∞

One of the women brought out a tray of cracked mugs of tea, an eclectic collection of chipped and colourful crockery. It was passed around the seated group. All had knitting or mending on their laps, which they set down to take a mug. The relaxed ease with which all helped themselves told Esther this was common practice.

'We take it in turns,' a woman to Esther's left said quietly. 'Sew, watch the children, drink. That's what we do.'

Children played in the dirt; chubby fists were slapped easily as muddy rattles neared mouths. Twin boys, fat and apple-cheeked, about the age of three, chased each other around a broken chair. Their mother, the high-chested woman who had first spoken to Esther when she ventured into the courtyard, ignored them, save for when one fell over and came running to her. She wiped his face with her skirts and sent him on his way with a hefty slap on his bottom.

'I don't raise whingeing children,' she said comfortably. 'You'll find that here, Miss Esther. Our colonial children have this land in their bones—they're never still. Mouths and all. Take some tea. Now, Bella is your sister?'

'Isobel, yes.' There it was, that name again. *Bella*. Esther took a mug of tea, fighting the urge to gulp it down. There had been a terrible accident with her box of stores on the boat—water had drenched her cabin during a storm, and while most of her possessions could be saved, her box of tea, dried fruits and biscuits was ruined. Sipping the tea now, she was reminded again just how much she had missed it. 'I landed this morning and took a nap. She must have gone out for a walk.'

'She'll be up Queen Street, looking for mending,' said a woman at the far end of the circle. 'I told her this morning which houses were sending out.'

'Isobel takes in mending?' Esther tried to keep her voice level. The image of her sister sitting in a smart townhouse—the one she had described in her letters to their mother—floated further away. Isobel mended other women's clothes for a living?

'We all do,' another woman spoke up and held up the shirt she was sewing. She had a large belly and returned her hands to her lap, cupping the rounded stomach. Esther glanced away, but not before taking in the swell of the woman's feet and the shiny red veins on bare ankles. 'Or else we're faced with asking the Hospital Board for relief.' She patted her stomach for emphasis.

'Have you a position set up?' The fiercely-chested woman again. The other women seemed to sit up a little at the question. Heads were cocked slightly.

'No. That is to say, I haven't sorted out employment.' Esther saw how the group exhaled at the news. 'I planned on living with Isobel and her husband for a while, until I get myself settled.'

'Let us know when you do,' the woman to Esther's left said softly. 'So you can tell us how it's done.'

There were a few titters at that, but then the women looked down at the ground gloomily. Esther examined them all, their shiny and patched clothes, hair that needed a good wash. Her heart sank.

'Don't let Rachel alarm you,' one woman said, the one who had spoken of Isobel going out for mending. 'I remember what it was like in Bolton, when the mills closed. This place is heavenly compared.'

'Is it heaven to work for a full year without pay, Hilda?' replied another, a woman who still looked to be in her teens. She turned to face Esther. 'I was taken on as a dressmaker at fourteen and it is quite common not to pay a girl in the first year of work.' She snorted. 'The payment is in the experience, you see.'

The stout mother of twins produced a pouch of tobacco and began rolling herself a cigarette. 'I haven't worked for a month. Milliner, by trade. Couldn't get a job at Smith and Caughey's so I'm on an enforced holiday. No trade.'

'You shouldn't be smoking those, Rose,' said Hilda. 'There was an article in the *Herald* this morning about tobacco affecting the heart and lungs.'

Rose pouted and lit the cigarette languidly. 'Don't you think the dust from Kauri's Mill affects us all enough? All that choking saw-dust, floating over the city. Bet the rich lot on Queen Street don't have to worry about dust coming through their windows or floor-boards. Not like here. One cigarette won't make much difference. Anyone else want one?'

The tobacco was passed around and the women settled into small conversations. Esther sat quietly, sipping her tea, whorls of talk and smoke rising and falling around her. Rachel, the woman to her left, had accepted Rose's offered tobacco and lit her own cig-arette. Items were transferred easily between hands. A child with a squint, very obviously the child belonging to a woman with a similar screwed-up look to her face, sitting some distance away, was admon-ished by another woman. No one seemed to mind. More mugs of tea appeared, passed around by someone else this time. The group in the courtyard picked up their sewing and eased into the day, glanc-ing occasionally at the gathering clouds above.

'So has the New Zealand weather startled you?' Rachel asked. 'The rain can be quite a shock at first.'

Leaning round to talk, Esther saw the woman was older than she'd first thought. Ash blonde hair was streaked with grey, and crow's feet straddled the corners of her eyes.

'It will take a while to get used to the heat,' Esther confessed. 'Back home, where I'm from, rain means cold, or a clearing of thunderstorms.'

'The heat makes for the beauty of the place,' Rachel said. 'Even Auckland—there's beauty here. The colours. So many colours of green. You should ask your sister to take you to the Domain or Albert Park. When Alfred and I landed in the fifties, Auckland was much smaller. The bush seemed to come up to our front door. We had to build our own house. It was a shambles, really, of timber and mud. But it felt wonderful, building a place together. It fell down, of course, in the storm of seventy-four.'

'Did you rebuild?'

The woman paused. 'I did. My sons helped. Alfred had died by then, dear. He's buried up on the gully at Symond's Street.'

'Rachel is our pioneer,' the young dressmaker interrupted.

'Oh, Helena.'

Helena laughed. 'It's true. You've been here for years, long before most of us. Long before my mother landed.'

'I suppose I have.'

'Have you been back at all?' Esther asked. The answer was suddenly very important to her. She held her mug tightly.

Rachel shook her head. 'To England? No. In the first years I wanted to. Before Alfred died, I tried to talk him round, to think about going home. I'd left my mother and sisters behind, you see. But Alfred said I should look around me—we had everything we ever wanted. Land was cheap back then. If you worked hard, you never starved, and there was hope. He was right, but ...' Rachel's hands moved helplessly. 'I had such a terrible feeling of being torn. Of being trapped between the hinges of what my heart wanted and

what my full stomach told me was true. And then he died. I couldn't
leave him alone here. Or leave my sons.'

Esther dipped her head and closed her eyes. The arrow of Rachel's
words pinned the centre of her and she felt the need to curl in, to hold
herself tight. Throughout the whole journey over, during those long,
rolling hours on the ship, she had swung between a great, great fear
of the unknown and a tender hope that, just maybe, New Zealand
would make everything right. Her belongings, packed so hurriedly,
gave little comfort; her mother had bought her a new trunk without discussing it and Esther found it in her room. There had been
no time to gather mementos, or order photographs from the stu-
dio. Not that she wanted one of *him*, particularly, even if she could
have one; more that the absence of such things thickened her loneli-
ness. Other first-class passengers kept images and keepsakes in their
pockets; walking the poop deck, Esther saw them bringing lockets
or charms to their lips. It was only when the sailor fell overboard on
that eerily calm day, just as they crossed the line, that Esther's mood
began to shift and the pain began to lift a little.

Rachel also bowed her head, staring down at the burning tobacco
in her fingers.

The women sat in the courtyard for a time talking, shouting
at the children, and Esther, with nowhere else to go, stayed with
them. Conversations lapped over her like water on a beach; a shout
at a child, a revelation about a husband that occasionally brought
the eruption of laughter. The women settled comfortably on their
improvised chairs while young children buzzed around them. The
older children, Esther learned, were at a free school a few streets
away.

It was the boy who called out that Esther was a new chum who
broke up the group. Not through his complaints that he was hungry, though many children did grumble as the dinner-time hour
approached. Instead the child came scooting up to his mother, sitting in the circle, and made an announcement.

'Mr Bellamy is coming!'

At that, the women scattered. They picked up their skirts and their mugs and, without a word of explanation, disappeared up a small alley that led away from the houses. Esther watched, agape, as they all moved as one—even Rachel with her creased brow and solemn expression. Within seconds, only Esther was left, sitting on a box, mug still in hand, looking around in amazement.

Moments later a man, dressed in brown corduroys and a black jacket, strode around the corner and into the courtyard. He was clean shaven, moustache-less. His face was pink. He made a face, a grimace, when he saw the courtyard was empty. His fingers clenched at his side.

Esther watched, confused. The speed of the women's departure puzzled her. Their movements that morning had been languid and unhurried, giving no indication of the way they could move together, like a flock. Or, indeed, why the haste and desire to be somewhere else. They had hurried up the alleyway, a flow of water, slimmer women tucked in beside bulkier frames, children scooped up and held on hips. Within seconds they had disappeared; only the circle of boxes—with Esther now at its centre—a clue to their presence.

The man spotted her. He tipped his head, studying her openly in a way Esther found disconcerting. He did not drop his eyes or raise his hat as men did on market day back home—in fact, his head was bare, light brown hair falling down to his neck. He strode toward her, stepping over wooden trains and one, lonely, upturned mug.

He stuck out his hand. 'Jack Bellamy.'

Esther leaned back, the man's forthright way of speaking making her feel unbalanced. She got up slowly, brushing down her dress and, with her fingertips, shook the man's hand. 'Miss Esther Carter.'

The man considered her again. He frowned, chin bouncing a little as he weighed up Esther's features. Then his brow cleared. 'Bella's sister?'

'Mrs Nelson is my sister.' Isobel's full title felt heavy in Esther's mouth.

'Bella is one of my better tenants. She mentioned you were coming.'

The frown slipped a little from Jack Bellamy's face. 'Sometimes I think I have imagined letting out my rooms—I never seem to be able to find those who owe me rent.'

Ah … Esther understood. The man was the landlord. That explained the women's urgent movements and their readiness to flee. She looked at him afresh. He seemed much younger than the landlords she occasionally encountered, when they came to speak to her mother. The ones Esther knew held themselves like swollen birds: they spoke of raising rents on miner's terraces, thumbs hooked in straining waistbands, cravats stuffed under corpulent faces. One squat little man, who met with Esther's mother at least once a month, had once allowed his fingers to linger on Esther's wrist when she shook hands. She had felt the grub of the man for days after.

'You are new here?' Jack Bellamy asked. 'When did you dock?'

'My steamer landed just this morning, Mr Bellamy. *The Lady Jasmine.*'

'Jack, please.' The man smiled. 'You'll find out here that titles are not so necessary. No doubt the rich at the Governor's House or in some of the big houses in Parnell would appreciate the usage, but not so in Freeman's Bay. You'll hear a phrase often repeated in New Zealand, I'm sure—"Jack's as good as his master."' The man shrugged. 'Naturally it's a phrase that I appreciate.'

Esther again felt the earth shift a little beneath her. This was not the New Zealand her sister wrote about in letters home. The life Isobel had described was one filled with parlour talk and walks in the gardens of Auckland Domain. She had not mentioned dirt and dry bread and beds made of packing boxes.

'Do you expect to see your sister soon?' Jack asked.

'I hardly know. I was resting and she went out for a walk.' Esther could not bring herself to say that Isobel had gone out to search for mending. Jack, though, nodded sagely, seeming to interpret her words.

'Well, it's like this—Bella is a little behind with rent, and we didn't exactly discuss terms—what with a new tenant staying in her cottage,

I mean. I have no objection if it is for a night or two, but …' He sighed. 'I'm no good at this. This chasing and pestering for money. It sits awkwardly with me. What I mean to say is—I expect you will be staying with your sister for a while?'

'I expect I will. Jack,' she said, forcing his name out. Esther glanced at him, catching as much of his face as she dare in the corner of her eyes. He grated his teeth and the brittle sound crawled up her spine. She dipped her hand into a fold of her dress, fishing out a small purse. 'Perhaps I could settle up with you now. To save Isobel the trouble later.'

She held the purse lightly in her hand, trying to keep the tremble from her fingers. She unclipped the clasp and shook some coins onto her palm.

At the light, tinny sound, Jack moved. He folded his hands over Esther's and, looking quickly over his shoulder, drew her down, back onto the boxes. She sat down cautiously, feeling the warmth of his fingers and the weight of velvet on her skin.

'You really *have* just landed,' Jack said. 'Never carry so much money around with you. You could easily be robbed.'

'By whom? There's no one here and the women were so friendly before.' Then she bit her lip, knowing she had given them away.

Jack snorted. 'So they *were* just here. Well, maybe some of them would never dream of taking a penny—unless their children were starving, of course. Unless they knew their husbands would come home with a thirst and there was no money for the bars or hotels.' He released his hold of Esther's hands and sat back. 'Find somewhere safe in Bella's room and keep it in there. Only carry a few coins. Never notes, not unless you have a man with you.'

Esther smarted at that. He does not know me at all! she thought, but she did not respond. Instead she looked at the young man curiously; youthful, wearing a high collar that obviously irritated him, for the skin on his neck was red. A man with a position of some importance but not comfortable with the role. She knew how the landlords back home would have acted, had she shown her purse.

They would have been inside it quicker than a fox in a hen house. Suddenly Esther wanted to be away, away from this courtyard and strange man, and back in the delicate safety of Isobel's room.

'How behind is Isobel? And what will you add for my staying with her?' she asked.

'She's two months behind. Twelve shillings per week, say thirteen shillings if we count your stay as well. But perhaps I should speak to Bella first.'

'No, don't.' Esther counted out a pile of coins. 'Here. Payment for two months.'

Jack looked at the coins she placed in his palm, eyes wide like he had never seen money before. He opened his mouth, as though about to speak, but seemed to think better of it. He coughed his thanks and slipped the money into a breast pocket.

A noise behind them—footsteps approached. It was Isobel. She held her coat tightly closed, and swinging by her side was an old, garish bag made, it appeared, from an old rug. She stopped when she saw Esther with Jack Bellamy.

Esther got up swiftly. She felt the longing to be back in Isobel's room more urgently than ever and, for a reason she did not understand, did not want her sister to see her linger with the landlord. She nodded a goodbye to Jack and, leaving him sitting on a box, walked over to her sister. She linked an arm through Isobel's and, before her sister had time to say a word, wheeled her around and back toward the cottage.

Isobel

Isobel had bought a meat pie from a butcher's on Wyndham Street—an extravagance—and it now warmed on the stove. She had kept it in her carpet bag, wrapped in newspaper, sitting on top of the mending. She had been careful on her walk back from Queen Street, holding the bag the way she might a child—cautiously, as though it might break apart in her hands. She didn't want to swing it and spill gravy and juices over the bundle of shirts and aprons collected from the stone houses; she had winced at the thought of such a disaster. One housekeeper, meeting her in the kitchens of a widowed ironmonger's house near to the junction of Queen and Wyndham, had offered a few crumbs of praise when handing that week's sewing over—the master had been pleased with the tiny, almost invisible mending of a favourite shirt. If Isobel kept it up, the housekeeper would put in a good word for her at the governor's mansion, *where she knew people.* She had muttered the words conspiratorially to Isobel, winking so grotesquely that Isobel had wanted to slap her face. Still, it was a remarkable opportunity. To return tablecloths and dress shirts that had been stained by gravy would be unthinkable, and put an end to any thought of working for the governor's wife.

But Isobel had nearly dropped the bag when she saw her sister talking to Jack Bellamy—*Jack Bellamy!*—in the courtyard. After discovering that Esther was not in her room, Isobel had gone to look for her, expecting that she had wandered out into the damp Auckland air. Not for Esther, the tight wadding of a closed room. Isobel could not think of her sister without recalling grass on the girl's hair or dirt on her shoes.

She wondered what Jack Bellamy had told her. If he had asked for rent.

But these were questions she could not ask, not when Esther sat in the one armchair reading newspaper strips lining the wall, while Isobel peeled a kumara and a few carrots. How had Isobel described the wallpaper in her imagined townhouse in her letters home, letters her younger sister read after their mother? Pale blue and yellow, almost satiny to touch. Blunt knife in hand, bent over the table, Isobel cringed.

The light was fading outside and Isobel lit the one gas lamp. Esther made a little sigh as the light fell over her face.

'Tired?' Isobel looked up from preparing the meal. 'I expect you are.'

'It's not that.' The yellow film of light sallowed Esther's skin, ageing her. She brushed the hair from her face and Isobel saw the skin around their father's ring, on the third finger of Esther's right hand, was swollen. 'I need something to do. I feel agitated. I can't sit here, waiting for—I don't know—*something*.'

'Brendan will be home soon, I expect.' Isobel finished with the last carrot and put a pot on the stove to boil. 'There'll be much to talk about then.'

'Has he changed in ten years?'

'Well ...' Isobel paused. 'I don't know.' The tight way he spoke to her, the pinch of his lips whenever she mentioned money or work ... she couldn't remember when he'd started to hate her, but it seemed like forever. Maybe he always had. 'You'll have to judge, I suppose.'

'What about your mending? Can I help with that?'

Isobel felt her cheeks pink. She had not said what was in her bag, or where she had been. A small part of her hoped that Hilda Riley and the other women had kept her secret. She had thought about telling her sister she had gone for a walk in Albert Park, and that she would take Esther there to see the fountain and Victoria's statue. But a voice, one that whispered defiantly in her ear as she walked up and down the 'right side' of Queen Street—the side with large houses and palm trees—told her there was nothing to be ashamed of in sewing other people's clothes. The voice whispered that life was what you made of it out here; as long as you were prepared to work, there was bread and sometimes a little mutton. Isobel had allowed the voice to deepen as she tapped on the servants' entrances along Queen Street, each mark in her pocket book upon receipt of clothing a new weight to her certainty.

She had come back to the house on George Street, determination expanding in her chest. She would tell Esther what it was really like out here. That no one thought ill of women looking for work—at least, not anyone Isobel knew. That in New Zealand women built homes with their bare hands and, in the back country, ran farms and homesteads, sometimes alone for weeks. And that there was a growing swell and push for women to be given the vote—that Isobel went along to meetings at the Temperance Union and listened to women talk about suffrage and the repeal of certain laws that were so unfair, so transgressive, that it made Isobel shudder to think about them.

Except Isobel found Esther sitting with Jack Bellamy, to whom she owed two months' rent, and she said none of those things. The words dried up on her tongue, burning her gums with unspokenness.

'Don't trouble yourself with my mending, dear,' she said quietly. 'I'll do it tonight, after dinner. Don't you have sewing of your own? Things to get ready?'

It was Esther's turn to look away, facing the door. She clasped her hands together. And then Brendan—of all people—saved the moment by turning the key in the door and entering the house, scuffed leather satchel in one hand, creased newspaper in the other.

∞

Brendan had shed flesh in the last ten years. As her husband slimmed, Isobel had taken in his shirts, and from his one good coat had managed to remove a panel of fabric so that the garment fell

about his waist and hugged his frame, just like the coats of the mon-
eyed who worked at the Bank of New Zealand, which was *definitely*
on the right side of Queen Street. Brendan's new shape suited him.
Prolonged periods on sparse rations had stripped the meat from his
English bones and, looking up as he stepped into the room, Isobel
saw him with new eyes. Taller than she, skin browned by the sun,
dressed in office clothes, Brendan was a confusing mix of labourer
and gentleman. A cat in a tiger skin, Isobel thought. A web of red
veins broke through the skin on his cheeks, and there was a slight
tremor to his hands when he dropped his bag and greeted Esther.

'Brendan.' Esther dipped her head in a curious movement. For a
second Isobel thought her sister would curtsey and a laugh bubbled
in her throat. *Stop it, Esther! Don't you remember how you used to
pull Bren's hair and climb on his back, those days he came courting to
our kitchen?*

Brendan took Esther's hand and shook it carefully, his lips pursed
in a way that an observer, other than his wife, might think of as a
touching constraint of emotion or an attempt to hold back tears.
Isobel saw something different, though, and knew with ugly certainty that her husband had been at a bar before coming home.

'We've been looking out for your ship for the past few days,'
Brendan said, slapping the newspaper down on the table and glancing at Isobel. 'One is never able to be certain about shipping matters
and when these new steamers might make their appearance. Did
you have a smooth crossing?'

The banal questions of a hotelier or barman, waiting to catch new
chums just on shore, eager to mop up their easy, naïve coin. Isobel
knew exactly where Brendan had picked up his easy patter. She
imagined him drinking words down along with the slop in his glass.

Esther, though, nodded and offered a small smile. 'I did, thank
you. But I was glad to get here. And thank you, Brendan, for letting
me stay.'

She had said exactly the right thing, Isobel saw. Brendan's lips
became fuller and he grinned back. 'That's quite all right!' A gust of

warm beer flowed throughout the room. 'When your mother wrote to say you were in a bit of a fix, Isobel and I immediately saw the logic in her proposal that you come out here.'

'Shall we sit?' Isobel asked in a hurry. She could not bear to talk about home and Esther's reasons for coming out, not with her husband full of beer and secret mending in her bag. 'I bought a pie from Gregory's—I know, I know'—a hand out to repel the look on Brendan's face—'it is a treat. A celebration of my sister, *our* sister, coming to live with us.'

Brendan fixed his wife with a hard stare but said nothing. He accepted a chair and watched Isobel motion Esther to the other seat before she dragged Esther's trunk over to sit on.

It was an excellent pie. They ate quickly and silently, Brendan making small grunts of approval. Isobel cleared her own plate and watched surreptitiously to see how Esther fared, gladdened by her sister's appetite. Esther ate it all, even a sliver of burnt crust. When they had finished, Brendan pushed his chair back and lit a pipe.

'A treat, as Isobel said. I suppose that's one thing you'll notice as you settle here.' He pointed his pipe at their plates. 'We're never short of mutton.'

'Mother has taken on a dairy back home,' Esther said. 'Ewes cheese sells well.'

'Mother has a dairy?' Isobel turned from the sideboard, where she was gathering the dishes.

'Well, she owns it. One of the men manages it.'

'I see.' Isobel shifted so that Esther could not see her face. Her tongue felt clamped to the roof of her mouth. Her mother had revealed none of these changes in her letters. What had Esther said earlier—that Mother's cousin had died and passed mining stock to her? The letters between them mentioned nothing. Isobel's hand stilled as she stacked the plates. She thought of her mother's spare words, the monotone voice that filled Isobel's head when she read. Mother wrote of marriages and births in the village, of course, and of visitors to the house. But nothing of the life behind such names, nothing of the wet sky that blighted a wedding or the curses of a birthing woman that could be heard all over the village. These were the gobs of currency that gave stories their flesh; Isobel remembered how her mother relished the telling of such tales, how she would repeat them in the kitchen or as they sewed in the parlour. 'The thatcher's new wife fell over on her way back from town, the split of her arse on show!' Isobel recalled her mother folding herself over, squealing at the tale, drunk with glee. And now, in her letters, there were no word-pictures of the thatcher's young wife caught tupping the colliery stallman.

It was possible, Isobel thought, taking the dishes out to the tap in the courtyard, it was possible that her mother's silence prompted her to fill her own letters with fancies and lies. That her mother's reticence and disapproval of Isobel's marriage created a space into which Isobel poured her daydreams. Into the gap created by her mother's reserve, Isobel wove tales of a townhouse with satin wallpaper. She painted Brendan into a job that required him to wear a top hat. Auckland, in her letters, was a city of pulse and push. Emigrants arrived, picked up their bags and made their fortunes. Streets were lit by gas, parks with statues of the queen gleamed like emeralds in the whorls and patterns of housing. Take a walk up to the top of Mount Eden, and any Aucklander could see across the harbour and shout a hello to the other side of the world.

'You'll wash the pattern on that plate clean away.' A soft voice at her elbow and Isobel turned around. It was Rachel Speedy, the eldest of Isobel's neighbours. Isobel smiled. She liked Rachel. The woman was gentle and had a mild way of speaking. Listening to her was like holding a mug of warm milk against the chest. Rachel had mud on her boots and carried a sack in one hand.

'I've been fishing at the foreshore,' Rachel said. 'Never forgotten how to do it, and it's saved me from a mighty pickle many a time. That's the truth.' Rachel pulled over a broken chair and placed the sack down on top. She pulled out a fat silver fish with black stripes. 'Parore. Caught a few. Want some?'

'That's very kind, Rachel, but, I ...'

'Don't want nothing for it. Besides, you darned my stockings for me just last week. It's the way things work round here, girl. Ain't you learned that yet?' Rachel handed her the fish and Isobel took it awkwardly, slippery in her hands like a newborn. 'Flesh is a bit tasteless so put plenty of pepper with it. Head is good for soup.'

'Thank you, Rachel.'

'Welcome.' Rachel wiped her hands on her skirt. Beyond the courtyard, the abattoir groaned and crashed, curses of men and the shrill pitch of an animal reaching up into the sky. Auckland gathered itself to shout again. Black clouds pooled together and there was the taste of a storm in the air. Static seemed to zip around the little courtyard while the women stood with fish in their hands.

'I'd best get inside,' Isobel said finally. Yet she found her body heavy to move. She wanted to speak more to Rachel, the rare, quiet woman with the sack of parore, who seemed to carry an air about her—not of contentment, exactly, nor of ease. That never really came to settlers born in the old country. Isobel had been in New Zealand long enough to understand it herself. It was impossible to experience true contentment in a land constantly held up against a memory, in a land pulled in on itself so that a man or woman might be reminded of a street or house from their English childhood. Public gardens were built, but not to celebrate what grew naturally in New Zealand. Instead they were populated with English plants and ferns that never properly took and had to be replaced, an ongoing replenishment of life.

Rachel seemed to sense Isobel wanted to talk. 'Your sister is in a tight spot, isn't she?' she said, speaking effortlessly, in that way of hers. 'It's not obvious—not like Felicia who lives in one of the cottages further down the road. Have you seen her recently? She must only be weeks away. I thought I saw the beginnings of it on Esther.'

It was bound to be spoken about, Isobel told herself, but the smoothness of Rachel's words and the ease with which Esther's secret was prised open made her chest hurt. She had looked for signs when

Esther landed, hating herself a little for pulling back when they first embraced, the hardness of her sister's stomach an unwelcome shock. Isobel set the fish down next to the water pump.

'You saw what you saw, Rachel. It's true. She's about four months along, I think.'

Rachel sighed. 'No man?'

'Not to speak of. Esther made some bad decisions.'

Rachel raised her eyebrows quizzically. 'Well, this is the place for straightening things out. It doesn't have to matter what baggage you come out with, not if you want to start again. But, Bella, how can having a child be a bad decision?'

'It isn't simple, even out here,' Isobel said. She thought of young Sally, her neighbour, and the men who occasionally came to call. More than once, Isobel had sat up rigid in bed, trying to close her ears to the low moan and bang of thighs in the room next door. Sometimes her eyes would stray to Brendan's snoring form beside her, the old longing creeping back into her stomach and between her legs. But envy would evaporate in the mornings when she saw Sally's bruised, tight face and the anxious way the girl ran back and forth to the latrine when her time of the month came around. So far, Isobel didn't think the girl had been caught out.

'New Zealand might give her the answers,' Rachel said. 'It did for me.'

'Were you …?'

'Lost the baby on the boat. Alfred and I weren't married but we planned to. Didn't seem important to wait and babies come along when they feel like it.' Rachel smiled sadly. 'Took us five children to have our two boys. Not one of them felt like a bad decision.'

'I'm sorry, Rachel, I didn't mean …'

Rachel waved a hand. 'We've never spoken of it, have we? There won't be a woman among us who hasn't lost a child in some form or another. Look at Rose who has the twins. She hasn't the money to keep all of hers now her husband took off—the eldest was sent to the industrial school just last month.'

Isobel gasped. 'That's terrible.'

'It's life, Bella.' Rachel looked around at the dirt on the floor and, unexpectedly, sat down. Thin bones stretched the skin of her neck and Isobel saw brown blotches, betraying the woman's age. She felt a great tenderness for her friend, for this odd pioneer with snake-skin and an easy way of talking.

'You're weary, Rachel.'

'I am, that,' and Rachel sighed. 'You know how it goes in this place. Remember the woman at Onehunga? It was in the paper. Everyone talked about it for weeks. They found her dosing babies with a sleeping draught and letting them die.'

'A wicked thing.'

'This isn't such a wonderful place that such things can't happen. Didn't someone from your Temperance Society discover it all? The sergeant dug up bodies in the garden. Imagine that, Bella. She'd been taking in babies for years. Women couldn't care for them so left them at her house.' Rachel rubbed her face. 'But I've seen women help each other, too. Rose, Hilda, even Helena—we've all taken soup to those on Sale Street who have little ones and no husbands and no money. We can live differently, here, if we want to. It seems to me we would all be happier if we stopped judging each other. There are worse things than being unmarried and having a baby.'

And Isobel, tongue like a stone in her mouth, feeling like she'd failed before she'd even begun, thought of her mother's letter. The letter tucked inside the shawl in Esther's trunk, and how she was not supposed to have read it. And she thought of how she hadn't returned the letter to Esther's trunk, but had hidden it under her mattress, pushed almost to the middle. There it lay; for how long she would hide it, she had no idea.

'I hope you're right, Rachel. I really do.'

Rachel sniffed. The hand she passed across her nose was wet from the fish, the ends of her fingers pointing like jabbing hooks. Isobel had heard the stories about how Rachel had built her own home with her bare hands, collecting driftwood from the beach to act as a roof and building the walls of her house with mud. That was before a storm blew it down. Isobel saw strength in her friend's thin hands, even now.

'There's a change coming,' Rachel was saying. She cleared her throat, her body seeming to make space for what she was about to say. 'Look what's happening in the Legislative—they reckon it will go through this time, don't they, giving us little women the vote? I signed the petition. You didn't need to persuade me when you brought one of your temperance friends round with the papers. What are they saying at your meetings?'

'We're hopeful.'

Rachel slapped her thigh, animated. 'The temperance lot are more determined about the vote than they are about drink, that's what I say. What a thing it would be, to finally have it! Women—us! Voting!'

'There's a long way to go yet, Rachel.' Isobel thought of the faces of the Good Templars just weeks earlier, when the premier, Ballance, had died. Despair dashed their flesh, creasing tired skin with desperation and the worry that their fight for the vote had suffered a terrible blow. Ballance had supported them—who, in the new premier's government, would speak for them now?

'Time has moved on since you lost Ballance,' Rachel said, speaking Isobel's thoughts. 'There seems to be a taste to the air these days. Can't you feel it? It reminds me of what it was like when we first landed in New Zealand, all those years ago. Such wildness, you would not believe—but raw hope. And raw hope has a flavour.' Rachel stuck out her tongue and then laughed. 'A crazy old lady, eh? I need my bed, Bella.'

Isobel helped her up, frowning, thinking what a beautiful oddity Rachel was. She held onto the woman's arm and Rachel leaned back against her.

'Make sure your sister has choices, Bella,' Rachel said. And with that she hauled herself away and disappeared into an alley.

Esther

The weeks passed. Brendan rose from his bed each morning, washed in cold water, and left for work. Esther heard him as she lay in bed behind the curtain, and also heard the small sigh Isobel gave each time her man left the house. It was not just because she was relieved to be free of him for the day, Esther came to quickly realise. Indeed, Brendan was still a presence even when he was not there, for Isobel talked about Brendan from time to time throughout the day; fragile bricks of words, marking out her hope that, maybe, he had found employment at which he could stick. No, Esther thought, lying on her lumpy bed—Isobel sighed out relief that he was gone and hope for what he might do. The look of bewildered pride on Isobel's face when Brendan passed over his first pay one evening made the phlegm catch in Esther's throat.

The sisters fell into a routine. Esther marvelled at the ease of it, how simple it was to share chores and sit with a person from whom she had been separated for ten years. After Brendan had left, Isobel would get up and dress. She would walk along Wellesley Street to the bakers, a coin from Esther's purse pressed into her palm. Esther insisted on fresh bread and, after trying one as a treat, some wraps of pastry stuffed with sweet butter. Isobel had never tasted anything so delicate, not in all her years in New Zealand, and she confessed to Esther that she had begun to look forward to them as much as her sister did.

While she was out, Esther would rise and dress before venturing out into the courtyard to fill the copper kettle. She would light the range and heat water so, by the time Isobel returned, tea would be ready. And it was tea that made Esther's tongue curl with joy; strong and pure, not like the soft tea she was used to. Isobel told her there was a law in New Zealand, banning tea that had been padded out with sawdust or bark. Esther couldn't drink enough, her body craving it. They would share a pot, taking it in turns to pour from their mother's rosebud set.

The teapot was obviously one of Isobel's prized possessions, but Esther struggled to recall seeing it at home before her sister left. She had no memory of her mother using it in her tiny drawing room, where she met the banker and landlords when their father was alive, not later when there was little money and no visitors. And yet Isobel's eyes shone when she poured tea, remarking daily on how carefully she had looked after the pot on their voyage out. Esther began to find her sister's pride unbearable. She could not bring herself to reply, so made small, soothing noises when Isobel spoke, remembering their mother's fury when Isobel left. It was quite possible she had packed Isobel off with a teapot she'd bought from a shop in their market town, purchased for pennies. One day, they were walking past a hotel on their way to Victoria Park, the windows of the bar crammed with items from a house sale. Esther spied a set of sideplates, similar to the rosebud teapot. She bought them for Isobel, shrugging off her objections. They ate breakfast from them every day.

One morning, Esther rose to find her sister out on her walk to the bakers, having left a note on the table. Esther was instructed to brew tea, for Isobel was going to buy them pastries with the pennies leftover from Brendan's pay that week.

After a while, as the day warmed up to itself outside, Esther heard Isobel put her key in the front door. She stood up, waiting to greet her sister. But Isobel lingered in the doorway, her head turned back toward the street. She was talking to someone over her shoulder. Esther craned her neck, trying to see. A man's voice, low but young, and an embarrassed cough. Still Isobel did not look round and Esther saw a crimson flush crawl up her sister's neck, beyond her collar and into her hair. Then the man made a slight movement with his head and Esther saw. It was Jack Bellamy.

Isobel bade goodbye and finally stepped into the room. Her face was ugly in its colour. She did not look at Esther. Whereas Isobel usually bustled in with a greeting, this morning she turned immediately to the stove and started to unwrap the flaky parcels from the bakers.

'Was that Mr Bellamy?' Esther said redundantly, needing to fill the silence. Isobel simply nodded and Esther found the words bursting from her. 'I'm sorry, I should have told you I'd paid your rent. But he caught me, that day—all the women ran away as soon as they knew he was coming, but I didn't know. I didn't know he was your landlord. Isobel, please, I was trying to help.'

Isobel still did not turn around but bowed her head over the range. Esther saw the cords of her sister's spine stand up and she thought of fishbones, white and sharp. Isobel had made stew from fish heads a few nights ago, given to her by a friend, Rachel. Rachel was always giving Isobel fish, and Esther knew her sister felt obliged to cook them. The dish she made was strong and stewed, and had sat warily in Esther's stomach.

She had to speak again, did Esther—such leaking of words shocked her. Her body had become fibrous in recent weeks, catching her out with dampness in all manner of places. It seemed words could not be contained either.

'I really am sorry, Isobel. But two months' rent! I could see you were not likely to be able to pay that, and I had the money. I *have* money, Isobel ...'

'Ah yes, you have money,' Isobel said quietly, finally turning round. 'Money for fancy plates, and the new drapes you keep suggesting, and proper wallpaper.' She wiped her hands on a rag and looked at Esther with such sadness that her sister felt her knees sag. 'Where does that money come from, Esther? From our mother? Maybe. But not all. I can't see Mother making sure you had enough to keep you and the baby comfortable. Her sense of outrage at you being caught out would be too great. Where, then? Who might give you money to make your journey to the other side of the world go easily?'

Esther's mouth fell open a little. She felt her chest prick with heat and shame. She had not had this conversation with Isobel yet, about the father of her child.

'You see, now I have a problem,' Isobel went on. Her colour had faded a little, but the skin around her collar looked mottled. 'Bren knew we were behind on the rent. After all, the money I make from mending does not cover everything and we were waiting for his first pay. Just what am I going to tell him now? That the man who got my sister in the family way has paid for his keep, as well as put food on his table and might even put drapes on his windows?'

Esther gasped. And then she felt angry. Her back ached, her knees felt weak. She had tossed and turned on the packing boxes the night before, the hard ball of her stomach rolling from side to side as she struggled to get comfortable. She had thrown her life into a trunk and left *him* behind, and her sister couldn't even give her a proper bed. She looked around, at the strips of newspaper covering the walls, and fury bubbled over.

'How dare you take such a high tone with me, Isobel! With the lies you've told—a townhouse! A parlour, a flower garden—that's what you said in your letters. Ha! Where are they?'

'Esther …'

'No, there's nothing you can say. It is what it is.' Esther took a long, shaky breath. 'But please don't adopt a superior attitude with me, simply for helping. Even I know you can't rely on Brendan, and who will pay your rent when he walks out of this job?'

Isobel was about to retort, her face aflame again, but Esther gasped and turned white. Her hands fumbled for her belly.

'Esther? What's wrong?'

It wasn't exactly pain, more a rolling kind of ache, but it surprised Esther with its suddenness. So far, apart from unwelcome dampness, the baby had made its presence known only in small ways—a knocking in her stomach, feathering movements that suggested a little secret was hidden away under Esther's clothes. Her body seemed to acknowledge the infant more through its flooding; underwear, soaked at the end of the day, damp circles on her shifts where her breasts had leaked. But the baby itself—that had stayed quiet and peaceful. Now it felt as though the child was turning on its head.

'Sit down,' and Isobel was beside her, hand on Esther's elbow, lowering her into the armchair. She leaned into her sister's face, troubled. 'Does something hurt?'

Esther shook her head and arched her back, stretching out her body. That helped. The baby settled again, not before sending a few kicks into her ribs.

'Tea is what you need.' Isobel nodded emphatically, but Esther could see she didn't really have the slightest clue what to do. Isobel handed her sister a cup and Esther saw the tremble in her fingers.

'Thank you, Isobel. It's passed now. Bigger movements, that's all. They sometimes take my breath away.'

Isobel looked at her, anxiety buried in the lines of her face. She looks older than ever, Esther thought. Is this what New Zealand does to you?

'I am sorry, Isobel,' Esther said. She set down her cup and saucer and caught hold of her sister's fingers. 'I'm sorry I didn't tell you I'd paid your rent. I'm not sorry I did it, not at all. But if you felt embarrassed in front of Mr Bellamy, I apologise.'

Isobel looked down at the fingers wrapped around hers, a sad weight to her mouth. 'He is so young. Jack Bellamy. Did you notice, Esther? Probably not much older than you. Younger than Brendan and I, certainly. Hilda said she'd heard that he had been sent north by his father—there had been some sort of family argument. He's been given a few houses along George Street to manage, to make something of himself.' She sighed. 'Can you imagine what it feels like to owe money to a person so much younger than you? It's awful. But, Esther, what I fear more is that Brendan will think of you as his ticket.'

'What do you mean?'

'I mean that you are the disgraced sister-in-law, taken in as an act of charity—that's how he sees you. And he thinks you are trapped and he might start to think you will simply have to pay all his bills. What if he gives up his job because he thinks you'll pay for our life here?'

'I wouldn't do that. I *couldn't* do that.'

Isobel shook her head. 'Bren gives himself over to temptation far too easily. He doesn't see past the moment.'

Esther sat silently for a moment. She felt the conversation had shifted into an area that, once entered, would be impossible to step back from. She was not a fool, despite what their mother had said that day months ago—she knew about Brendan. The smell from him when he returned from work; a smell that came from a bar, not an office with a desk and ink and paper. The shake of his hands, the lace of veins across his face. They all shouted of enthusiastic hours in the drink. It was a wonder he had stuck at his job at the gas company for the time that he had.

Suddenly Isobel stood up. She pushed her chin outward, in a way that Esther had not seen for a long time, not since landing in the country. Isobel held herself still, and Esther thought of the times they accompanied their father on his walks, when he sought specimens for his drawings. She heard his smoky whisper—'Hush Esther! Down, Isobel!'—and she was back in a memory, crouching down in the grass and brush, out of sight of a hare or a kite. 'Tell every muscle in your body to stay as still as night,' their father used to breathe, one of his favourite phrases Esther found herself repeating after he died. *As still as night, as still as night.* But the girls would dutifully tighten their limbs and become rigid statues. Father would, silently, pull out a notebook and sketch and, when the animal or bird had finally taken off, he would tap them gently on the head. 'Well done, girls. Keeping still is the surest way of seeing.'

Isobel was always better at keeping still. Esther could do it for only moments before her arms and legs became filled with restlessness. She watched, now, as Isobel tightened herself up. A decision had been made, Esther saw.

'We won't tell Brendan,' Isobel said. 'That's what we'll do—we won't tell him. I'll have to speak to Jack Bellamy and ask him not to say anything to Bren, either.'

'I would like to help you, Isobel,' Esther said. She folded her arms under her stomach, still aching a little. 'The bed you made for me—well, it won't do for much longer. I'm getting bigger now and I can't rest so easily on it. Might we buy a frame and a mattress?'

'Those things are expensive.'

'But, still.'

'What about Bren? Rent is one thing, and no one can complain about the better food. But a new bed? He'll have something to say about that.'

Esther felt a small flame of anger; that she should sleep on a box to protect her brother-in-law's pride! But there was Isobel. 'Tell him ...' Esther cast about the room. She spotted the bag of mending next to Isobel's bed. 'Tell him I've started to help you with your sewing and saved up to buy a bed. He'll believe that. And it doesn't have to be a lie—I *could* help you. I learned to sew while you were away, if you can believe it.'

'I *can't* believe it.'

'Who else would do it after you'd gone? I'm good, too, especially at repairs. Let me help you.'

Isobel sighed. 'If you like. But what about your own things? You need to start sewing for the baby.'

'I know.' But the truth was, Esther didn't really know. The gaps in her knowledge about what a baby needed panicked her at times, whenever she allowed herself to think far enough ahead. She was as helpless as Isobel, she realised. Mother had had no more babies after her; Esther was the youngest. No younger brothers or sisters to dress or feed or run after with a damp cloth.

After she was certain that a baby was coming, that spring day when the wind shuttled around the house torn between two counties, Esther had taken the weather under her skin and paced the floorboards in the room above the kitchen. Bubbling, roaring acid in her stomach seemed to travel to her legs and her thighs burned. She wanted to run, she wanted to lift her body up into the sky and flap, bird-like, to a place a hundred miles away where her secret could grow without judgment or shame. She didn't know the first thing about babies. She knew how to get them, of course—her mother had taught her that—but didn't know how to stop them coming.

'There's plenty of time to get things ready for the baby,' she said. She stood up and poured more tea. 'I'm so hungry, Isobel. Shall we eat? And then we can take a walk along Queen Street and see what mending we can find.'

❧

After they had eaten, Isobel insisted on clearing away and washing the dishes. She shooed Esther back into the armchair, pausing to smooth down a strand of her sister's red hair. 'Father had red hair, you know,' Isobel said, and smiled in such a way that Esther felt a throb around her heart.

'I only remember him bald.'

'He was nearly bald when you were born, but I remember how thick it used to be. He used to let me cut it.' Isobel touched Esther's head. 'You have the same crown. There, to the side. Yes, almost the same colour as his. I remember being tiny and sitting on his shoulders and pulling it. I was cruel, but he never complained.'

'I can't believe you were ever cruel, Isobel.'

Isobel sniffed. 'I'll wash the dishes. We'll take a walk after.'

It had rained through the night and the ground was steaming when they left the house on George Street. Sun pressed down, and clouds seeped from banks of earth from where carts had struggled through and churned mud into mounds. Isobel closed and locked the front door and turned to face her sister.

'Shall we walk to the temperance meeting house on the way?'

'If you like, Isobel.'

'It's across the street from the gas company where Brendan works.' Isobel now looked at the ground and Esther was struck by the memory of the time her sister first brought Brendan home to their mother's house. The shy, furiously proud look on Isobel's face when she showed him into the kitchen, and the way she folded her bottom lip under her teeth when introducing him to their mother. Esther felt a rush of love for her sister, glaring at the sodden earth beneath their feet, and wondered how many jobs Brendan had had over the past ten years. How many times had Isobel forced her feet to the doorsteps of the well-to-do on Queen Street?

'It would be interesting to see where Brendan works,' Esther said, hoping her voice sounded kind. 'You must be proud of him.'

Isobel swung her bag of mending into the crease of her elbow. She offered her empty arm to Esther and, limbs locked together, the sisters set off through the maze of brown streets into the roar of the city.

The blue of Freeman's Bay blinked from the west as the sisters picked their way along Wellington Street. Esther felt the water's presence as they walked, a shadow in the distance. The ebb and roll of the emigrant ship was still fresh in her mind. And now the water banked around her, around Auckland, and she felt the lines of her body pushed and breached.

And yet, and yet—the sea of Auckland felt different. It was not like a sea Esther had ever known. The water seemed to neither encroach nor retreat—an odd observance, Esther knew, remembering Rachel Speedy's words about a storm destroying her house. But that's how it felt to her. It seemed as though the water of the bay held itself back patiently. Esther strained to see the boats and steamers, a fluttering beneath her waistband.

'Do you remember when Father took us to Grimsby?' she asked. They were passing a dairy and Isobel was looking up at the advertising signs, painted red and green. Metal urns were propped against the wooden building and baskets of cheese wrapped in wax paper rested on a table.

'Grimsby? What made you think of that?' Isobel dropped her mending bag and dipped her hand into her pocket, pulling out a purse. 'Would you like a little cheese for supper? Rachel says this dairy is one of the best. It might not be as good as the cheese Mother produces in her dairy, but still …' Isobel's lips thinned and Esther could see she was angry at the thought of Mother's dairy.

'If you like.' She looked away, seeking the harbour, but the view was obscured by Waite's Dairy. Beyond the store, on the slope down to the water, stood hundreds of huts and cottages. Churches and larger, grander buildings jostled for space on land closest to the quayside. Auckland was a pitted mass of green and brown, supplanted industry fighting for space with trees and bush. And still the water hung back.

Isobel paid the moustached storekeeper and made an arrangement to collect the cheese on their way back from Queen Street. 'I do remember Grimsby,' she said, looping Esther's arm through her own again. 'We went to see Father's Aunt Maud.'

Esther shuddered, remembering an old woman with sour milk for breath and hair on her top lip. The aunt's house had been a mile from the port—a grey terrace among many like it. But the smell … a salty, brackish odour that clung to the furniture and the curtains. The weight of Grimsby's fishing industry and the taste of it on glasses and forks had twisted Esther's young stomach, and she'd been unable to eat Aunt Maud's cake, despite her father's apologetic embarrassment.

They were nearing the end of Wellington Road. Ahead, the street separated and Isobel guided Esther to the left, down another gnarled track. A painted wooden sign hammered into the ground announced they had entered Pitt Street. A large stone building looked at the end of the road, its ornate window frames and solid brickwork incongruous with the timid-looking shacks surrounding it.

Isobel pointed at it. 'The offices of the gas company. That's where Bren works.'

As before, she glanced away and Esther saw her sister's mouth fight for control. The building faced out on all sides of the street, sheets of glass blinking solemnly, benevolent and all-seeing. Somewhere in that body of stone sat Brendan. Esther pictured him behind a desk, fingertips wet with ink, ledgers open in front of him. He would be wearing his red cravat, the one into which he sweated as the day wore on. Esther had helped Isobel with the washing one day, and the dampness of Brendan's neck tie when she picked it up had brought her small breakfast back into her throat.

They approached the building, Isobel's arm twitching against her sister's body. For a moment Esther thought Isobel had changed her mind—that they were no longer going to the temperance building but were going to the gas company, to see Brendan, to check he was there and really working. But Isobel pointed to a simple wooden building, directly opposite the gas company's offices. 'The Methodist Church,' she said. 'Where the Templars meet.'

The proximity of the two buildings was jarring. Only a few dozen feet separated the church, where temperance was preached, and the building where Brendan worked and counted down the hours until he could run to the bar. Esther wondered if her brother-in-law had even registered what was yards from his desk; if he ever looked out of one of the windows overlooking Pitt Street and gazed down at the church, or if he heard the hymns and prayers.

Isobel led them inside the small wooden church. Thin strips of glass ran along the walls and let in light but the belly of the church was in gloom. Esther squinted, making out pews crammed in together, barely any legroom between them. Simple framed prints lined the walls between the narrow windows, and at the far end of the room stood an altar, decorated with purple flowers, the type of which Esther had not seen before. There was a door to the right of the altar. Esther heard a low murmuring as Isobel led her down the aisle.

The door opened out into a small room. A table stood in the centre, topped with what appeared to be an intricate tablecloth, against which a woman stood with a child of about five years in her arms. They were talking, girl child and woman, and the woman was pointing at the table. She looked around as Isobel and Esther entered the room and lowered the girl quickly to the floor.

'Bella! It's been over a week! And is this she, the sister who has kept you from us?'

Bella. That name again. Esther watched as the woman embraced her sister, throwing her arms up and exposing patches of different fabric under her arms. The hem of the woman's skirt also did not match the rest of the garment. Her hair was wildly pinned. But Isobel hugged the woman back and then dropped down to gather the child into her arms.

'Miss Dottie. It is good to see the colour in your cheeks again,' Isobel said, and the girl smiled bashfully, ducking behind the woman's skirts.

'She's much better, Bella,' the woman said. 'Stewart thought we'd have to send for the doctor, but the fever broke and she slept for two days. And is now back to the Dottie we know so well.' She smoothed a hand along the girl's cheek and, with an abruptness that startled Esther, turned around to face her. 'Bella has told me all about you. I am Elizabeth Ellis. Oh!' And the woman put her hand to her mouth and blushed.

'Not Ellis, Mama,' the girl hissed, and Isobel laughed. Another staggering thing, Esther thought. She hadn't heard Isobel laugh so easily since she arrived.

'Elizabeth keeps forgetting she remarried,' Isobel explained. 'She's now Mrs Peter.'

'I'm still not used to it,' Elizabeth said apologetically. She smiled at Isobel, a sad passing of understanding, and Esther felt excluded. 'And you're Esther.'

'I am.' But Esther felt unsure for a second, giddy at swirl of feelings.

'You must sit down and have tea. Please.' Elizabeth turned back to the table and picked up the edges of the tablecloth, which Esther could see, now she was nearer, was not a tablecloth at all. It was a map, a huge one. A spider's web of streets and tiny writing threaded over the paper.

'Is that a map of Auckland?' Esther asked.

'It is. Dottie, will you fetch the tea cups, my sweet?' Elizabeth folded the map over, clearing the table and making space. 'Best to keep this out the way—imagine if we spilled on it!'

Dottie laughed, a twinkly sound, and Esther saw the round apple of her face and the thick curls bouncing on her shoulders. She wondered if Elizabeth tied the girl's hair in rags at bedtime, and imagined quick hands working through the locks.

Elizabeth had now moved to a stove in the corner and was setting a light under a tin kettle. 'We're going to struggle to collate all the signatures before Kate needs them. All the Templars are out gathering them now. Some have been up since dawn.'

'They came to George Street last month,' Isobel said. 'I took them around the cottages.'

'Did everyone sign?'

'Of course.'

Esther watched as Dottie brought the tea cups over, the girl pouting with concentration as she placed cups on top of saucers. 'You did that very well,' she offered to the child, astonished to feel an urge to pull the girl into an embrace. She breathed deeply, the zip and tremble of her body difficult to fathom.

Isobel pulled over some chairs and they sat. Elizabeth poured water onto the tea leaves, but became distracted and started scribbling on a piece of paper, leaving the tea to steep in the pot. Isobel smiled and shook her head, and served the tea herself. Esther wondered again at the ease of her sister in this room. Isobel, the girl she remembered moving awkwardly around their mother's kitchen, reluctant to go calling at the houses of her mother's friends. Esther wondered what this land had done to her sister over the past ten years.

'What is the map for?' she asked when Elizabeth had put down her stub of pencil. The woman's nose flared and Dottie giggled.

'You haven't told her?' Elizabeth asked Isobel. 'Oh, Esther, what a time for you to come to our land!'

'We are gathering a petition,' Isobel said. A smile curled at the corner of her lips and she lifted her chin slightly. 'Members of the

Temperance Union are gathering signatures, which we'll parcel up and send to Kate Sheppard in Christchurch.'

'*We are?*' Esther turned the words into a question. Her feeling of astonishment deepened. Isobel was working on a petition? 'A petition for what?'

'The vote!' Elizabeth Peter's hands flew like birds and she gestured to the map. 'We're walking every street in Auckland, asking women to sign.'

'The Temperance Union down in Christchurch are gluing the sheets together,' Isobel added. 'It's said that when they've finished, the roll could reach the sea from the far end of Queen Street.'

Esther thought of water again, of the silent, sallow roll of blue and green; the careful, watchful way the sea seemed to hug the coastline. What a land this was. 'You're petitioning for women?'

'Votes for women!' Dottie sat up straight on her chair and shouted, giving a gap-toothed grin as Elizabeth and Isobel clapped. Elizabeth scooped the child up and held her to her breast.

'You are my sweet darling,' she said and buried her face extravagantly into the child's neck. Esther watched, enthralled.

'Do you really think a petition will bring you the vote?' she asked after Elizabeth had returned the child to her chair.

'Oh, yes.' Elizabeth nodded emphatically. 'We're on the cusp of a great moment, we all believe that. Women *will* have a voice in this country. Just think—the first boats were filled with women who helped build this country. Women have cleared bush and hammered timber alongside their menfolk in order to put a roof over the heads of their children. They've worked with men in settling this earth. Finally, we'll have a say in how our society should be run.'

'It's real,' Isobel said quietly, oddly. 'New Zealand will let this happen.'

'It will be like—oh, I don't suppose I'll ever really know, but I expect it will be like a birth,' Elizabeth said. Like Isobel, her skin shone. 'The birth of a new nation—*our* nation.'

Confused, bewildered by the passion the women felt, Esther

stared at Elizabeth. What did she mean, she'd never know what a birth felt like? She has her own child sitting next to her! And what of Isobel and her unexpected role in all of this? Esther shook her head, marvelling. In her belly, her secret rolled and flopped, and then settled again.

Isobel

The day was getting away from them. Elizabeth talked some more about the streets the Templars had yet to cover and Isobel saw her sister tire. She had expected it; Elizabeth could be wearying for even the most energetic of her friends, but those in Esther's condition could not expect to keep up with the woman's vitality for long. Even in grief, Elizabeth did not keep still, and Isobel thought back to that time when Elizabeth was had stumbled into the church after her discovery at the house at Onehunga. The dead babies, the ones Rachel remembered. Isobel had sat beside her friend as Elizabeth wept and talked about the one baby who had lived. Elizabeth had rubbed her hands over her skirt constantly as she talked, oblivious to the shocked faces around her, jabbing at the fabric, as though she were trying to push the memories away from her body.

Light streamed through the window into the room, announcing the afternoon. They had yet to reach Queen Street. 'We should go now,' Isobel said, and pulled Esther gently to her feet. Esther's jacket flared open at the waist. The bulge of her stomach was apparent and Isobel saw a stricken look pass over her sister's face.

But Elizabeth could have moments of gentleness, alongside the surge and motion of her unquiet limbs. She stood up too. Dottie had gone to play on the carpet with a flaxen-haired doll.

Elizabeth spoke softly. 'Having a child doesn't have to be frightening.'

'Is it so obvious?' Esther asked. Her eyes shone. Isobel slipped her hand under Esther's palm.

'I think we make it so women don't feel as though they have the right to want their child,' Elizabeth Peter said. 'It's terrible—feeling desperate is terrible. It leads to sinful decisions.'

Isobel saw the crease of her friend's brow and knew Elizabeth was back in the house in Onehunga. Elizabeth had gulped down cup after cup of sweet tea after making it back to the church that day. If one of the men had had their pipe, Isobel was sure Elizabeth would have smoked it, and been glad of it. Instead, Isobel had refilled Elizabeth's cup and given her cake; helpless acts those at the church clung to as the horror of the story seeped out. Babies were found buried in the garden and swaddled in an upstairs room, and the newspapers spoke of a trunk, full of trinkets and letters left by mothers. The woman of the house had taken an overdose of a sleeping draught—the *Herald* said it was the same draught she'd used on the children which, if true, seemed to Isobel to add a sorrowful, sensational twist to the story.

'I have no husband,' Esther said.

'I had no husband when I took in Dottie.' Elizabeth smiled, but her eyes were wet. 'My husband had died in England, as well as our baby. I left them there, buried under an oak tree—and do you know, I cannot for the life of me remember the name of the churchyard. They were buried near to my husband's family, you see.'

'I'm sorry.'

Elizabeth's face was serene. 'I had nothing when I came out to New Zealand, and then I found the Templars, and then I found Dottie. She had no one either, and then we had each other. You have more than I, Esther—you have your sister, and you're young—you have the strength of your body and your mind.'

Isobel thought of white paper, a flow of familiar writing. Her mother's letter—that she should not have read—was still hidden under the mattress. Isobel blinked the thoughts away and made herself speak. 'Of *course* she has me. I'll see her through this.'

Esther looked away, not comforted, and Isobel saw her unease and how much her sister wanted to run away. Esther was more like Elizabeth than she realised.

Rebecca Burns

'What if ...' Esther began, her lips folding into themselves, 'what if, after all this, the baby ... something happens to it? After coming here, being thrown out of my home by my mother, after the man ... I should have stopped it, I know that. I was foolish. What if, after all that, the baby doesn't live—what then?'

Elizabeth looked over her shoulder at Dottie. 'You can save each other, your child and you. Dottie wasn't meant to be here either. But we found each other.'

It was then that Isobel became unaccountably sure of something she had always suspected. Dottie was the child who had survived at Onehunga. She had never asked Elizabeth about Dottie's true parents, but she knew now with certainty. Elizabeth had taken the baby in.

Esther seemed on the verge of tears and the thought of her sister crying was weighty and awful, so Isobel said a hurried farewell and steered Esther back through the church and into the glare of sunlight on the street outside. Esther seemed dazed. Shouts and bangs from the docks washed over them, carts rattled along Karangahape Road nearby. The church had been a cocoon from the thrum of Auckland life, the noise of the city folding over the building in a way that was comforting. But now Isobel and Esther were back in the midst of life. Isobel tucked Esther's arm under her own and led her to the end of Pitt Street, where they turned, briefly, onto Karangahape Road. Housewives and shop boys on bicycles scurried between draper's shops and bakers, and the sisters paused to let a man by with a box of boots, all with heels flapping like drunken tongues. They watched as he disappeared into a bootmaker's store and then waited again to cross at the intersection leading onto Queen Street.

The cemetery at Symonds Street spilled over onto the Queen Street side and, as they watched for a lull in the cars and buggies passing by, Isobel looked out at the graves. A few cypress trees and shrubs obscured the view, affording the dead some privacy. A dry stone wall acted as a boundary between the living and the dead, though Isobel heard from maids handing over their mistresses' mending on Lower Symonds Street that there had been trouble with cemetery water draining into the domestic supply. Isobel had had trouble eating dinner the night she was told that, fish soup lying bitterly in her mouth. Rachel Speedy's husband was lying out there, somewhere.

And then they were on Queen Street. They passed the stables on the corner just as a cabbie hauled his carriage into the stable courtyard and yelled for his animal. Further along, large painted houses were set back from the road. Ornate wooden staircases led away from the street and up to the entrance porch. Pots of roses and pink camellias stood at strategic points, balconies opened out from first floor bedrooms. Isobel heard Esther gasp as they walked, knowing her sister was shocked at the contrast between these houses and the one-roomed shack on George Street.

'Just a little further and we'll get to our first stop,' Isobel said.

'Who lives here?' Esther asked, coming to a stop a few paces later. The house she stared at was the grandest yet; three storeys, brilliant white in the afternoon sun. A thick green lawn was wrapped smugly around the house like a cat. Isobel was fearful of setting foot on such velvetiness whenever she visited the house, and always jumped onto a small, hidden path leading to the rear.

'It belongs to a music teacher,' she said. She opened her bag and rummaged for the mending—several shirts with replaced buttons and new, monogrammed breast pockets. 'A German, I believe, though I've never spoken to him. The kitchen staff tell me he teaches the governor's daughter and the children of others in the Legislative.'

'He must be doing well for himself,' Esther muttered.

Isobel hummed. 'I daresay he is. Would you wait here while I take these to the kitchen? It's where the housekeeper prefers to see me.'

'Couldn't have you marching up to the front door, eh?' Esther nodded. 'Will I not come with you, though?'

Inwardly Isobel winced, and hesitated before speaking. Elizabeth had seen the evidence of Esther's body; the maids would too. 'I think you should stay here, Esther. I won't be long.'

Esther smiled ruefully. 'You're ashamed. I know you are. It's all right, Isobel.'

'I'm sorry, Esther.' Isobel felt a pain in her chest and tears gathered in her throat. 'But you don't wear a wedding band and the girls will ask and …'

'It's all right, Isobel,' Esther said again. Her face had pinked, but to Isobel she looked more beautiful than ever. A strand of red hair had come loose and it flapped wildly in the wind. Esther made no attempt to hide it away. 'You wouldn't want to write home to Mother about a scene, would you? I can't imagine she'd like to hear of a scandal in your townhouse.'

Her words stung and Isobel had to turn away. She followed the gravel path round the back of the house to where it dipped down and led to a set of stone steps, a plain wooden door at the bottom. She knocked and a young girl, duster in hand and a weary shine to her skin, answered.

'I've brought the mending, miss,' Isobel said. She held out the packet of shirts, wrapped in brown paper. 'For the master.'

'Wait here, please.' The girl took the packet and closed the door again and Isobel stepped back. Some maids were friendlier and let her wait inside while the housekeeper was fetched. One kitchen, on Lower Symonds Street, even welcomed her with a cup of tea every time she came through, but since overhearing the maids speaking about cemetery water getting into their supply, Isobel hadn't liked to take it. This house was run differently and Isobel adopted a demure, patient look as she waited, suspecting that the housekeeper was peering out of an upstairs window into the garden and watching her.

After a short while the maid returned and handed over an envelope of coins. 'The missus was pleased with the job, thank you,' she said. Her accent was thick and Irish, and Isobel had to listen carefully. 'Will you be able to take some more next week?'

'Shirts or something else?'

'Dresses, probably.' The maid was new enough to roll her eyes, unreserved scorn seeping from her. 'There's another ball at the Governor's House, so the missus and girls will need their dresses taken in. Or let out. They eat so many cakes.'

Isobel smiled. Now able to look at the maid for more than a few seconds, she could see that the girl was older than she first thought. She hadn't seen her before—the friendly kitchen who gave her tea was also free with gossip, and Isobel knew that maids were difficult to keep. Many stayed with a family for a few months and then married, setting up their own home or striking out for the South Island in the hope of buying a strip of land.

'You're new here?' she asked.

'Docked a few weeks ago with my brothers.' The maid glanced over her shoulder, but seemed reassured that she had a few moments to talk. 'One of them got a place at Partington's Windmill, just along the street. The other is at a timber mill in the Coromandel, somewhere. My eldest brother found work as a miner in Otago.'

'Scattered to the four winds already,' Isobel said. She felt sad for the girl. New Zealand was a wide space, threaded together by only the thinnest of telegraph wires or men on horses delivering mail. Families were stretched like cobwebs over such vastness. 'Do your brothers write?'

'My Otago brother does,' the maid said. 'Not Bertie, who's at the timber mill. Never took to writing, even though our father tried to thrash learning into him. I see Liam once a month. He's the one at the windmill. We go for a walk at Albert Park and feed the ducks. He has a terrible cough all the time, from the flour.'

'It must be different from home,' Isobel said.

'It is.' The girl sighed. 'At home we had three rooms and we lived on top of each other, with my parents. Sure, I share a room here with another girl here, but there's more space. It's not the same. I can't imagine when my brothers and I will be back together again.' She bit her lip and looked past Isobel, toward the dark stone steps leading back into the garden.

Isobel's sympathy deepened; ten years in New Zealand had not done much to dampen the ache for family, for those who shared her blood. Even with a mother like hers, she still felt sorrow at the distance between them. The chance of a better life in a new land came with a severing with the past. Isobel had seen how, for some, the cut was too deep and they sank into booze, or melancholy, or sought out a boat to take them home.

'Will you make a go of it here, do you think?' she asked, the words out before she could shape them and smooth away the edges. 'Will you work here for long?'

The girl's eyes narrowed suspiciously. 'Why do you ask that? Has the housekeeper been talking to you?'

'No, it's just …'

'I'm content, thank you!' Sharpness to the girl's tone belied a childhood with three brothers. Isobel expected the girl had learned how to be tough from an early age.

'I'm sure you are. I didn't mean anything by it.' Isobel deposited the envelope of coins in her pocket. 'It's just that women who settle here don't stay as maids for long. They look for something else, something new to try, and New Zealand usually offers it. So I've heard, anyway.'

'Like mending?' The girl raised her eyebrows, but seemed to soften.

'Not like mending.' Isobel grinned. 'I take it you're not married? It's harder to break free when you're married.' She shook her head a little, marvelling at the words spilling from her mouth, and put it down to the hour spent with Elizabeth Peter, who was probably still waiting at the church for women to return with signatures for the petition. Elizabeth always seemed to have an impetuous effect upon Isobel. In the first years, when Isobel still hoped for a baby, she would leave Elizabeth and return to Brendan in an assertive mood.

The maid straightened up. 'I'll be called back to work soon enough. There's always something to dust.'

Isobel nodded and turned to go. But spontaneity took her again and she thought of the map on the table in the church, and Elizabeth standing over it, frowning. So many streets to walk and gather signatures. 'Did you sign the petition?' she asked.

The girl had her hand on the door and was getting ready to close it. 'What petition?'

'The one that's going to be put to parliament, asking that women be given the vote. It's important.'

'Oh, someone came to the door a few weeks ago. I heard the cook talking about it. The missus wouldn't let her in the house.'

'Is that so?'

'Cook said the missus thinks it isn't natural for women to vote. The missus told Cook that women will give up caring for the children, or the home, if they were to get involved in politics.' The maid looked down at her fingers, the nails jagged and torn. 'Not that the missus cares for the house or children herself.'

Isobel sighed. 'It isn't true, you know. Women aren't going to abandon their babies and protest every hour of the day if they get the vote. If anything, they want the vote so they can protect their homes and families. We want to be a steadying influence.'

'Well, I don't know about that. I'm not long here and I'm keen to keep my job, if it's all the same. Sure, there are people out of work wherever you go—I've seen them. My brothers have had to go where work is.' The maid suddenly looked worried. 'Now, you won't be saying anything to the cook or the housekeeper about our little talk, will you?'

'Of course not.'

'Because I can't afford to lose my place. I have to go now.'

The girl retreated and shut the door with a firm click and there was nothing else for Isobel to do but make her way back up the stone stairs and follow the garden path onto the street. She told herself to remember to call back again in a week's time to collect more mending, wondering if she would see the girl again, or if being a maid would become intolerable and the girl would disappear.

Esther was waiting for her. She stood with her hand on her middle, unconsciously, and from the side the egg of her belly was clear to see. She smiled, over-brightly, when Isobel approached.

'Done? Where now?' Her cheeks were two red spots and Isobel could see how tired she was.

'Just a few more houses, if you can manage it? This one has

promised me some mending next week. You might help me with it, if it isn't too much for you.' Isobel looked closely into her sister's face and Esther pursed up her lips.

'I'm all right, Isobel. Please, don't fuss over me.'

~

It rained for much of the following week. Water leaked through the seal around the cottage window and every morning Isobel used yesterday's paper in a futile attempt to stem the flow. Her hands turned grey with ink, the words of the colony staining her skin. Her habit of brushing her fringe from her eyes left dirty streaks on her face; one evening, when Brendan came home from work and they turned on the lamp for the first time, he erupted into high-pitched laughter and told her she looked like a coal miner. Esther, hemming skirts belonging to a mistress further along Queen Street, said nothing, but Isobel saw the line of anger in her sister's tight face. They hadn't noticed the ink on Isobel's face, trying to conserve gas by sitting in the growing dark.

A month or so after Esther arrived, a fire broke out on Sale Street, not far from the gasometers supplying the city. Isobel and Esther heard the bells ring out, a constant, insistent sound that sent their neighbours out onto the street. The sisters joined them, watching fire brigades from several stations gallop their engines along the rutted roads. Someone spoke of a hotel elsewhere in the city that had burned down a few years before through lack of water for the hoses, and the nearness of the fire to the gas reserves had the crowd on edge. Yet, like a tide, the people flowed toward it, some holding buckets in pretence, others openly jostling to see. Once on the street, it seemed impossible to go against the flow, and Isobel and Esther found their feet marching in the same direction. They held hands tightly, Isobel trying to position herself in front of Esther's belly wherever possible.

A couple of wooden houses on Sale Street were aflame. There were soft, breathy noises of appreciation from the crowd as a woman jumped from a first floor window of a house and was caught in a large sheet. There were gasps as a man, in a state of undress, tumbled out of the same building, followed soon after by a bare-breasted woman. Women onlookers shielded their eyes and clucked delightedly; someone pretended to faint. Men shared knowing looks, aware of what kind of house was burning. The crowd was overjoyed. It roared when the fire brigade turned on their hoses, and hung around to be sure there was no more scandal or heroics. Fellows from the local newspapers scribbled in notepads, trying to go unnoticed as policemen wrestled shouting, smoke-streaked women back into their clothes.

It was just as they were about to leave and fight their way home that Isobel saw Brendan. He was stood near the burning building, staring up at it with a frightened, bewildered expression on his face. His hair was unkempt.

But of course he's there, Isobel thought. Someone will have sent him from the gas company to make sure the fire is put out properly. She watched him gape and hold his hands to his chest, and she felt an uncommon prick of pride for her man; she wanted to run across the street and embrace him. A wonderful, crackling feeling grew in her stomach—her husband was working hard to protect and provide for their adopted city.

But then she saw. He wasn't wearing any shoes. Or socks. His shirt was undone at the throat and the buttons of his trousers were open. As she watched, he tucked himself in and turned away to see to his trousers. The warm feeling in her body became like fire itself and the world seemed to shimmer around her.

She looked from her husband to the women gathered on the street, their breasts loose in their clothes, mouths open and wet with colour.

Breath was tight in her throat. She did not want Brendan to see her. She edged Esther around, turning her sister's body away from the house. Esther looked at her curiously.

'What is it, Isobel? Are you afraid? Don't be—it looks as though everyone made it out safely.'

'It's the crowds. Too much for me. Please, let's go home. There's nothing more to see.'

'Of course.' Esther moved, as though she was about to take one last look at the burning shell on Sale Street, but turned quickly back when Isobel tugged her hand. 'I'm coming, Isobel.'

Isobel pulled her sister along the street, past the rising stacks of the gasometers the firemen were so fearful for. One fire engine had been stationed beside them, probably as a precaution in case the fire from Sale Street spread. Isobel saw the engine's horses harrumph and stamp their feet as the crowd milled by. She wondered what good the firemen could do if the stacks really did catch fire, and if water would be enough to subdue the flames before it ate the whole city. She lengthened her step.

Beyond the stacks glittered the water of Freeman's Bay, darts of blue whipping the harbour wall, leaking into Isobel's sight as she hurried her sister along. The water seemed like a thick rope around her, had done since the moment she made landfall all those years ago. In the ten years since she had arrived, Isobel had not left Auckland. Instead she had walked the edges of the city, seeking work or seeking Brendan, but never beyond. The brisk salty tang of the sea had been her companion, a belt holding her in place, containing her to the city. She knew Esther found the sea restful, now that the ordeal of the crossing was over. Esther sometimes dozed in the afternoon, head turned to the open window where the lull and throb of water could be heard faintly. But Esther had always been drawn to water. She loved the pressure of it, the push of ice on her narrow ribs. The immersion of her body in the brook near their mother's house and the flood of brackish water in her ears.

Isobel did not see think of water in such a way. Water was to be respected and, if possible, avoided. As the sisters reached College Road, Isobel heard the crash and whoop of ships docking and goods being uploaded. She wondered, again, what the New Zealand shoreline must have been like before she and all the settlers before her made the place their home.

By the time they reached the cottage on George Street, Esther was winded and held her stomach. Isobel settled her down on the bed she shared with Brendan, a riot of emotions fighting to control her throat and drying up the spit in her mouth. She had hurried Esther back from Sale Street unfairly and now her sister was exhausted. Her own skin smarted at the memory of Brendan, his bewildered face staring up at the burning building from which he had just exited. She tucked the blankets around Esther's legs and sat down in the armchair, waiting for her sister to fall asleep.

Brendan's hair. The memory of it flooded back to her. It had been tousled and unkempt as he stood, blinking on Sale Street, rubbed free of the oil he used to keep it in check. During the first few months of their marriage, before leaving England, Brendan's hair was like that each morning. Wild and free. She had loved to plunge her hands into it as he bobbed above her. Her mother had explained the mechanics of married life, but nothing of the pleasure a husband could give. It had shocked Isobel and Brendan both: the sweetness of the embrace, the ache at the split of her thighs that exploded into light when Brendan touched the exact spot. The satisfaction of holding handfuls of his hair when he shouted his way to his own end, leaving them both wet and giggling.

But that had been before, so long ago. She wondered if Brendan thought about giving the women on Sale Street pleasure, but suspected the transaction was abrupt and focused on his needs. It had stung to see him standing on the street, shoeless and flapping. Had he finished what he started before the fire broke out? Had whichever woman who serviced him brought him to the end, to the point where his lips made that tight circle and his eyes squeezed shut? Isobel could remember his face at such a moment, and it hurt to think of it.

She felt foolish. Since they came to New Zealand and drink took hold, Brendan had rarely touched her. Sometimes, after spending time with Elizabeth, Isobel would feel the old need and hope, and thought of a baby. But Brendan was usually too far gone in whisky to offer more than a few, half-hearted thrusts. They grew used to their sides of the bed, bodies cupped by the sagging mattress, arms and limbs distinctly untangled.

But Brendan's presence on Sale Street shouted out that he had those desires still. And that Isobel was no longer the woman from whom he sought them.

Esther moaned a little and, through the thin blanket, Isobel saw her sleeping sister's belly move; the slightest ripple, the slightest movement as the hidden child pushed out a webbed hand. Isobel clutched her face and wept.

Esther

When Esther awoke, she did so with a jerk. Her belly ached in such a way that she thought she had fallen. Her insides felt bruised and sore, and she felt the quick throb of panic—was she back on the ship during a storm? She braced herself and instinctively wrapped her arms around her stomach. But the baby was quiet and still, and the bed did not sway with the sea. Esther sat up and saw she was in Isobel's bed. Beside her was Brendan's pillow, a soft divot from the weight of his head.

Esther got up hurriedly, wanting to be away from a place Brendan had laid his body. Outside it had grown dark but, just as she stood against the window and looked out, a gas light was switched on. The street became a box of shadows. Black and white shapes dotted the pathways.

The light woke Isobel, resting in the armchair, and she came over to join Esther at the window. 'I thought you would sleep better in my bed,' Isobel said. 'You could barely stand when we got back. Oh, they've put up a new street light. The gas company will be keen to show that all is well after the fire.'

The fire on Sale Street. Esther had never seen such a thing. There had been bonfires in their village when they were children, and they'd circled the common square and cooed with the rest of them when Guy Fawkes was burned. But today's fire on Sale Street had been magnificent. The crack of splintering timber, the shriek of a smoking, naked woman—Esther had felt a rush of urgency to move with the crowd. The push and throb of people spilling down the streets to the scene had thrilled her. She had felt powerless and urged along, but the sense of motion and recklessness it gave her was intoxicating.

Esther had seen Brendan outside the burning building. She caught a glimpse of him just before Isobel turned her away. She saw his unhooked clothing and his bare, shameful feet. She had felt anger herself briefly—that Brendan would do such a thing and betray Isobel in such a way … but that feeling evaporated as readily as the smoke. Esther had knowledge of married men, after all.

'Should we prepare something for dinner?' she asked. The larder was well-stocked now and Isobel had purchased horse meat from the knacker's yard near the harbour just that morning. 'I could make a stew.'

Isobel shrugged. There were creases around her eyes.

Esther put a hand on her sister's wrist. 'Why don't you sew?' she said. 'I can make a meal for when Brendan comes home.'

At her husband's name, Isobel's left eyelid flickered, something Esther had not seen since their father died. Isobel had twitched throughout his funeral, infuriating their mother, who eventually made Isobel wear a patch over her eye. Esther remembered her sister making up an excuse for curious mourners that she had scraped her face on thorns, gathering roses from the garden for their father's casket. It was a lie that filled Esther with both fury and sadness.

There was a movement on the street outside and Isobel let out her breath in a hurry. 'There's Rachel,' she said. 'I must step outside to speak to her. Can I leave you to make supper then?'

She didn't wait for Esther to agree and hurried out. Esther saw her wave a greeting to her friend, and then both women walked slowly around the cottages to the shared courtyard. Rachel Speedy had Isobel's arm and was nodding. Esther wondered if Isobel was telling Rachel what had happened on Sale Street.

Esther had learned to find her way around the small room and easily found a knife and a chopping board. She rummaged around in a basket on the floor and picked out yesterday's vegetables—a few potatoes, carrots, a pale squash, and an onion. The dark, offal smell of horse meat filled the air and she covered it with a cloth, faintly nauseous. Pulling up a chair to the kitchen table, she began to peel and slice.

The fruit and vegetables in New Zealand had shocked Esther with their size and ripeness. In the first weeks, she had lingered at the grocers on Karangahape Road, startled at the way potatoes and vegetables seemed to swell under their skin. The carrots she prepared now were bright and thick, wetting her fingers with a nutty scent. They were unlike the thin, hardened vegetables back home. She remembered forcing a blunt knife through a pile of turnips on her first day in the big house where she met him. He had taken the knife from her hand and sharpened it on a belt.

She had been eighteen. Her mother's cousin was yet to die and her mother was yet to become wealthy. The master at Gallerton House further over the border into Derbyshire needed a girl to help in the kitchen. Esther was to stay in the servant's quarters during the week and walk the five miles back to her mother's house each Saturday.

The man said to the cook he had come to see how the new girl was settling in and Esther, sweating into her flannel smock, caught the older woman's look. She hated the uniform and the way it pinched under her arms. She hated that it was all one colour and the plainness of it, and she hated that her new master had been a friend of her father's. His oldest child, a girl only a few years older than Esther, had visited with the master when they came for a portrait by Esther's father. Esther remembered watching the girl play with a doll, fascinated and appalled that she would find such a thing so engaging.

The master had watched her struggle to slice and peel and, when the cook had stepped outside to speak to the delivery boy, he folded his hands over Esther's. 'Here. Like this.'

She knew power then, at that moment. His hands were over hers, fixing them in place, but Esther knew her strength and the magnet of her body. No doubt he had tried this before, with other girls, but Esther was not a girl easily frightened. Later that day she lingered, pivoting a toe on the back stairs, letting him see more than he ought.

Those were breathless first weeks, a time when blood pounded in her ears and in her breasts. He was as helpless in her arms as a rabbit in the mouth of a dog.

She had let him take her to bed on May Day, while his wife and daughters watched men dance around the pole and place flowers in their hair. He was unwell, he said, and needed someone to stay behind to keep the stoneware bottles topped up with boiling water. He'd looked at her with damp eyes and she felt the glorious thump of her wet heart, the mild attraction of his body nothing compared to the surging power she would feel later, sitting astride him.

The carrots and onion chopped, the squash carved into odd-shaped chunks; only the horse meat left. Esther unwrapped it and looked at it again. The flesh was dark red, liver-like. A year or so ago, she hadn't been quick enough with the vinegar water after he'd finished inside her. Either she had been too slow or life had refused to be washed away. He had paid for someone to see to her, in Derby. The pain of the curled hook, the feeling that she was being emptied—she trembled in her bed for three days after, changing the cloths between her legs every hour. She would not go back to the woman in Derby when she was caught again, not even when, whispering and crying, he said he would not divorce his wife.

The Esther in New Zealand wanted nothing more but to parcel the slippery red horse meat back in its paper and find a place in the garden to bury it. But it was their supper—Brendan's supper—and he would be hungry after his afternoon's exertions. She had a sense he would be on edge when he came home, and sharp with his tongue. Idly she wondered what it would be like to aggravate him, but knew it would be Isobel who would feel the consequences. So Esther sliced the horse meat quickly. She poured water in the pot and lit the stove, and pushed the armchair as far away as possible.

A cat yowled outside and a slip of black hurried by, rat in mouth. Misty, too, had been a good catcher. The cat had been Esther's flighty friend for most of her childhood. Misty had come home when she was hungry, sometimes with a present of a mouse or a bird, but for most of the day was nowhere to be seen. One the odd occasions Misty would allow her mistress to pet her, Esther would bury her nose in the cat's neck and offer up a prayer that they might change places, so she could stalk the hedgerows and leap onto roofs in the thick of night. She had slept badly the week after she killed the pet just after Isobel left for New Zealand, but Misty had seen off another of their neighbour's hens, and Esther couldn't bear the thought of someone else doing it.

It was quiet outside. No sign of the women from nearby cottages, no children playing in the dirt of the courtyard. She wondered if they were still on Sale Street, watching the fireman spray the smouldering building, gawking at the unclothed women and their sullen, shamed clients.

Her trunk was at the end of the bed. There hadn't been enough room to keep it behind the curtain next to her own camp bed, so Isobel had tried to turn it into a piece of furniture. Esther's two books, stolen from her father's library, sat on top with today's folded paper. The trunk squatted like an obstinate child.

A moment of panic when she couldn't find the small key in her bag, but finally her fingers hooked onto it, tucked away inside the lining. Such things always seemed to hide from her. She removed her clothes and books from the trunk, and her mother's shawl that she did not like to touch, setting the pile on Isobel's bed. Then, key in the lock of the false bottom, Esther opened a secret compartment. It was a thin space, only suitable to keep papers and letters. A single sheet of paper lay in there, as undisturbed as the day she hid it. She took it out.

The master had been pitiful when he gave it to her, a week before Esther set off on the *Lady Jasmine*. He had taken her into the sitting room, his wife and daughters out for the day, servants somewhere else. Esther had sat down on the horsehair sofa, looking around. She had been in the room many times. A year after working in his kitchen, her mother's cousin had died and they suddenly had money. The master's wife, keen to right the wrong of employing a girl who had become her equal, had invited Esther for tea several times. A blurred photograph of the wife was perched in a frame above the fireplace, a rubbed-away, unimportant image. Esther had balanced primly on the sofa while the master sat opposite. He was holding a tumbler of whisky and poured one for her.

'You have to leave,' he told her, eyes again wet and averted. 'My wife knows. You know I won't leave her, but I had hoped we could make some sort of … arrangement. I am sorry. My wife has spoken with your mother and it's been decided. You are going to New Zealand, to live with your sister.'

Esther remembered that bemusement was, at first, the stronger feeling—that he would act in such a way! This man, who was helpless beneath her body in bed and who cried and whimpered at his time of crisis, who spent long minutes caressing her neck and back … this man who would sometimes only want to be near her body, to sleep with his chin hooked into the dip of her shoulder … *this* man would tell her she had to leave for the other side of the world when she was carrying his child. It was a wonder he even knew how to string such words together.

But then came the shock. Her mother knew. Isobel too. Esther could not run away to a place of her own choosing, as she'd hoped in the weeks since her situation became apparent. Her road, or sea, was now set out before her.

Not even the thought of months on the free wild of the ocean could prevent what happened next, there in that parlour. She had felt the ever-present acid in her chest boil into a tight knot and, with sudden ferocity, vomited on the carpet. A rope was being put around her life, so her body was rebelling, pushing against its borders, spilling out in with hideous force. And Esther did not feel embarrassed. The man had seen every part of her, he had touched every tucked away, coiled secret. He could have the vomit and the shame, and the burning insides too.

The master stood up and, hand trembling, handed Esther a sheet of paper. 'I bought you this. It wasn't so hard to obtain. Land is still available, if you know the right vendor. And I'll see to it you'll have money. Enough to keep you comfortable.' Then, his body moving mechanically, as though it was not his, he walked from the room.

The paper was yellow and discoloured against the red blanket on Isobel's bed, and as fragile as a bone. Esther frowned over it, her belly pressing down on the tops of her thighs. She had not read it since stashing it away in the secret drawer.

It was a title deed to a piece of land in the Hatcher Valley, South Island. A hundred acres of land. The appellation, written in tiny copperplate, informed the buyer that the land was bracketed by mountains and a lake, subject to occasional flooding and snowstorms, but hardy.

He had given this to her, her lover and bringer of pain. With his hand blocking the smell of her vomit, he had given her a solution to the problem, a kind of independence, but only if she disappeared and made his life fatly comfortable again.

The vendor of the sale had added his signature to the land deed in an affected swirl, making it impossible to identify who it was. The thought had crossed Esther's mind on the boat that maybe the document wasn't real, that there was no sale and no ownership. But such doubts were pressed aside by the move and stretch of the hidden child. The paper was similarly folded away.

There was noise outside and the sound of a deliberate, heeled step. Esther moved swiftly, returning the deed to the secret drawer, turning the trunk back into a secret. A man walked in the courtyard, young and lean. It was Jack Bellamy. He turned and saw Esther by the glass and lifted his hand in a greeting.

Esther hesitated. She was bigger now, her belly a hard reality against her dress. He would see it and it stung to think that his talk of New Zealand being a land of chance and hope would fade away at the sight of an unwed woman in a pickle.

But she went outside to meet him anyway and when he turned she saw a black smear on his cheek. The knee of his trouser leg was torn.

'Are you hurt?' she asked. He turned to face her, the almonds of his eyes widening as he looked over her dress and her huge, unmistakable belly. He seemed as if he might say something and Esther tensed, ready. But then Jack sighed and pulled at his trousers.

'Caught it on a piece of timber,' he said. 'Were you out at Sale Street? The whole building came down. Bit of a panic, all that wood and brick on fire.'

'Isobel and I went to see, but we didn't stay long.' Esther saw the red glaze of his knee. 'Sit down. I'll fetch a cloth.'

She turned back to Isobel's room and, when she returned to the courtyard, found Jack sitting on one of the upturned crates in the courtyard, gritting his teeth. He had pulled his trouser leg up so that the fabric bunched together mid-thigh.

Esther approached slowly. The man's slim white calf seemed barely strong enough to support him. Her father had been slender too, the dough of his muscles slapping sickeningly from side to side as they walked the hills together. But the frame of this New Zealand man was different. His skin looked soft and smooth, and Esther wanted to touch it. She wondered if it would be warm under her palm, like the master's had been. *His* body had been thick and sturdy, sometimes brutal in his movements. Esther shook away the memory and crouched down slowly beside Jack Bellamy.

He reached out immediately. 'Let me. You can't be sitting like that.'

The gentle acknowledgment of her condition made Esther burn a little. 'It's quite all right. Let me see.'

The cut to Jack's leg was light and superficial, despite the blood, and Esther was soon able to clean the wound. She heard Jack hiss through his teeth occasionally, but did not look up. With another dry cloth, she stopped the bleeding.

'Here, hold it in place.' Esther finally stood up, cramp shooting like ice through her feet. She clenched her fists and sat down heavily.

He looked over. 'Legs hurt? I remember my mother suffering with cramp when she was carrying my brother.'

'It will pass,' Esther said. She heard the uneasy intonation in Jack's voice, his hesitation to refer to her condition, and she wanted suddenly to pull off her boots and show him her swollen feet. Look! she wanted to say. Look what carrying the children of men does to us! Instead, she wound her ankles around slowly, making circles. 'Sometimes it comes in the night for no reason at all, but it fades away before long.'

'Would a warm bath help?'

Esther cocked her head at him. The calamitous, wild feeling hadn't left her bones. She saw the soot in Jack's brown hair, the ash on his collar. He wasn't wearing a cravat today. How old is he? she wondered. There were tiny faint lines at the corners of his eyes, which suggested he had a year or so on her, but not much more. Esther wondered if Jack had drawn many baths for women in his time, and she suddenly imagined him helping her slide into milky white water, slipping in behind her. She knew he would have a soft scutter of hair across his chest. She imagined her back against it. She twitched the image away; the last few weeks had been odd and heady, nights disturbed by unspeakable dreams.

'And where, Mr Bellamy, would I be finding a bath around here?'

Jack shrugged and moved on his perch. He had transgressed and spoken too far, and she could see he was sorry. This land still holds onto English insistence of being shocked, she thought.

'You have a point,' he said. 'Out on Queen Street, with the maids and boilers—yes, there are baths to be found there. But here—with the pump in the courtyard? No. No, no.'

He spoke as though a memory had occurred to him. Esther waited. He carried on.

'My father used to take a hot bath every Saturday night, to be clean for Sunday. Not so unusual, except that there was no one to boil the water for him but my brother and I. We would have to leave our work an hour early and boil water in these huge copper pots.' Jack held out his hands for emphasis. 'The ribbing we took from the other men—leaving the shearing or the muster just to boil water for our father to take a bath. Like we were his housemaids.'

Sometimes the master at Gallerton Hall spoke like Jack; meandering, memory-drenched. It occurred during the rare moments when they could rest after a frantic exchange and meeting of their bodies. It grated on Esther to hear the man speak in such a way. She heard indulgence and pity in the maze-like circle of his words. He spoke about his mother, an invalid living some miles away, and the harsh, remembered treatment of school teachers. Esther wanted to rise up from his bed and tell him he was a little boy after all.

But such feelings did not occur when she listened to Jack. She did not feel the quiet tick of rage against her ribs, nor long to clamp her hands over her ears. Instead she felt sympathy. Another marvel, she supposed, another change that had occurred as the child grew inside her.

'I imagine my father will be managing without me just fine,' Jack said and blew out air noisily. He looked into the distance, where smoke still rolled across the city from Sale Street.

Isobel had said there had been a family argument. Esther waited, wondering if Jack would say more. She realised she wanted him to. She wanted to listen again to the clipped accent and the sharp, hard finish of his words. But Jack had no more to say and sat in silence.

The ice had melted from her feet. Esther could stand, so she did, swinging her skirts around her belly.

'I'll be on my way now, Mr Bellamy. Take care of that knee and see it doesn't become infected.'

'Oh, it will be right.' He smiled. 'Such a scrape was commonplace when I was a child. A proper little colonial, I was, wild and always in trouble.' He looked away again, a glass screen falling over his eyes, and she could see he was remembering again. Then he was back, blinking away whatever thoughts distracted him. He made to move and Esther wondered if he would get up to make a proper, gentlemanly farewell, the kind she had seen visitors to her mother's drawing room make. The master was a great one for formalities too, in the spaces beyond his bedroom. She had seen the master raise his chin in a lofty, false farewell many times.

But Jack did not. Instead he nodded from his seat, and for this common, easy touch, she was strangely glad.

❧

An hour later, Isobel returned and then, an hour after her, Brendan came back. He swung open the door to the cottage, almost bouncing it against the kitchen table, the cold of the evening air funnelling about him. Isobel, sitting on the edge of their bed with mending on her knee, glanced up, tight-lipped, and looked down again.

Her sister would not greet her husband, Esther could see, and the threat to the calm bubble of the cottage alarmed her. So she got up from the easy chair and reached for Brendan's hat. 'Good evening. Are you hungry?'

Brendan squinted around the room. His clothes were where they should be. Socks and shoes were on his feet. His hair was smooth. But the sweat of beer rolled from him. Esther felt sour air lap against her and she was, momentarily, grateful for the open door.

'Did you hear about the fire on Sale Street?' Brendan said, his voice a boom. 'Too close to the gas works for comfort.'

Esther put Brendan's hat on the shelf above the stove and went to the stew. 'We did.'

'We were there, Bren,' Isobel said, looking up from her sewing. 'It was quite an adventure. I trust no one was hurt?'

Brendan blinked at his wife. Esther felt a ripple of unease between them and she wanted to run, pulling Isobel after her. Instead she made a show of setting plates on the table.

'I think the firemen rescued everyone,' Brendan said eventually. 'The building came down but the girls got out.'

'Girls?' said Isobel.

'We'll eat, shall we?' Esther suggested. Strips of newspaper fluttered on the walls. Wind tugged at printed reports of drownings, gala dinners, women marching for suffrage. Isobel said nothing but instead stared at her husband.

Seconds passed, during which Esther thought they would never join her at the table. But then Brendan sighed, closed the door, and shakily pulled up a chair. Isobel put down her mending and, without a word, perched on the edge of a crate ready to eat. The meal passed in silence.

Later, Esther took the pot and plates out into the courtyard to wash them. Isobel returned to her sewing, taking the easy chair that Brendan usually occupied when he returned from work. He had glared at her and then laid out the newspaper on the table, sucking the horse meat from his teeth. Whether he was reading or not, Esther could not be sure.

A few of the women had returned from Sale Street and were talking excitedly about the fire. A couple Esther recognised; Helena, the young dressmaker, stood with hands on hips, speaking to Rose, who had her arms crossed over her ample chest, smoking.

They raised their chins in greeting. 'Did you see it, then?' Rose asked.

'I did. Isobel and I went along. We didn't see the building come down.'

'It made such a crash!' Helena's eyes widened in her pale face, and she flicked out her fingers. 'Boom!'

'Did you see the women?' Rose added.

'Yes,' Esther confessed. One woman had been wearing a night-dress trimmed with red lace, and clutched a brightly coloured lamp, obviously grabbed as she made her escape. The nightdress had torn and the woman's stomach was exposed. Esther had stared, unable to look away; the woman's belly was wrinkled and saggy, and Esther knew the woman had had a child. She had wondered where the child was, if the woman paid for its care by selling her body. Now, in the courtyard, Esther felt compelled to say something in the woman's defence. 'Such places are to be found in every city, I expect.'

'Oh, I should think,' Rose said. Her arms fell to her sides and Esther saw new patches on the sleeves of her dress. They were bright coloured squares, out of place with the faded brown fabric.

'Wherever there are men there will be houses like the one on Sale Street. And wherever there is money, there will be folk—like those in the big houses on Queen Street—spluttering their outrage at such a thing.'

'Women have to eat,' Helena said simply. She paused, seeming to wait for Rose to nod, and then continued. 'It's women who are checked by inspectors for diseases, but men who give it to them.'

'*Forced* inspections,' Rose added solemnly. 'Checking all parts, if you catch my meaning. Well, if we get the vote, we might be able to change that. The Sale Street fire will be talked about for a time to come, I expect. You might think yourself lucky, Miss Esther. This land has shown you her under-britches and entertained you at the same time.'

Esther did not know how to answer the woman. There was anger in Rose's voice, and an ownership of sorts. She did not know if the woman expected her to be critical, to sneer at a land where such events occurred. But then Rose, the patched woman, glanced at Isobel's window, glinting in the evening light. Esther knew that Rose had seen Brendan. Helena probably had too.

'Mr Bellamy came by earlier,' Esther said after a pause. 'He'd hurt his leg.'

The women were disinterested, Esther could tell, but made a vague show of concern. 'How did he do that?' Helena asked.

'Timber from a burnt building caught him. Nothing serious. I cleaned it up.'

Rose looked at Esther curiously. 'You saw to him?'

'It was just a scrape, really. Nothing worse than a child does climbing a tree.'

'But you *saw* to him?'

'Yes.' Esther gathered the crockery together, annoyed to find her face getting hot.

'I imagine Mr Bellamy appreciated your administrations,' Rose said dryly.

There was no reason to linger and Esther now wanted to be away,

away from the gossiping women and back with her sister. She picked up the plates and cups and, smiling a quick goodbye, hurried back toward the cottage.

∽

A jerking awake. Open eyes to a dark room, save for a yellow glow somewhere near the ceiling. Esther lay in her lumpy bed, breathing quickly, hair damp at her temples, hands twisted in the sheet. She had been woken by something—the baby? She slid her hands under her nightdress, cupping her belly, but the baby was still. No pain in her legs, no ache at her back. She squeezed her eyes shut, trying to calm, trying to settle whatever it was that had disturbed her.

The sound came again. A small cry, a pleading 'no'. Then a harsh whisper and a bounce of springs. The noise gathered, more urgently.

It came from beyond the sheet, in the room separate from her. Esther listened, eyes shut. She knew now what it was, and heard her sister gasp and Brendan curse.

Esther did not need to pull back the dividing sheet to know Brendan was on top of her sister, lurching back and forth. She knew that Isobel was lying on her back, an arm thrown across her face, the other pinned above her. The movement on the bed became frantic, Brendan reaching the end. Then a sharp intake of breath—she was not sure from whom—and a groan. A rolling away. And then the unbearable sound of Isobel weeping. The guttural, animal sound of Brendan snoring.

And Esther kept perfectly still, teeth clenched, tears of her own falling into her hair. She lay silently until she heard that Isobel had fallen asleep. Morning light slid under the door.

Isobel

Brendan left early for the office. Whether it was a headache or his conscience that drove him from the bed, Isobel did not know, but she stayed furrowed under the blankets, her face to the wall. She felt him stand over her at one point before he left, but she kept her face hidden, a sheet pulled over her eyes. She wondered if he would speak to her, if he would touch her shoulder. She did not know what she would do if he did. But Brendan left without a word. Esther, too, lay silently behind her curtain.

There was a knife between her thighs, a pain so sharp that Isobel gasped as she swung her legs round to get up. A streak of blood on the nightdress and bedsheets. It had been over quickly, Brendan's insistent body addled with drink. He had told her what he wanted and that it was her duty to give it. When she had not wanted to, he had taken it.

Isobel did not know she was crying until her neck became soaked. She thought of Rachel, and wanted her friend badly. She glanced again at the sheet masking Esther, her sister seeming an eternal distance away rather than a few steps. She dressed carefully, easing on clean drawers and folding one of her monthly cloths to put between her legs. As quietly as she could, she let herself out of the cottage and walked, not really sure of where she was going, into the courtyard.

The relief to find Rachel crouched over a basket brought fresh tears, ones Isobel could not wipe away before her friend saw. Rachel looked up, knife and twine in her hands, and quickly stood up.

'Isobel?' Rachel dropped her things and held out her arms. Isobel went to her. The older woman embraced her. 'What did he do?'

Isobel shook her head, unable to speak. She bowed her head and
set it on Rachel's shoulder—an awkward task as Rachel was smaller
than she. But the feel of the old settler's rough dress on her cheek
was comforting. She thought of her father and the scratchy bark of
his unshaven face.

'Did you tell him you saw him on Sale Street?' Rachel asked. Her
hand fell in Isobel's hair. 'There now.'

'Why did I marry him?' Isobel said, the struggle of the past ten
years laid out in the toneless, awful question.

At this, Rachel took her friend by the shoulders and glared in her
face. The question seemed to infuriate her. She shook her head and
was about to say something, but then sighed. 'Come with me. We'll
walk on the shore and dig for shellfish. A breakfast of pipi will see
you right.'

It did not take long to walk along St Mary's Road toward the harbour and the bay. The smell of sulphur hung in the air, remnants
from yesterday's fire. But the morning was bright. As Isobel and
Rachel walked past the girls' college and convent, they saw pupils
scurry, coatless, into the chapel, the spire looming over the street.
Some, dressed in black tunics, wore their hair in plaits. Others, older
and more daring, had hair pinned up. Rachel nodded a curt good
morning to a nun who watched her charges gather for prayers, and
then they were at the beach at St Mary's Bay.

The shore was separated from the city by a line of myrtle trees
with bare trunks and red, spiky flowers. Houses and shacks were
set against the rock, workshops and shipbuilders crowded together.
Sails rounded the bay, others sailed beyond. Boats broke the calm
water. The air was sharp and salty, and seared the throat.

Rachel moved with surety and ease on the sand but Isobel, unused
to the shore, stepped clumsily. The shifting earth alarmed her. She
splayed out her arms, trying to keep her balance, and Rachel laughed.

'Don't take such big steps!' the old settler said. 'You can't stride
around here like you do on land. You have to adapt. Tread carefully.
There, that's better.'

There were some early morning gatherers on the beach. A group of Maori had strung up a wooden frame and were smoking fish. Women stood in the water, bare-legged, shaking out baskets. A small child played with a pile of shells.

'Ever dig for pipis before?' Rachel asked. She squatted down on the wet foreshore, the heels of her boots pressing into the sand. Isobel watched, entranced, sand creeping up the sides of Rachel's feet. Isobel wondered if the earth would suck her friend down into the depths.

She sat down awkwardly, the pain in her lower belly still sharp. Rachel watched silently and then dipped her hand into her pocket, handing Isobel a blunt-bladed knife.

'You should learn how to use this,' she said, holding Isobel's gaze for a second too long.

Isobel took it and turned it over in her hand. It was a simple thing, a knife she had seen Rachel use on fish many times. The blade was rounded.

'Won't take much to sharpen up,' Rachel said. The older woman's eyes glinted. A spell seemed to have come upon her and Isobel heard the rhythmic thrum of the sea, in and out, in and out. Then Rachel took the knife back and slapped it on her knee. The moment was broken. 'Watch.'

There was a small mound in front of her, about the width of her palm. Rachel plunged the knife into the top of the mound and made a circular motion. She cocked her head, listening. 'Hear that tap? The blade has found one.'

She made a shovel with a cupped hand and, moments later, produced a pale shell, the shape of a small, smooth fan. 'A pipi. Not much to look at, is it? Not one of your fancy, fake shells that sell so well on Queen Street and are sent back to the old country as a bit of memorabilia. No, this is the real stuff. Inside, it's perfect. It will need to be soaked to remove the grit but it's mighty tasty when boiled and dipped in a bit of vinegar.'

She put the shell in Isobel's hand, who looked at it curiously. She had seen shells like this on sale outside the grocer's, baskets of them, stinking in the sun. It had never crossed her mind to buy some. She would not have a single idea as to how to cook them, or to eat them. Standing at the grocers, she would move the baskets aside on her way to the counter to purchase bread and cheese.

Rachel laughed. 'Will you trust me, Isobel? I'm not out to poison you. Here, have a go.' She handed the knife to Isobel and pointed to another small mound nearby. 'That's where there'll be one.'

The women edged over, Rachel crawling on her knees, not caring about the sand sticking to her dress. Isobel got up slowly and stepped over to the mound, bending down gingerly again. She forced the knife into the sand. 'Like this?'

Rachel nodded. 'Turn it round. Wait till you hear that click. The blade will find it out.'

Isobel concentrated and a second later felt the knife scrape something. She scrabbled with her hands and pulled out a pipi, holding it up triumphantly. 'There!'

Rachel clapped her hands. 'Well done! Another dozen more and we'll have ourselves a breakfast.'

There was another pile of sand closer to the water and Isobel shuffled over, excited now. She repeated the same action and found another shell almost immediately. She squealed. 'Look!'

A Maori woman, twisting her bare feet in the water, glanced over. She said something to her companion and they turned to look at Isobel, bent over the pipi mound, dress trailing on the wet sand.

'Here, you do it.' Isobel said, suddenly embarrassed. She held the knife out to Rachel.

'But you've got the idea of it. You're doing well.'

'I'm getting wet.'

'So, take off your jacket,' Rachel said softly. 'And your boots.'

'I can't.' Tears gathered in Isobel's throat. Here, outside in the clean salt air, she felt hideously exposed.

'Of course you can. There's no one here to see and, even if there was, you're getting wet—you said so yourself.'

Isobel shook her head, aware that the Maori women were still watching her. She got up and folded Rachel's hand over the knife. 'I can't.'

Her friend sighed. 'Well, I will. There's another way to find pipi. Like them,' and she nodded over to the Maori family. 'You can find them with your feet. That's what I'm going to do.' She bent down and stripped the boots and stockings from her feet and, with a smirk over her shoulder, waded into the water to gather shellfish.

In the end Rachel found over two dozen pipi shells and, pockets stuffed, they walked back to the cottage on George Street. Rachel strolled with her stockings draped over her shoulder, boots swinging from her hand. For a moment, Isobel thought her friend was going to walk like that the whole way home, and she winced, not sure what she feared more: the looks of people as they went by, or Rachel's hot tongue if she asked her to put her footwear back on.

Rachel sat down on a bench at the point where the street merged with the beach. She unfurled her stockings back up her feet, gritting her teeth as wet wool rolled up her calves. She tied her boots with a sigh. 'There, now. Uncomfortable enough for society.'

They went back to Rachel's room on George Street, arriving back just as the carpenter opened for business and began, noisily, to saw and hammer wood. A dray rattled by and the sound of the timber mill wafted along the street. Auckland was awake.

They sat around Rachel's kitchen table as the pipis were soaked and boiled. A kettle sat contentedly alongside the pan. The cottage was of the same size and order as Isobel's, but, with a single bed pushed against the wall, there seemed to be much more space. An embroidered quilt lay snugly over the bed, lace squares over the backs of the two easy chairs. Isobel touched them enviously, remembering the pieces of lace she had brought with her from home, all those years ago, and how quickly they had been sold.

Rachel tipped a pile of pipis into a bowl and set it in front of Isobel, along with a small bottle of vinegar and a cup of tea. 'Eat. You won't believe what they taste like.'

The gobs of steaming, salty flesh were delicious, unlike anything Isobel had ever eaten. She prised open the shells one after the other, eating without speaking. Rachel, swallowing slowly, laughed.

When she had finished, Isobel sat back in the chair and sipped her tea. She could smell the beach on her fingers and brought them to her nose, breathing it in. The pain in her stomach eased. She felt her body slowly beginning to gather itself together again.

'Has Brendan treated you that way before?' Rachel asked. It was an unexpected but gentle question. She did not look away when she asked.

Isobel paused over her tea, remembering the ache and the insistence of him, the sour blow of her husband's breath as his weight threatened to crush her. She had stayed as quiet as she could, not able to bear the thought of Esther waking and hearing it all.

'No. Last night was the first time.'

'And before that? Were …' Rachel swallowed a gulp of tea, and Isobel could see her friend considering how to frame her words. 'How were relations before?'

They were wonderful, when they happened, Isobel wanted to say, and was filled with an idiotic desire to giggle. Before the drink turned everything upside down, Brendan was a tender lover. She wondered what her friend would say were she to declare that she, Isobel, buttoned-up as she was, had known passion.

But instead she said, 'They were normal, I suppose. Quite normal.'

'I ask, Isobel, because of children. There are no children, are there?'

In all their long years of friendship, they had not spoken of it. 'No children. Not a single one, even for just a little while.'

'But relations were normal?' Rachel asked. 'Forgive me, Bella. We women never know how to speak about this part of life, do we? We'd do well to learn, I think, not least so we can tell those who want to control such private moments to mind their own business. There's nothing wrong with wanting pleasure and knowing how to say it.' She put her cup on the table noisily.

'What was it like—for you? With Alfred?'

'Oh, that part was always rather splendid.' Rachel clapped her hands, a broad grin. 'Once I knew what on earth he was trying to do. Of course, my mother never told me what to expect—well, she didn't expect us to start with those games before we were married anyway. My sister wasn't very helpful either. She told me a considerate husband would see a child on me and then pay for his needs to be met elsewhere. What horseshit! In the early years when we built the house and struggled to feed the family, there were days when a roll in bed was the only thing to look forward to.'

It was impossible not to laugh and Isobel did, feeling her heart lift, feeling the band around her chest loosen a little. She took more tea and tried to balance the cup on its saucer. 'Last night was the first time in months.'

Rachel's laughter abruptly disappeared. 'What happened last night was not about love or desire.' She leaned over and grabbed Isobel's hand. 'It was about dominance. You had shamed him, seeing him on Sale Street in that state. Brendan wanted to take back control. Don't ever think he took what he wanted out of desire. And it wasn't his to take.'

'I have duties,' Isobel said sadly.

Rachel made an exasperated, blowing sound. 'What a contradiction you are, Bella! You knock on doors and petition for the vote, and you run around with your Templar friends, but will you stand up to your husband? No, you will not.'

'But a good wife …'

'A good wife would slap her man's face the moment he laid an unwelcome hand upon her.' Rachel made a swiping motion. 'A good *husband* would see to it that his wife's body is respected.'

'You won't say anything, Rachel?' Her friend's anger panicked Isobel. 'Please.'

Rachel glittered on her chair and Isobel could see it was an effort for her to find the right words. But Rachel eventually nodded. 'I wish you would be a little braver, Bella. It's up to us how we manage our lives. It's not down to everyone else. Leave that kind of life to those who care about calling cards and dyeing every piece of clothing black when a member of the royal family dies. Such utter, wasteful nonsense. Who cares what anyone else thinks? New Zealand is the land where women can define themselves, if only they had the courage. Oh, Bella, I wish you had screamed last night and followed it up with a punch to Brendan's tender areas.'

In spite of feeling as though she was being admonished and resenting it a little, Isobel laughed.

Rachel held up her hand. 'Hilda Riley sent a drunken fool on his way just a fortnight ago, by administering a kick in a painful area. He'd tried to grab her on her way back from collecting her mending. Bella, did Esther hear anything of what Brendan did to you last night?'

'I hope not.'

'Well. It's been different, hasn't it, with your sister here?'

'Esther keeps out of his way. She does everything she can to be helpful.'

'That's not what I mean. I mean there's been more money, hasn't there? Better meals? Hilda says you have doubled your mending from Queen Street.'

'Esther is a wonderful sewer. You would never have thought she could sew, if you'd known her as a child. She was so wild. But she's really excellent.'

'And Brendan is jealous.'

'Oh, Rachel, I don't think so.'

'I think he is. That would be another reason for how he acted last night. Putting himself back in charge, at least over you. If you can, kick him out before that baby comes. There will be one person in control when that tiny thing arrives and it won't be Brendan.'

Three months. That was how long they had before Esther's baby made its appearance. As ever, the thought of her sister's child pulled Isobel's stomach in opposing directions so that her breakfast seemed to leak back into her throat. Words burned in her mouth. There was something she wanted to say, badly, but she did not know how to start.

'What is it, Bella?' Rachel watched her closely.

'There was a letter,' Isobel said after a moment. 'From our mother. She wrote a letter to Esther and I don't know if my sister read it. It was wrapped in my mother's shawl in Esther's trunk—Esther wouldn't have worn my mother's shawl, I'm sure. She wouldn't have even touched it. I don't think she knew the letter was there. I found it and hid it away.'

Rachel leaned forward. 'Why would you do that?'

A simple question, but Isobel could not answer. She remembered holding the letter in her hand and seeing the instruction on the envelope—that Esther was to open it in September when the baby had arrived. The black script tolerated no nonsense. Spikey, sharp, the arrows of their mother's body contained in the slant and prick of the letters. What was it that made Isobel ignore her mother's demands and open it? She had slid a finger under the envelope's seal and popped the paper open. She had read the words, every one, and understood.

'It was a strange sort of letter,' she heard herself saying. The salty sweet of pipi came back into her mouth and she swallowed it down thinking, bemused, that the baby must have a similar, gross effect on Esther's body every day. 'Our mother is not one for an excess of kindness. Sometimes I wonder how she and our father came to make us. She embraced me only once in my life, I think.' Isobel paused and looked at the half-moons of her nails, white crescents split by grains of sand. 'I had a wild hope that she would write loving things in the letter to Esther—about what it means to be a mother, or such. But, of course, my mother is a creature of habit.'

'What did the letter say?'

'But maybe she does love me, after all. She talked about me having my heart's desire.'

Rachel shook her head and touched Isobel on the knee. 'The letter. What did the letter say? What would make you hide it and keep it from Esther?'

'It said …' Isobel sniffed. 'It said that Esther should give the baby to me and return home to England, as though nothing had ever happened.'

Esther

The baby seemed to have been awoken by the fury pumping through her veins. Esther strode about the small cottage, pacing between bed and easy chair, and the child bounced with her. She felt it roll and kick, deliberate, pronounced movements now. The spike of an elbow, the jab of a tiny, perfectly formed foot.

Esther was dressed. She had risen sometime after the sun, knowing immediately she was on her own in the room. There were the usual sounds outside. Women chatted outside in the courtyard, and she listened intently for her sister's voice. But Isobel was not there.

The master at Gallerton Hall had not been Esther's only lover—an apprentice at the smithy had left black traces on her body—but she had never given in against her will. Hearing Brendan with Isobel the night before incensed her. She had lain awake for hours after, hair tear-damp at the temples. How dare he? *How dare he?*

She was glad he was gone for the day. If she had risen to find him in the cottage, sitting at the table or sweating into the armchair … Esther tapped her stomach. Better he had left. She would have too much to say, and a man who hurt his own wife might think nothing of hitting a woman carrying a child.

She expected that Isobel was with Rachel, and a little pang ignited around her heart. She pictured them walking together, arm in arm, pausing to talk and bow heads. She wanted to be the person Isobel walked with. The person Isobel turned to. Bella.

Bella. Not a name Esther had imagined to hear when she first arrived in New Zealand. But the women in the courtyard used it easily; Bella was helloed in that oddly colonial way from the end of the street, a whooping sound and a brisk wave. Elizabeth Peter had called out 'Bella' when they talked about gathering signatures for the petition. Esther had heard the talk about her sister and a neighbour delivering a baby born a few streets over, and the idea seemed preposterous—Isobel, delivering a baby! But *Bella* had. *Bella*, the woman formed after ten years in New Zealand.

And yet *Isobel* had written letters home to their mother with fanciful tales about a townhouse and Brendan's well-paid job, and Isobel kept her pregnant sister on the pavement when picking up mending from the wealthy on Queen Street. Esther sighed. Her head hurt.

The door opened slowly and her sister stepped through. Her eyes were pink and red-rimmed, and her skin looked burnished and raw. She hasn't been crying, Esther thought. No, I know that look. She's been walking.

'Where have you been? With Rachel?'

Isobel pulled a handful of shells from her pocket and clattered them on the table. 'We were at the shore. These are pipis. Delicious. How silly to not have tried them before. Would you like some?'

Esther looked down at the pale shells. 'No. How are you?'

Isobel didn't answer, but instead pulled off her coat. She sat down in the armchair and closed her eyes.

Esther pulled a crate over and perched, though her belly threatened to topple her. 'Isobel?'

'Hush, Esther. I'm tired.'

But words spilled out in a rush. Esther could no more keep it in than she could hide the swell of her stomach. 'I heard what happened. I heard it all. Oh, Isobel. I hate him! I want to kill him. I swear, if I had a knife, I'd ...'

Isobel held up her hand, eyes still clenched tightly shut. She did not speak. A tear snaked from the corner of her eye. Esther could smell salt on her sister's clothes. There was sand on her boots.

'I think,' Isobel said softly, 'I think we should decide what to do before Brendan comes home.' She finally opened her eyes and slumped forward, her shoulder blades sharp against the fabric of her dress. 'Obviously you can't kill him, Esther. I don't think the prisons out here are equipped to hold a baby.'

Unbelievably, Isobel was trying to be humorous. Esther felt sick.

'I don't know what is best,' Isobel said. 'Rachel tells me I have choices and all I have to do is grab them.' She made a clenching motion with her fists and Esther wondered if her sister was miming her friend. 'But I don't know how. I don't know how I can make a man leave his own home. I've seen women on this street try to do it over the years. They've barricaded the door against men who are cheaters, or liars, or drunks, and all the husband has to do is fetch a policeman. I don't want that humiliation as well.'

Esther sniffed. She shuffled down onto the floor and lay her head in her sister's lap, breathing in the scent of water and Auckland. She felt Isobel's hand drop softly into her hair.

'You used to sit like this when we were children,' Isobel said, her mouth sounding full. 'Not often—only late at night when you were tired but didn't want to go to bed.'

'You had a way of soothing me.'

'Did I? I thought you hated my playing with your hair.'

Esther reached round and caught her sister's fingers. 'No.'

The noise of the courtyard lapped into the room. A child was admonished and they heard a slap. Someone else rattled over the dirt with a tray of mugs. There was chatter. A scrape of a packing crate being pulled up to the conversation. It was the kind of day that Esther had come to learn was normal for those on George Street.

Isobel sat quietly for so long that Esther thought her sister had fallen asleep. Her legs ached, spikes of pain flaring up her calves, but she didn't want to move. Isobel's hand rested beside her ear, her fingertips beside the flesh of Esther's earlobe. It was a sweet, comforting touch. Esther sighed and breathed in the wharf from her sister's clothes.

'I don't think I could bear to see him again.' Isobel's voice was slight but clear.

Esther sat up, pain flooding her feet and, wincing, hauled herself up to sit on the side of the bed.

'I cannot tolerate the thought of him coming home after he's finished at the gas works, stinking of grog, marching back in here like last night was nothing.' Isobel stared straight ahead at the torn newspaper lining the walls. The tone of her voice was different. Darker, heavier. Esther had heard her talk in such a way only once before, the day she left home and sailed for New Zealand. Isobel had returned to the kitchen after speaking to their mother in their father's old study. Esther remembered standing beside the table, making the coffin for Misty, the cat. Isobel had dropped down to quickly embrace her sister. 'I will write to you, little Esther,' she'd said, but her voice was cold and dark.

Isobel stood up. She walked unsteadily to the far end of the room, to the corner furthest from the window and bent down. Esther heard a rustle and a rush of breath as Isobel pulled at something—a floorboard. Then she stood up and Esther saw she held a bottle in her hand.

'Brandy,' Isobel said. 'Brendan stashed a bottle under the floorboards a year or so ago, in one of his stupors. He'd taken it into his head that the money was running out and he'd need an emergency supply. Of course, he had no memory of hiding the drink when he woke up. I never told him.'

She grabbed two mismatched teacups from the cupboard above the stove. 'First pipi, now brandy. Seems to be the day for trying new things.'

She sloshed pale liquid into the cups, almost up to the brim and handed one to Esther. A sharp, brazen smell stole around the cottage. Esther peered into the beige sun of her cup, her stomach shifting a little.

'Let's see what it's all about, shall we?' Isobel said. Her face was an ugly, forced grin, like the gurn of a Christmas puppet they had seen as children. Esther wanted to stop her drinking; she wanted to throw the brandy in her sister's face and wash away the manically smiling creature inhabiting Isobel's mouth.

But Isobel was too quick and, with a flick of her head, knocked the brandy down her throat in one go. She gasped, her eyes watered, and she threw out a hand to steady herself against the table. Then, lurching away, she flung open the front door.

The hard ball of her stomach and the needles of pain in her feet slowed Esther, and when she made it round to the courtyard, she found Isobel gulping down water from the pump, soaking the collar and hem of her dress. A group of women sat nearby in silence, watching. Esther laid the flat of her hand on Isobel's back and, when her sister began to retch, looked up helplessly.

Rose made it over first and forced Isobel to stand up straight. 'Something sitting badly in your stomach?' she said, and Esther saw the woman puff out the barrel of her chest. 'You need to let it have a way out—scrunching over like that won't help. Come on, stand up straight. You're not a little woman tending to a fire in one of the posh Queen Street houses. Let your body do what it needs to do.'

Hilda came to stand with them. She took Isobel's arm and kept her standing straight while Rose rubbed her belly. Isobel panted and a look passed between the women as they took in the unmistakable whiff of brandy fumes. They tutted with grim satisfaction as Isobel leaned forward again and spilled the contents of her stomach into the dirt.

It was over quickly. The women pushed Isobel onto a seat and curled her hands around a mug of tea. Esther, breathless and fighting tears, sat beside her. She wanted to hold Isobel's hand, but her sister seemed free of discomfort now and sipped her tea quietly.

'Well, I guess I'll be the one to say it,' Rose said, casting a look at Hilda. The other women looked on curiously, and at the edge of her eye, Esther saw Rachel enter the courtyard and stand close to the backs of the cottages. 'I never took you for a drinker, Isobel. Don't try to tell me it wasn't grog that you chucked up over there—we've all been married and know the smell from our men. I can't say I expected it to be a habit of yours, that's all I'll say.'

'Oh, it was brandy, I won't deny it.' Isobel's voice was shaky, but still Esther heard the line of darkness from before. 'Brendan has a secret stash. So secret he's forgotten about it.'

Someone—one of the younger women—tittered, but the rest stayed silent.

Isobel sighed. 'I'm not about to hit the drink, Rose, so please don't worry about that. The men doing it is bad enough, but I remember too well what happened to Verity.'

There was a communal sucking of teeth and a few nodding heads. Esther looked around, confused. Whoever this Verity was, she had left a distressing memory behind.

'Why then, Bella?' Hilda asked. 'I bet there's not one here who hasn't thought about emptying a bottle from time to time—but why now?'

Esther kept her eyes on her tea. She could not trust herself to look at Isobel; she knew her sister would silently plead with her to say nothing. Such a mute appeal, on top of what Esther had heard last night, and the indignity in the courtyard was too much to bear.

Isobel coughed a few more times, clearing the morning from her throat. 'I wanted to see what it would be like, that's all. I've never tasted brandy.' She gave a sudden shout of laughter. 'I don't even know if it's what Brendan drinks!'

The women were watchful as Isobel hooted hysterically, her laughter distilling wildly into tears. Esther put down her cup and wrapped an arm around Isobel's shoulders. She pulled her sister to her, glancing up to see unsurprised weariness on the faces of those nearby.

Rose clapped a hand on Isobel's shoulder. 'It gets to us all, dear.'

There was a movement to Esther's right, where Rachel was standing, and Esther saw the old woman make a fist and strike the brickwork.

⁓

'Isobel, I need to show you something.'

They were back in the cottage. An hour or so had passed since Isobel had drank the brandy and she was now at the table, a pile of sewing in her hands. Esther hadn't seen her needle move, however. The waistband of the skirt belonging to the music teacher's wife had yet to be let out, stitches were yet to be unpicked. When Isobel moved the fabric, Esther saw wet patches left by her sister's palms.

But Isobel seemed calmer. A little pale, but there had been no bouts of retching for a while. She had refused water or food.

Esther got up and went over to her trunk. She found the keys to the hidden compartment in her pocket. 'Help me lift this onto the bed, will you?'

Isobel did, seemingly disinterested, but she set the trunk in the centre of the bed where it was in no danger of toppling over. She stood back and watched as Esther opened the secret bottom.

'This is what I want to show you.' Her tongue felt thick in her mouth as she opened the compartment, suddenly grabbed by a frightening thought that the paper would not be there—that it was all in her imagination. That the master at Gallerton Hall had played her for a fool.

The paper was real enough, though, and still in the secret compartment. The title deeds to land in Canterbury sat on the bed in Isobel's dilapidated cottage, and the women strained to read it in the poor light.

'You own a piece of land?' Isobel blinked back into herself and colour returned to her cheeks. 'Am I reading this correctly?'

'Yes. Well, I suppose so. Of course, I've never seen the land itself.'

'Why didn't you tell me this before?'

'I wasn't sure what to do with it,' Esther said. 'And I didn't want Brendan to know.'

'How did you come to get it?'

Esther said nothing. The baby lay asleep beneath her ribs but her gaze fell, just for a brief second, and Isobel understood.

'Oh. *He* gave it do you. The father.'

Esther winced at the description; she did not think of the man from Gallerton Hall in such a way. The baby, becoming more real and present every day, was wrapped around *her* heart and lungs, not his. The child throbbed and pushed at *her* skin, it brought brine to *her* brow just to walk from George Street into the city—the child was bound to her and her alone. It had announced its presence on the ship over, through explosions and sickness. The sea had created it.

'The man gave the deeds to me, yes,' she said. 'As for where he acquired it—I have no idea.'

Isobel touched the edges of the paper, her forehead a crease of curiosity. 'This land, Esther—it could be your future.'

'Only if I went there.'

Isobel glanced at her. 'Are you afraid to? It is easy to understand your fear, Esther. After travelling so far to get here.'

Esther sat down on the bed. Her belly balled up on her thighs and she had to lean back, resting her weight on her hands. 'I am afraid of the journey, yes. There's no train to speak of—not from Picton to Christchurch, as far as I know. I'd have to ride or go by coach. And being as I am ...' She looked down at her stomach. 'Yes, I am afraid.'

Isobel looked at the document, but Esther could see she wasn't reading it. Her sister was thinking of something else again. Maybe Brendan? The air stilled and Esther could hear her blood pound in her ears. She tasted metal, the astringency making her mouth water.

'If you were with me, Isobel, I wouldn't be afraid.'

Isobel

The clock rolled around to midday, and Isobel set out bread and cheese for them. Esther made tea and they sat around the table, but Isobel did not eat. The slop of pipis spilling from her throat and the burn of brandy had stripped her appetite. She watched as Esther ate and sipped tea, hiding the fact that she did not eat by talking about the sewing they were to take back to Queen Street.

She had not responded to Esther's remark about accompanying her to the South Island to see the land. Her thoughts were elsewhere and it was difficult to focus. She could only think of the baby and what the land papers might mean. Owning land might give Esther hope, and she might want to keep the child.

She knew land still had power. She'd overheard some steerage emigrants on the boat out to New Zealand, another lifetime ago, speak of heading down to the plains where work was available. Others had talked of setting up stores and businesses in Otago, where towns still lingered after the gold rush. But none owned land. They had gone out to New Zealand to work, with maybe—*maybe*—the hope of saving enough to buy a piece of land. None had a piece of paper such as the one lying in the bottom of Esther's trunk, hidden beneath clothes and books.

Isobel could not think clearly. She could not see what she was meant to do. The longing to hold Esther's baby had grown inexplicably since the morning with Rachel. Her friend had been the first person she had told about their mother's letter and, since saying the words out loud, she knew she wanted the baby. She wanted what her body, or Brendan's body, could not give her.

The longing was strong and fierce, and frightened her. The only safety lay, she thought, in routine. Normality. In undertaking chores that were safe in their familiarity.

'We should take the mending back to the music teacher's family,' she said when Esther had finished. 'Will you finish the skirt while I clean up?'

Esther took the clothing to the easy chair and sat down, fingers flying across the fabric. Isobel watched out of the corner of her eye, between wiping the table down and wrapping the cheese in paper. The speed and accuracy of Esther's work with a needle still astonished her—the girl she remembered from ten years ago frowned and objected when it came to needlework time, and Isobel recalled their mother using all manner of threats to keep the girl in place. But now Esther could sew and fix and mend. She was fearless when it came to snipping away threads or material, and had altered dresses in a way Isobel would not have dared. Isobel had been given more mending than ever before—over the past few weeks, the maids on Queen Street had even begun to hand over their own clothes for alteration.

Esther finished fixing the skirt quickly and shook it out. She smoothed the clothing over her knee. 'There. Will it do?'

'It will do.' Isobel pulled on her jacket and reached for Esther's coat. 'Will you manage the walk to Queen Street today? You aren't tired?'

Esther shook her head and wrapped the coat around her shoulders. There was no hope of it closing over her belly now, so she had purchased a strip of black fabric from a haberdashers on Karangahape Road and had tacked it to the inside of the coat, fastening it across her stomach with the aid of buttons. To the unobservant, the fix looked a deliberate fashion, but Isobel resolved to ask her sister to wait on the pavement again while she delivered the mending.

The wind had risen when they went outside again and the courtyard was empty. Dust swirled in circular funnels, casting out dirty shards and handfuls of gravel. To the east, where the harbour foamed and waved, darkening clouds gathered.

Esther pointed them out. 'There's a storm. Should we wait until it passes?'

Isobel shook her head. 'I promised the mending would be back today. We can hurry. We'll be back before the rain comes and, if we get caught out, I'll buy us a bun from the teashop at the bottom of Queen Street.'

The sisters locked arms, as had become their way, and hurried as quickly as they could along the uneven streets. There was an unusual taste to the air; thick and beery, like vegetation left to spoil. A dog trotted nearby, rangy and young, and lifted its nose to sniff before whimpering and running off.

By the time they made it to Queen Street, the rain had come. Heavy, bulbous raindrops fell like eggs onto the pavements. Esther had an umbrella, a pitiful thing better suited to decoration only, and they ducked under it as best they could, quickening their step even more. Above there was a ripping, rendering sound, and thunder came down upon their heads.

'You'll have to wait here,' Isobel said desperately as they reached the music teacher's house. She looked through the garden, along the paths to the back door where servants came and went. There was a little cover, just over the doorway, but nothing to those standing on the street.

'Oh, Isobel, even in this weather you want to keep me hidden away?' Esther's hair was plastered to her face, making her look impossibly young. Isobel remembered how she looked on bath nights, when their father filled the tin bath in front of the fire and Esther stayed in the water until it became completely cold, her wet hair pressed to her head. Isobel used to want to pull her sister close, to wrap her arms around Esther's fragility.

But now they stood on Queen Street, outside the house of the wealthy. Isobel handed Esther the umbrella. 'I'll be as quick as I can.'

Esther took the umbrella and said nothing. The tiniest shake of her head, and Isobel knew her sister was thinking of the night before, and of Brendan. Isobel almost buckled. Brendan had risen that morning and dressed himself for work, hurrying onto the street as though nothing had happened. His spite was draped in the uniform of respectability and Esther, with her honest, swollen belly, who had never hurt Isobel, was being forced to stay out of sight of those easily offended.

Even so, Isobel hurried away, leaving Esther on the sodden street.

The same girl from before answered the door, the Irish maid with the impenetrable accent. The door was snatched open the second Isobel finished knocking and she stood back startled.

The maid peered around the door, eyes darting over Isobel's face rapidly. It was as though she could not make her out, as though she did not recognise Isobel. Then the maid spoke, her voice cracked and odd.

'It's yourself, is it? You have mending?'

'I do.' Isobel began to take out a parcel of mending from her bag, glancing up curiously. She heard snuffling sounds from the kitchen. 'Is anything wrong?'

'You might as well tell her, Bessie!' came a shriek from over the maid's shoulder. 'Everyone will know soon enough!'

Isobel handed over the package, shocked. She recognised the voice: it was one of the music teacher's daughters, the eldest. She had spoken to Isobel the Christmas before, about a holly and ivy pattern she had wanted to be added to the trim of a dress. The girl's voice was shrill and high-pitched. Bessie, the maid, tutted and turned back inside.

'Hush, miss! Lord, you don't know what you're saying.' Bessie even raised a finger in the daughter's direction.

Isobel gaped, her bewilderment increasing. She had never seen a servant speak in such a way to a mistress before, even if the mistress was not much more than a child. Bessie, now facing her, saw Isobel's surprise and slumped against the door.

'You'd better come in,' she said. 'I'll need you to understand so you don't go off, repeating what you've seen here.'

'No, that's not necessary,' Isobel said, beginning to back away into the rain and sludge of the garden. Whatever drama was happening at this house could stay in the kitchen.

But Bessie swung the door wide open, exposing the kitchen and the music teacher's daughter sitting at the table, her head in her hands. Her shoulders shook. The girl was sobbing. A chair had been overturned and a knife lay on the table.

'Come right in,' Bessie said. 'It's quite a sight, I'm sure.'

Isobel hesitated in the doorway. The music teacher's daughter wiped her face and Isobel could see her more clearly. One of her cheeks was red raw. What appeared to be a slap mark blazed over her face and neck.

'Please, come in.' Bessie grabbed Isobel's hand agitatedly. Isobel looked down, confusion growing.

Outside a thunder clap tore across the sky, and the garden was lit up. Bessie smiled triumphantly. 'See, the weather! Surely you'll not want to be going back out in this.'

It was true, Isobel did not. The rain bore down relentlessly and cold sent shivery fingers around her wet ankles and damp legs. The kitchen smelled of mutton and kumara, and Isobel's appetite was awakened. She thought of Esther, standing alone on the pavement.

'I can only stay a minute. My sister is waiting for me on the street. May I invite her in as well? I would hate to leave her outside in this.'

She saw Bessie's eyebrows raise but, whatever it was that was occurring in the music teacher's house, whatever it was that caused the maid to drag Isobel inside and speak so sharply to her mistress, also dampened down any misgivings she might have had. Bessie nodded.

Isobel retreated to the street hurriedly before Bessie could change her mind. She found Esther leaning against the low wall dividing the house garden from the pavement, water pouring over the bedraggled umbrella. Isobel felt a wave of longing and guilt build inside her; she had kept her sister hidden, had forced precious Esther to huddle in the rain like a cat. Without a word she wove an arm around Esther's waist and steered her down the path to the kitchen door.

Bessie stood back to let them in and, as Esther stepped uncertainly into the room and unfolded herself, water puddling at her feet, her stomach was jutting and bold. The rain had pasted her clothes to her frame. Her breasts, now round and firm, stood out proudly but were dwarfed by the boulder of her stomach. She glanced around, confusion on her face, unsure of why she was in the room. Isobel slipped a hand into hers, unseen, and squeezed.

'Esther, we have been invited in out of the rain. Isn't that pleasant?'

The overturned chair had been righted and pushed under the kitchen table. The music teacher's daughter sat silently, staring at Esther's belly. The girl looked to be around seventeen. Her hair was pinned up, though strands were coming loose. Blonde curls fell by her temples. She was not pretty, not in the sense that Isobel understood beauty. Her eyes were set too far apart and a gap appeared between her teeth when her lips parted. But her skin was fresh and clean, and her dress, cut a little too low for her age, revealed a smooth bosom.

The girl's unblinking stare at Esther's stomach became unnerving. Bessie noticed it too. She leaned across her mistress and picked up the knife. She put it on the sideboard.

'Please, will you sit?' Bessie said, and Isobel felt again how upside down things felt in this room. It was not correct for a maid to offer a seat to a guest when the mistress was there. Isobel glanced at the girl and waited, but the music teacher's daughter continued to bite her lips and look away. Isobel cleared her throat and sat down, nodding at Esther to do the same.

'Perhaps I should introduce myself, miss,' Isobel said. 'You have been gracious enough to invite us in, but you may not know my name. I am Mrs Isobel Nelson and this is my sister … Esther.'

The moment Isobel started on her clumsy speech, she knew immediately she had blundered. With Esther's state so obvious, she should not have drawn attention to her unmarried status. At least, not before they'd had a chance to dry off from the rain, whispered a wicked voice in the back of her mind, sounding rather like Rachel.

It was a large colonial kitchen, almost perfectly square in shape.

Pots and pans and oversized serving plates rested on a rail above head height. A large tray on a pulley hung above them too, crowded with cooking equipment, most of which Isobel didn't recognise or see the use for. There was a bucket of timber in the corner for the stove and a basket of bread on the sideboard. An earthenware sink and a drying rack was positioned at the side of the room, upon which sat cups and plates, presumably the remnants of the servant's lunch. Coloured glass bottles lined the window looking up into the garden, and brief flashes of greens, reds, and blues loomed on the wall. It added a dazzling effect to the room and when Isobel looked away, blocks of light danced in her eyes.

'Cook's out buying fish at the harbourside,' Bessie said. She bounced her fingertips together before forcing them down to her sides where they tapped out a rhythm against her uniform. 'I expect she'll be back before long.'

The girl jerked at this and Isobel was puzzled even further. Just what was happening in this kitchen, and why had they been invited in to witness it? It was not a household that had invited her in before, and the room was odd and unsettling, for all its attempt at homeliness. It was so square shaped, just like a box. It was a room equipped for industry and work, with all those spoons and pots and tureens. And yet they were sparklingly clean, as though they were not to be used and were for display only. A suspended room. Isobel felt trapped, like a fly in amber.

In the silent room, water gathered at Isobel's feet. Esther, too, was circled by rain sliding down her clothes and out through her boots.

'Be careful,' Bessie said. She had yet to sit down and her feet edged the pool of water. 'A wet floor is a devil's tongue.'

Miss Joanna snickered softly. 'Another of your sayings, Bessie.'

'What if it is?'

Again, that sharp tone. Isobel could not fathom it—servants did not speak to their employers in such a way, especially not now work was harder to find. In the first years of living in the colony, she had heard the stories of servants laying down the law to ladies and gentlemen. She'd heard about the maids who would not bake or churn, or care for children, knowing they could walk into a house just next door and have those conditions met without question. But the lean years of the Depression had put an end to such demands. Isobel remembered how Bessie had turned abruptly away the last time they met, when she feared she had said too much and might lose her employment. The country had seen a change.

'I suppose you're wondering what all of this is about,' Bessie said, as though she had read Isobel's mind. 'The truth is that our Miss Joanna'—she nodded over to the girl discourteously—'has taken rather a shine to my brother. The one I told you about who works at Partington's Windmill? Liam made a delivery here one afternoon when the miss was in the kitchen, probably asking Cook to bake those little cakes she's so fond of.'

Scorn crept into Bessie's voice. Miss Joanna looked down at the tablecloth, brilliant white except for the corners where it had been seared by the iron.

'I understand there have been meetings between them,' Bessie went on. The sneer in her voice grew stronger, and within it Isobel heard hissed curses and repressed objections to a thousand pointless, mundane tasks. Bessie had been waiting for such a moment, Isobel sensed. The hours she had spent dusting and polishing and wiping the smear of rich arses from privy seats had come to this.

'There really is no need to tell us any more,' Esther spoke up. Isobel looked at her in surprise. 'It seems indelicate, if I may say so.'

'Indelicate?' Bessie's eyebrows arched. '*Fancy.* Perhaps you would know more about that than I.'

Esther's mouth fell open at that, but she closed it quickly, as though swallowing back a retort.

Bessie went on. 'If I hadn't been in this kitchen today, the whole street would be knowing about our indelicate Miss Joanna.'

'What do you mean?' Isobel asked.

'An agreement had been reached,' Bessie said emphatically. 'An agreement between Miss Joanna and Liam—that they would run off together and be married. Only, Liam wasn't where he said he would be when she went to meet him this morning.'

'You were going to elope with him?' Isobel looked at the music teacher's daughter with astonishment. The girl began to weep again.

'She was,' Bessie said with satisfaction. 'They'd arranged to meet at the bandstand at Albert Park, if you can believe it. In front of all those people, taking the air! That Liam wasn't there is no surprise to me, let me tell you. If I'd known any of this before today, I could have warned her. It's not the first time Liam has had his entertainment and then taken to his heels. When Miss Joanna went to his lodgings to track him down, he was gone. Belongings and all. He will have left Auckland. I don't know if I'll ever hear from him again.'

At this Miss Joanna sobbed noisily, covering her face, and Bessie bit her lip, finally looking downcast. The women were bookends to their distress.

Esther's head was bowed. Isobel reached over and squeezed her sister's fingers and, pausing for only a second, leaned across the table to also take Miss Joanna's small hand. The girl's fingers were soft and white, the nails clean and neatly clipped. They did not look like pianist fingers to Isobel and she wondered briefly if the girl had not inherited her father's talent. She held Miss Joanna's hand, forming a chain between herself, Esther, and the girl.

Seconds passed and they broke off. Bessie gathered herself and handed Miss Joanna a handkerchief. The girl hiccupped and wiped her face, and calmed.

'Perhaps,' Isobel began hesitantly, 'perhaps you are better free of him. If he has played a cruel a trick as this, better you know it now than later. Was there any ... I don't know how to put this, but what kind of meetings were they, exactly?'

Miss Joanna looked confused, but Bessie understood perfectly. 'Nothing like that, miss, from what I understand. I don't think ...' She turned her body a little, away from Miss Joanna. 'I don't think those matters have been explained to her.'

'I see.' Isobel thought of the conversation she'd had with Rachel only that morning—was it only hours ago?—concerning women's lack of knowledge when it came to matters of the body. It did not surprise her that a young, unmarried girl would have no knowledge of what Liam might have wanted.

'He kissed me, if that is what you mean,' the girl said falteringly. 'Just once, last night. I don't think you can get into trouble from that.'

'Depends who sees,' Bessie said darkly.

'Was anyone else aware of your arrangement?' Isobel asked.

'Well, that's the problem.' Bessie turned back round to glower at Miss Joanna, who shrank in her seat. 'Our little miss wasn't exactly discreet when she went marching over to Liam's lodgings. I understand she made a bit of a spectacle on the street. One of the maids happened to be on an errand nearby—her day off, you see. She brought her back here, which was a stroke of fortune. And then Miss Joanna threatened to harm herself if I didn't somehow magically find Liam.' Bessie's eyes narrowed. 'I had to be a little stern with her, if you see what I mean.'

That explained the knife and the slap mark on Miss Joanna's face which, as Isobel looked closely, became deeper and crimson. It also, Isobel realised, explained why Isobel and Esther had been invited inside. They were witnesses. A maid slapping a mistress was certainly a sacking offence, and most likely enough for a policeman to called. Whether the girl had waved the knife around, Isobel could not be sure—Miss Joanna looked dramatic enough, sitting there with a blotched face and a wet handkerchief. A witness being prepared to swear they saw a knife might be enough to save Bessie's job, should the girl complain.

'Have you ever—have you *ever* loved someone so much your mind seems to have turned to jam, and you can't think straight and all you can do is wait for the next moment you will see them?' Miss Joanna's voice was breathless and she wrung her hands together.

From her place near the sideboard, Bessie rolled her eyes.

'Whatever your feelings, it does not seem that the young man felt the same way,' Isobel said gently.

'He did!' The girl banged her fist on the table and Isobel saw a little red line on the inside of her wrist. Maybe she had tried to hurt herself after all.

Isobel continued cautiously. 'I understand that you think he cared for you. But it would be best for you if you put the boy out of your mind. And no more silliness about hurting yourself.'

Miss Joanna cast about the table again, chastened. She had the look about her of someone who had stood at the edge of a deep pond and stepped back at the last moment. Her hand strayed to her cheek. Isobel wondered just how many slaps Bessie had landed on the poor girl's face.

Still, Esther was silent. Isobel inclined her head, inviting her to talk, but Esther looked away.

It was time to go. Bessie kept glancing at the little clock above the stove, as though afraid that Cook would return at any moment. Her feet were still sodden, but Isobel got up anyway and helped Esther. She wanted to be gone, away from the craziness, away from the crying and raw emotion, away from all that feeling.

They bowed a goodbye and Bessie held the door open.

'Thank you,' the maid said, and the sisters climbed the steps back up into the garden. They heard the door close behind them and Isobel had the strong sense that she would not receive mending from that house again. Then they were back out in the street where, mercifully, it had stopped raining.

'I didn't want that horrid woman to tell us any of it,' Esther said. They were tramping south along Queen Street, away from the harbour. Muddy streets sucked at their boots. Men hauled carts through the sludge, women picked up their skirts and leaped over puddles. A group of young women nearby, clutching baskets of white flowers, giggled and shrieked as one fell to her knees in the dirt.

'Do you mean Bessie?' Isobel hopped across a wide sluice of water and reached out to help Esther.

'She couldn't wait to betray the girl, could she?'

It was impossible to march, not with the weight of her belly and the malevolence of the streets, but Esther pounded her anger down into her boots. She had sat in the kitchen on Queen Street with an old familiar pain in her chest, the type she used to feel when the master at Gallerton Hall returned to his wife after a morning with her. The knowledge that he would be with the mistress, laughing or smiling, or sitting and listening to her chatter was enough to impale Esther—and she hadn't even loved him. She had felt none of the passion that Miss Joanna evidently felt for Liam, but she felt the scorch of the music teacher's daughter in her windpipe and breast.

'It sounds as though Bessie saved the girl from doing something foolish. She and the other maid who saw her outside the boy's lodgings,' Isobel said.

'We only have Bessie's word for it. Confound it, Isobel! It's the women who are left behind to put the shattered glass back together again, isn't it?'

'You might have said something to her. Offered her a few words of comfort.'

'I?' Esther laughed bitterly. They had reached the intersection of Queen Street and Wellesley Street, and she stepped aside to allow a man with a basket of eels tied to his back to pass, heading for the fishmongers. A horse hauled a wagon toward a furniture store, chairs and beds piled in the back. The beast strained and farted with the effort. 'I don't expect advice from a woman in my situation would have helped. I am *indelicate*, after all.'

'But you know something of thwarted love. The—the father, I mean, of your baby.'

'Oh, Isobel.' Esther stopped and caught her sister's hand. 'I didn't love him.'

'You didn't love him …?'

'No. Oh, I hated that he would go back to *her*, his wife. How could he stand it? She was so dull. But I didn't love him.' Esther tucked her arms around her belly. 'It was a need, that's all.'

Isobel stepped back, shocked.

'Come, Isobel,' Esther said, saddened. 'I'm sorry. It is unfeeling of me to speak to you like this after—earlier.' She meant what had happened through the night with Brendan, and she sensed Isobel tighten.

'I don't suppose you will believe me, but I do know something of that kind of love,' Isobel said. She untangled Esther's fingers from her own and sighed. 'I seem to have spoken more about the exchange between a man and woman in the past twelve hours than ever in my life before. But that girl nearly made a terrible mistake, you must see that. Maybe she has already.'

'I don't see that, actually.'

'But you *must*, Esther. The music teacher's daughter isn't like you. She doesn't have somewhere to escape to—at least, I don't think she does. If she were to marry that young man, she'd have nowhere to run to.'

'But why should she run, Isobel?' Esther felt anger bounce like an egg in her stomach; she wondered if the baby could feel it, knocking against its ribs. 'I wish I had not.'

'Do you?' Isobel wore an odd, tight look. 'Do you wish you had stayed at home and had the baby? You would have been ostracised.'

'Oh, Mother would have thrown me out, there's no doubt about that. But there are other ways to deal with my kind of problem.'

'What do you mean?'

What Esther meant, she could not find the words to say. She had been seen to by the woman in Derby, with the curved hook and hot water, and it had hurt her terribly, in ways she had not imagined. She couldn't go through it again. But babies could be given away.

She didn't say these things to her sister, though. Instead: 'You are such a contradiction, Isobel. You march about the streets gathering signatures so that women might have the vote—which, I must tell you, after getting on a boat and coming out here is the bravest thing you've ever done. I still can't believe you are involved in politics. But then you keep me away from the easily shocked in the big houses not a hundred yards from the reality of life out here.' She gestured toward the poor horse pulling the cart of furniture, wheezing audibly as the wagon was unloaded. 'And you tell little Miss Besotted that she's wrong to have fallen in love with a poor man. It's as though you can't see what this place is.'

'What place? Auckland?' Isobel's face was contorted. It was impossible to tell if she was furious or not.

'Yes!' Esther swept her arm around, taking in the street, the dirt, the boys playing with sticks in the mud. Stores and timber houses rose precariously in tight formation, wedged against each other for balance, and sluiceways of muck flowed down from the higher ground toward the sea. Yet the streets thrummed. She could feel it. Carts, feet, dogs, men driving horses—they tore up the earth, shaping and reshaping it, over and over. Shouts broke the damp air, with storekeepers hollering about the latest delivery of honey or fabric. Voices overlapped with voices; a thick plait of accents, cries of opportunity.

'It's crept up on me, but I have the strongest feeling that this is a place where you can decide just what kind of life you want,' Esther said. She felt a grin seize her face maniacally. 'We're so far away from all those ridiculous customs and rules, and the little glances that put ropes around us. We can be free to love whom we want, or reject those who don't love us. Half of you can see it and half of you wants to hide.'

A curious look from Isobel and she seemed on the edge of saying something. But she did not. Her attention was gripped by a crowd gathering just to the east. There was a large building on the corner with wooden columns holding up an ornate, carved front. A painted sign above declared it to be the opera house. The doors were flung open and a crowd bustled outside the overcrowded building, people standing on tiptoes straining to see inside. There were hisses and calls for quiet, and a voice shouted in frustration.

'Of course, how could I have forgotten?' Isobel tugged Esther's hand. 'It's a public meeting. The Franchise League called it. It's been in the papers for the past week.'

'What meeting?'

'About the bill. They say they'll put the petition before the House of Representatives again. I can't believe I forgot. Elizabeth Peter will be there.'

'The bill to give women the vote?'

'What else? Come on. We might be able to hear some of it.'

As if overtaken by sudden urgency, Isobel joined the back of the crowd, standing on tiptoes as well and craning her neck to hear. Esther followed, baffled at the sight of her sister leaning carelessly against the man in front, desperate to hear the speakers.

A couple noticed Esther's swollen belly and a little space was opened up in the crowd for them. Up ahead, near the door, a young man was hooked off a seat and room was made for Esther. She sat down, and Isobel edged in beside her.

They could not see into the room but they could hear. A woman nearby hushed for silence, and an announcement was made that a new speaker was about to begin. There must have been a stage up ahead and Esther heard words threading out. A woman's voice.

'... how can parliament reflect the wishes of the electorate when half of us are not represented? Laws are passed that are said to benefit women, and yet we have no say in them. It is a matter of justice, not sentiment, for this bill to go through.'

The crowd murmured its approval and some clapped softly. Esther felt Isobel bounce on the seat beside her, nodding her head emphatically. She turned to look, increasingly bewildered that her sister could be so enraptured and yet, this morning, when such a wrong had been done to her by her very husband, she had either sat mute or tried to drink away her pain.

The crowd about them was young—men and women. Some wore factory clothes and rough, torn shirts. Others were better dressed, with polished boots and brooches pinned to their breast. It was a mixed, eclectic crowd, but all reached out for the white flowers handed out by young girls hovering at the back of the crowd. Esther recognised the girls from earlier; the girl who passed a flower along to her was the one who had fallen in the mud. Isobel fastened the flower into Esther's coat.

'White camellia,' she said. 'The symbol of the suffrage cause.'

The speaker continued and the crowd became more vocal in their agreement. They packed in closer and a man's calves brushed Esther's knees. The air felt tight and warm. She felt the breath choke in her throat, though the sensation was more exciting than alarming.

'And there may even be a woman mayor before the end of the year!' A man's voice from inside the building and the crowd nodded as one. He was a good orator, Esther thought. His words were slow, almost teasing. He spoke with a rise and fall, rolling the listeners with him. Esther felt herself yearn to hear more. 'Our friends in Onehunga are watching closely, waiting for their chance to vote for a woman candidate.'

Onehunga. Isobel had taken her to the temperance meeting place, and she had met Elizabeth and her daughter. Hadn't the child,

Dottie, come from a house at Onehunga? Isobel had told her a little
of the story, though Esther had the sense her sister had held back on
details. Elizabeth had found the girl in Onehunga in danger, and had
taken her in.

'There are some who say a woman cannot be mayor. What do you
think I say to that?'

The crowd laughed, dirtily, hungrily.

'What do you think I say to those who argue that women should
be excluded from all representation?'

'You say poppycock!' a wag yelled, and there was a moan from
those around him. An audible release. Others tittered.

The man on the stage had not heard and his voice dropped,
steadying himself for delivery. 'I say women's minds are as keen as
the men around them. And women are needed in parliament and
voting for parliament. They are *needed*.'

There were gasps and screwed-up faces of pleasure. A couple,
obviously newly in love, turned and kissed passionately. Someone
sighed; another whooped in celebration.

Then there was movement. A woman pushed her way out of the
opera house, looking at a pocket watch anxiously. A space opened up
and suddenly Esther could see through a window. There was nothing to observe though, except for bodies standing upright, straining
to see the stage. She looked closely. In the reflection of the glass, she
could see the figure of a man staring at her.

His cloth cap was pulled down over his brow, but she knew the
nose and shape of his mouth. It was Jack Bellamy. He was at the back
of the crowd, tall above those in front of him. He wore an open neck
shirt and the hair at his temples was spiked. Perhaps he had been
caught out in the rain, perhaps he was hot from the throb of the
crowd.

He did not know she could see him. He did not know that Esther
knew he was observing *her*. She kept her head still, her body positioned toward the window and the opera house. An electric current
thrilled in her chest, sending a line between her stomach and throat.

The agitation of the crowd had already infected her. Now her skin lit up to think he was watching her, while she was watching him.

'It is said that New Zealand should not follow but lead. Where better than to lead in the area of justice and fairness?' A woman spoke now and her voice from inside the building was high and full of passion. 'It is also said that those selling drink will see their profits fall should women be given the right to vote. I say—good! I say—hurrah!'

A few women nearby punched the air. Esther felt Isobel shift beside her, but she did not turn her face away from the window.

'Sir John Hall will be putting our petition to the House shortly. I know so many of you good people here marched the streets and gathered signatures, and for that the Franchise and Temperance Unions are grateful. We've been here before, have we not? We hoped our petition would pass last year. So we must keep our hope. And our fight!'

The crowd roared back to life at that, thumping like a wild heart, boots pounding the ground. Esther felt the brazen energy of the men and women around her, and the shake of her sister as Isobel trembled. Esther felt her own veins pop with urgency. Her breasts swelled and ached.

The woman's speech seemed to have been the final one. The crescendo had been reached and the crowd began to ebb away. Some wiped their faces. Esther saw one woman with damp patches under her arms and she glanced away, embarrassed. The leaking of bodies shamed her, as it always did as the baby grew.

It was then, the body of the crowd melting back onto the street, the fervour over, that she turned to look, to stare at Jack fully in the face. Unblinking. He, too, cautious at first, then hungry. He raised his own eyes to bear down on her.

⁂

'Mr Bellamy? Why, what are you doing here?'

Jack stood before them. Men and women were thronging from the opera house back into the steaming street, and Esther and Isobel watched them from their seat. Esther peered up at Jack's face. He must have been caught in a shower, she thought, for his jacket was wet and the flannel of his trousers was smeared over his thighs.

'Mrs Nelson.' Jack bowed his head toward Isobel politely. His eyes, though, did not stray far from Esther's face. 'It is a momentous time, after all. I was on my way back from the bank on Queen Street when I saw the meeting. Did it interest you, Miss Carter?'

'The speakers?' Esther smiled. 'I only heard a little. But their passion! The passion of the crowd! It is infectious.'

'Yes.'

Isobel looked between them, back and forth, brow creased. Then she moved away hurriedly. 'There's Elizabeth Peter. Ah, she has Dottie with her—I wondered if she would bring her. Please excuse me.'

Esther watched as her sister slipped from the seat and wove her way over to Mrs Peter, who stood holding the hand of her daughter. Dottie's sturdy wide legs bounced and Esther saw Isobel swing the girl up onto her hip. She saw Isobel wince as the child wrapped her legs tightly around Isobel's waist, her sister's hand straying to her stomach.

Fury overtook Esther all over again and she saw Brendan's red, smirking face in her mind's eye. She gritted her teeth and, when she turned back to Jack Bellamy, realised he was staring intently at her.

'Mr Bellamy ...'

'Jack, please.'

'Jack, then. Can I ask you a question about your family? It may seem odd and I apologise if it is unwelcome, but there's something I wanted to know.'

Jack waited. He seemed poised, cat-like, and Esther felt her skin itch. She knew the look; the master at Gallerton Hall had looked at her the same way in those early days. She felt a familiar, melting sensation in her stomach.

'I heard that your family settled in the South Island.'

'That's right.' He shifted at this, the question unexpected. His eyes narrowed and changed, and Esther was reminded of the shutters that came over him when they spoke in the courtyard on George Street, the day of the Sale Street fire. She plunged on regardless.

'Where on the South Island?'

'A valley between Christchurch and Dunedin. It's quite remote.'

'I have land in that area. In the Hatcher Valley.'

Jack raised his eyebrows. 'You have land?'

'Yes.'

'How did you come to own land?'

Esther shook her head. 'I cannot say. But do you know the area?'

Jack studied her. 'I do. The Hatcher Valley is within half a day's ride of my father's farm. But tell me more about the land you own.'

A firm shake of her head. 'Maybe later. Isobel and I are thinking of taking a trip to see it. I'm not sure if I'll keep it, truth be told. It would give me an income, for when the baby arrives. But I need to see it first.'

'You would need a guide. Or a chaperone.'

It was impossible not to snort at the word. 'We don't need a chaperone. I've heard there are many women who travel around on their own in this land, or travel with a female companion. No chaperones—I left the last one on the boat over here, thank you.'

Jack stared at her.

'No, we don't need a chaperone, but we do need a guide. Someone who could help us get to where we're going.' Over Jack's shoulder, Esther could see Isobel hugging Dottie and chucking the child under her chin. Every now and then Isobel's hand strayed to the small of her back, and eventually she put the girl down on the ground.

'Are you asking me to accompany you, Miss Carter?'

Esther paused. The crowd around the opera house was streaming away into the city, but there were some who lingered, like them, to talk with friends. Pockets of people gathered around the speakers, who were striding out into the sunshine breaking through the clouds. Groups laughed. Someone shouted and one woman began clapping her hands rhythmically. The energy on the street was warm and pressed against Esther's body.

'I would like it very much if you could accompany us,' she said, the words tumbling from her hurriedly, as though they were afraid she would take them back. She did not look at Jack's face, but instead stared at his boots and waited for his reaction.

He was silent for a few moments and she wondered if the shock had been too much. It was scandalous, after all, for a woman—a new settler, at that—to invite a man to accompany her on a journey. But, Esther thought, the idea of a scandal was a very English thing, and England was thousands of miles away.

'I would have to take a leave of absence from my work as a land-lord,' Jack said eventually. His voice was contemplative, and any fear Esther had that she had shocked him evaporated. 'We would need at least a month.'

'Is that something you can arrange?'

'Perhaps. I'm sure my tenants would not object at all if I disappeared for a month.' He smiled ruefully. 'I collected rent only two days ago, so being away for a while would not matter so much.'

'You'll consider it?' Esther looked at him hopefully.

'When do you plan on leaving? If you don't mind me saying, are you capable of travelling right now?'

Esther glanced again at Isobel. Her sister was wiping her brow, nodding and listening to Elizabeth Peter. Isobel was smiling too, and Esther saw how Mrs Peter lifted her sister's spirits. Isobel pushed her hair out of her eyes in that old way of hers, and Esther was embraced by love for her. She saw the patches on her sister's dress, the strip of fabric that had been used to repair the hem, the patches of grey at Isobel's temple.

'We should leave while there is still time. We want to go today, Mr Bellamy. This very day.'

Part Two

Esther

They had a bag each. Not nearly enough for a month of travelling, especially in the back country where grass was burnt, and dust and sweat stayed on the body for days, but a bag apiece was the most they wanted to carry.

Back at the cottage, the thrill of clandestine planning zipped between the sisters like a wild flame and Isobel emptied her bag of mending on the bed recklessly. There were no shirts waiting to be darned, thank goodness—they had left the music teacher's house on Queen Street without a new parcel of clothes—but spools of thread and offcuts of fabric scattered over Isobel's quilt. Esther eyed them sadly, realising her sister had used odd pieces to patch her own dresses and line the hem of her skirt.

'At least we won't be delayed by taking mending back to Queen Street,' Isobel had said, handing the bag to Esther. 'Here, you use the bag. You've only got that big trunk of yours, and there's no way we can drag that the hundreds of miles down to the South Island.'

Persuading Isobel to go had been remarkably easy. As the crowds dispersed outside the opera house, Esther had walked over to Isobel, who stood talking to Elizabeth Peter. Elizabeth bobbed from foot to foot animatedly, reaching out to touch Dottie's cheek or smooth down her hair, clapping her hands together at certain points.

'What a wonderful meeting!' Elizabeth said, glittering. 'Can't you feel the power of the moment? I can—it's like the very air knows a change is coming.'

Isobel laughed and rolled her eyes, teasing her friend. 'Let's see what happens when they vote on it.'

Elizabeth flapped her hand. 'I have faith and so should you. Change is on its way!'

Jack appeared at Esther's side. 'The speakers were uplifting, that is true.'

'Elizabeth, this is Mr Jack Bellamy, my landlord,' Isobel said.

'Good afternoon.' But Elizabeth was distracted. She stood on tiptoes, peering over the heads of those still left. 'My husband should be somewhere about. He said he would come along to listen.'

'Isobel, can I talk to you?' Esther whispered. 'About an idea. Jack might be able to help us.'

And it had been simple to set out her idea. Elizabeth had moved slightly away, still looking for her husband, and Dottie held Isobel's hand while kicking at stones in the dirt. Esther had laid out her proposal, paring her thoughts back to the most basic. She wanted to make her plan sound clean and unfussy, giving Isobel nothing to pick over. The idea was simply to take a trip to the South Island to see the land Esther owned, with Jack as their guide. They would leave immediately.

Esther saw her sister hesitate and knew that well-worn excuses were poised to slip over Isobel's shoulders like an easy coat. She waited for them, bracing herself for Isobel's strangled attempt to explain that she could not leave and that going back to Brendan was the only way.

'Don't you think it would be an adventure?' Esther said desperately. 'You told me once you had never left Auckland, not in the whole ten years you have been here. What do you say to exploring New Zealand together? Say yes, please, Bella.'

It was deliberate, to use that name. Never before had Esther called her sister by her New Zealand name. It sat clumsily on her tongue but, once said, seemed perfect and whole. Esther saw surprise open Isobel's face, and then the sisters noticed, together, that Elizabeth Peter had finally spotted her husband and dashed to him. They watched Mr Peter wrap protective arms around his wife and hug her close, almost lifting the woman off her feet.

Just behind them, at the opera house doors, someone started to sing—a lilting, up-and-down melody that most of those left on the street knew. Many voices joined in, singing along to the end; a song of New Zealand and God. Isobel joined in and, when the singing stopped, turned to Esther with shining eyes.

'The national anthem. Of here, not England.'

'I don't know it.'

'No, I don't expect you do.' Isobel smiled. 'I'm glad someone started singing it now. Esther, I'll go with you to see your land. If Mr Bellamy can help us find our way, I'd be glad of his company.'

And that was it. They would go.

After a hurried return to the cottage to collect the title deeds to the land and the money Esther had left, and after loading two small bags with clothes for the journey, they left. A few of the women on George Street were in the courtyard when they returned, and Isobel spent some moments with Rachel Speedy in the courtyard. When she returned, her eyes were pink and Esther knew her sister felt the parting from her friend.

They set off. Jack was waiting for them at the end of George Street, away from neighbours' eyes. Isobel had suggested he wait out of sight, on their walk back from the opera house and Jack, seeming to sense how delicately Isobel was balanced, agreed without protest. Isobel's decision to leave had been swift, but she was tense and nervous. It would not take much to push her from the knife's edge and back onto the side of respectability, and Brendan.

Jack had a bag of his own and a pair of scuffed riding boots that swung as they walked. 'Do you know anything about the journey?' he asked, when Esther looked at the boots quizzically. 'There may be a tourist route now, and trains to most cities on these islands, but we'll be tramping or riding for some of it.'

'I can't ride,' Esther said, a little panicked. The ache in her belly doubled in protest.

Jack shrugged. 'You might have to.'

They walked back toward Queen Street, toward the harbour and the railway station built near the water. The evening cooled and darkened, and they walked as quickly as Esther's gasping frame would allow. Some stores made use of new gas lights and yellow orbs lined the brown streets. A haberdasher had strung up a swatch of gauze over his store light, and Esther and Isobel walked through a puddle of pink as they passed by. Esther paused, holding up her boot, letting the soft glow wrap around her foot. At the corner, where the street and store ended, another light and another wrap of fabric threw green shapes onto the earth, soaking away dirt and foulness. Esther lingered again but then hurried her step as they marched on.

They would take a train south from Auckland station; the building an old, grey colonial, stained by gulls and the salt of the harbour. Esther gave Jack money to buy their tickets and she waited with Isobel while he fetched them, standing close together as passengers milled around the station's two platforms. The noise in the building was deafening. Goods and parcels were being loaded, men in oiled trousers running from engine shed to train with last-minute items. One young lad, likely an apprentice, stumbled with a box of tools and received a clip round the ear for his trouble. Esther watched sympathetically as the lad shook his head and rubbed the pain away, before picking up the tools and sprinting for a departing train.

Their train took them to Cambridge, a few hours south, where they were able to find a room in a small hotel near the station. The place was crowded and they elicited a number of curious stares from fellow travellers. There was just the one room and Jack insisted that Esther and Isobel take the bedroom, with its narrow cots and sour smelling sheets, while he slept in an armchair in the parlour downstairs. In the morning, when they came down for breakfast, they found Jack slumped with his neck at an awkward angle. Isobel returned to their room to soak a bundle of handkerchiefs in the hot water set out for a morning wash, and Jack held the wet poultice to his neck while they ate.

From Cambridge, they were forced to take a Cobb. They picked up a bright red coach and, until Taupo, were the only passengers.

'Maybe we'll make quick time,' Jack speculated as he helped Isobel swing herself up into the carriage, pointing out thin leather straps that hung from the ceiling. 'Hold onto those. The road down to Whanganui is well marked and used—you should see stone sign-posts every few miles or so—but it will still be a bumpy journey.'

The journey, in fact, passed by in a blur for Esther. Almost as soon as the driver whipped the horses and cooed to other coaches nearby, the carriage was thrown around. The seats were padded and wide, but that did nothing to ease the discomfort. Isobel wedged herself against Esther, who was nearest the carriage wall, and shouted across at Jack.

'Was it like this when you journeyed north?'

Jack smiled ruefully. 'Worse. The rains were heavy when I travelled, and we almost lost a passenger trying to cross the Whanganui River.'

The Cobb changed horses where possible and, at night, when the passengers rested in coaching houses, Esther felt the shudder and swing of the day's journey in her muscles when she lay down on her narrow bed. Her flesh felt threaded with motion and memory. Rain pounded the corrugated iron roof of their accommodation, and the baby turned and stamped. The roar of weather filled Esther's ears. When she should have folded herself in sleep, she lay awake on the thin mattress. Her nightdress moved with the baby. She felt as though her body was about to crack open.

After taking a train from Whanganui they reached Wellington, and found themselves in a city as big and noisy as Auckland, though alien and strange. City folk walked with an urgency they both recognised, but spoke of places they did not know: Lower Hutt, Karori, Thorndon.

Wellington intrigued Esther and she would have liked to have lingered. But the Hatcher Valley pulled her, throbbing across the water. They bought tickets for a boat to Picton and, on a calm day five days after leaving Auckland, their odd little group crossed the Cook Straits and found themselves on the South Island.

Isobel

'It will be tough going from here until Kaikoura,' Jack said.

They were at breakfast in a small Picton hotel. They had arrived the day before after a smooth, uneventful crossing but, by the time they docked at Picton Harbour, Esther was exhausted. She tried to go on and made attempts to persuade Jack to seek out a carriage for their onward journey, but Isobel, asserting herself forcefully, instructed their little party to find accommodation for the rest of the day. A few hours rest turned into an overnight stay, and Esther struggled to wake in the morning.

Their breakfast table was set plainly but plentifully: bread, tea, thin slices of mutton, and a bowl of cream cheese. The landlady, a suspicious Scotswoman with a rather magnificent moustache, bustled in the background, seeing to other guests. Isobel and Jack lingered at the table, waiting for Esther. She had eaten a small plate of food and then returned to the room she shared with Isobel, excusing herself by saying she needed to replace the lace in her boots. She must have thought she was out of sight, but Isobel saw her sister pause and lean against the banister at the bottom of the stairs, a hand pressed to her stomach.

'How tough will the going be in the south?' Isobel asked. 'Or do I want to know?'

'There won't be a public coach to speak of,' Jack said. He looked down at a newspaper, folded over at the advertisements. 'We'll need to see if we can hire one locally. There are plenty in the paper. Then we pick up a Cobb at Kaikoura. There's no train until we're just outside Christchurch. Luckily the railway runs almost to the Hatcher

Valley and then it's a just a few hours ride to Esther's land. We might be able to rest the horses at my father's farm for a spell.'

'Did you telegram ahead to let him know you were travelling south?'

'No.' Jack glared down at the paper, avoiding her eyes. 'You should know that whatever private carriage we manage to hire, this next part of the journey will be hard on Esther.' He pinked a little, cheekbones taking on a hot sheen.

Isobel considered him. She was not sure if he was embarrassed about referring to Esther's condition, albeit obliquely, or if something else troubled him. 'She's weary already.'

'I can see that.' Jack sighed. 'There hasn't been the opportunity to speak to you about this, not in the weeks since we left Auckland …'

'Yes?' She wondered if he would ask about the father of Esther's baby.

'I can't help but think it was a foolhardy time to take a trip of this distance and challenge when Esther is so … when the baby is …'

'She has a few more weeks yet.'

'But babies can come early.'

'You know about these things, then?' Isobel peered over her teacup at the young man, taking in the worn, tired cuff of his shirt and the life-lines starting to creep around his eyes. She knew she was embarrassing him with her questions and stares. Jack blushed deeper and she felt cruel. He did not deserve it.

She was also unexpectedly sure of one thing. Isobel scoffed a little at herself—how could she have been so blind? It was obvious, really; the discomfort the man felt at bringing up the subject of Esther's pregnancy was not because of the indelicacy of the issue. It was, instead, far simpler and cleaner—the boy was in love.

She felt wistful and sad and jealous and empty and—oh, so many things all at once! Her belly and heart danced. *Esther, you lucky girl, you poor soul.*

Isobel breathed shakily and put down her cup of tea. 'I'm sorry. Of course, I don't expect you have much experience of babies. Nor do I. But I think the baby is content where it is at the moment. Esther would say if she thought there was any danger it would arrive imminently.'

'Yes, quite. But the question remains. Why take such a trip now? Forgive me, Isobel, but it seems you are doing more than merely sightseeing.'

Isobel picked up Jack's newspaper. 'May I?'

'Of course.'

She pushed aside their breakfast dishes and folded the paper out. The *Marlborough Express* expanded over the table. Amid articles about the best way to see off rabbits and recommendations for new health pills and tonics were advertisements for transportation further into the island, or across Arthur's Pass to the west coast. Jack was right—there were many private carriages available, at wildly different prices. Other pages provided news from across the colony, Sydney and London. She skimmed over the Women's Section, with its news about garden parties, a debate about the wearing of trousers, and medical treatments, until she reached a page near to the back of the newspaper with local announcements. She read through them, just as she had done with every paper she had come across on the journey.

She was looking for something and it was not there. Isobel exhaled noisily and sat back in her chair.

Jack watched. He poured himself another cup of tea and sat quietly, waiting.

'You really do want an answer to your question, don't you?' Isobel said, both irritated and amused.

Jack merely raised an eyebrow.

'Very well,' Isobel sighed. 'You are right, we're not just sightseeing. I was looking in the paper for a particular kind of notice. I'm sure you have seen them—women appealing for news about disappearing husbands, tempting announcements about an unclaimed fortune, with a request that so-and-so contacts the editor. That kind of thing.'

'I have seen them.'

'Desperately sad, aren't they? Imagine the humiliation a wife must feel to make it public that her husband has abandoned her and left her destitute? Or to try to trick them into contacting them by advertising a non-existent inheritance? I wonder if these notices ever have a positive effect. That is, if they flush out the bounders or bigamists.'

'Is your husband missing, Isobel? Is this what the trip is for—to find him?'

Isobel burst out laughing, loud enough for other diners to turn around. She held up a hand in apology and leaned forward on the table. Jack shook his head softly, puzzled.

'No, Jack, Brendan hasn't high-tailed it and left me all alone. Perhaps if he had we wouldn't be here—but I am confusing matters more. No, *I'm* the missing spouse. Esther and I departed on this trip without his knowledge, and I've been checking the papers every chance I can get to see if he's decided to make it public. I don't expect he'd put a notice in the paper in order to convince me to come home—no, I suspect that if he chose to make my desertion public, his motivation would be from a darker, angrier place. To humiliate me, I expect.'

The contours of Jack's face changed, surprise bringing an old man to his skin. 'You left your husband?'

'I did.' Isobel discovered that it was satisfying to say the words. 'Perhaps temporarily, I don't know.' She glanced over her shoulder at the others in the dining room. They were all couples, save for two men sitting with large trunks at their feet. They wore brightly coloured cravats and waistcoats, and Isobel was convinced they were salesmen.

'Would you tell me why you left him if I asked?'

'I would not.' Isobel smiled. 'There may be women all over the empire leaving their husbands—these are times of change, after all. Women are riding bicycles and wearing trousers, and all manner of modern things. But I won't share the details of my marriage. I'm sorry, I know you are not being discourteous by asking. The last few weeks have taught me that you are not a discourteous man.'

Jack tilted his head, accepting the compliment.

'But I'd rather not say why I left Brendan. And, of course, we want to see Esther's land. It may mean a future for her. A way out of her predicament.'

Again, a gap of silence from Jack, in which the baby's unspoken presence was acknowledged.

'Are you worried that Brendan will come after you?' Jack asked eventually. A couple nearby finished breakfast and stood up. Jack dropped his voice. 'Could he?'

Isobel paused over her teacup. She had considered such a thing, of course, in the days since they left Auckland. Whenever those thoughts occurred, whether sitting next to Esther in a jerking, swinging carriage or as they edged together in a train south, a snake of panic curled around Isobel's windpipe, threatening to choke off her breath.

Panic was not the strongest feeling, however. She had told Jack that Brendan might want to humiliate her through the newspapers, but a creeping voice persisted in giving her feelings their true name: embarrassment. It stung to think of the failure of her marriage and the flight from her home. She did not know if Brendan would follow her—his actions that night in their bed wiped away all certainty she had about him. She no longer knew him. She wondered, too, if he had been mortified by what he had done. Perhaps too mortified to follow her.

Mortification had a colour, Isobel had learned. Black, the colour of stout or ale or beer. Black for the lines that slashed the skin on Brendan's brow when he stomped home, bereft of another job. Black for the clothes Isobel dyed, a colour to last between wash days. She remembered wearing a dress for two weeks until she had sewn herself a replacement, and when she plunged the dress into the washtub on George Street the water turned black too.

So, yes. Brendan might follow them, find her, and embarrass her further by making her come home with him. Isobel looked into Jack's young face and felt like weeping.

'I am worried. I don't think Brendan will follow me, but it depends how angry he is.'

'Does anyone know where you and Esther are headed?'

'Only Rachel Speedy. I told her just before we left.'

'I know her. She's one of my tenants.'

Isobel recalled how Rachel had bobbed her head hurriedly as they talked in the courtyard, encouraging Isobel in her babbled plans. 'Go as quickly as you can,' Rachel had said. 'Before he comes home.'

'Would Rachel tell Brendan where you were going?' Jack asked.

Rachel had caught Isobel's arm just before she turned to go, the old woman pressing something cold and metallic into Isobel's hand. It was Rachel's knife, the one she had used to clean pipis only hours before. Rachel said nothing but her meaning was clear. Isobel had stared at it, sickened by the thought she might need it and the reality of what Brendan, her husband, had done to her. But she had not tried to hand the knife back to her friend. Instead she had pushed the knife under the sleeve of her dress and hidden it. When they reached Auckland train station, she had transferred it surreptitiously inside her boot.

'No, Rachel won't tell Brendan a thing,' Isobel said. 'I'm more certain about that than anything.'

'Well, let us continue,' Jack said, draining his cup of tea and taking a final mouthful of mutton. 'I'll see about getting us a carriage as far as Blenheim. The newspaper seems to indicate there are many vendors to choose from, though who knows what they will charge. Give me an hour, will you?'

'Of course.' Isobel watched as the young man excused himself and left the room. A couple of women at nearby tables glanced at him surreptitiously, angling their gaze over the newspapers burying their husbands. Jack was a handsome man. His eyes were wide set where Brendan's were small and close, and the younger man was in desperate need of a haircut. Thick hair fell past his ears. But he held himself easily; the tapered city coat that came down to his thighs had been discarded soon after they left Auckland, bartered along the way for a heavy tramper's jacket, and he had taken to wearing a pale blue cotton shirt and breeches. He looked more like a swaggie or farmhand than a landlord, and the transition suited him. At Wellington he had picked up a straw hat, and he put that on now as he left the boarding house, bidding farewell to the aggressive landlady and stepping out onto the street.

Isobel left the breakfast room and made for the room she had shared with Esther. The women who stared at Jack now transferred their gaze to her, and she felt their questions. Was she his wife? Sister? Something more secretive and improper? Words were on the tip of Isobel's tongue, explanatory words, phrases that she could use to dispel all curiosity and smooth away any thought of impropriety. But Isobel held them back and merely nodded as she passed by. As she walked she knew that there would have been a time, only weeks before, when the perception of other people mattered a great deal. Enough to leave her sister on a sodden wet Queen Street.

Isobel of the Picton boarding house felt ashamed. The rattle and surge of carriages and Cobbs had started to shake a new woman from her bones. She hurried up to the bedroom without a word to her fellow diners.

She found Esther sitting on her bed, unlaced boots still on her feet. Esther was frowning at a bundle of white linen in her hands.

'Esther?'

A tremble to her sister's fingers and the linen was folded away and dropped into the old mending bag at Esther's feet. 'Are we ready to leave, Isobel?'

'Not quite. Jack's gone to find a wagon or a Cobb to take us to Blenheim,' Isobel said. She eyed the white fabric bunched in the bag, but Esther stood up, blocking her view. 'Are you unwell?'

'It's nothing.' Esther gathered a hairbrush and small mirror from the table beside the window. Her brow was beaded with sweat and her skin seemed waxen, but she smoothed her dress down purposefully, hands rounding the bulge of her stomach. 'Let's make sure we're ready for him. I don't want to linger here any longer than necessary and we still have a long way to go.'

'We have some time. Maybe an hour. It will take Jack a while to find a man able to take us further south.'

Esther sighed at that and sat down again on the edge of the bed. She closed her eyes wearily and Isobel noted again how pale her sister was. 'Perhaps I can rest a little longer then.'

'Of course. Here, swing your legs round and get comfortable.' Isobel reached down for Esther's boots and made to lift them up onto the bed, but Esther gave a shout.

'Don't, please Bella!' Esther pulled her sister's arm away and then cringed back, hands returning again to her stomach. 'I'm sorry.'

Isobel stood back, shocked. She had dropped Esther's feet at her sister's cry, and waited now, bewildered. 'What is it, Esther? Is it the baby?'

She gasped, appalled, as Esther began to sob. Something terrible had happened, Isobel was convinced. She was sure the baby was being strangled by its cord and that her sister could feel every thrash of the child but was helpless to assist.

But it was not that. Esther gathered herself, sniffing back tears, and pointed to the carpet bag. 'I felt a change in the night. I didn't want to wake you. The baby feels lower.'

'Lower?' Isobel blinked.

'Oh, Bella. You've been married so long and know so little.' Faint exasperation in Esther's voice. She cupped her hand at the point where her legs met beneath her dress and Isobel stared, repelled but fascinated. 'The baby has moved further *down*,' Esther said deliberately. 'When I woke this morning, I found I could breathe easier, the easiest I've been able to breathe in months. But then, when we were at breakfast, there was a show.'

Isobel hesitated. 'I don't know what you mean.'

'A slight bleed. My body is getting ready, that's all. It can happen a few weeks before the baby is born. There's nothing to worry about, but I have to be careful. No sudden movements, not until my body settles down again.'

Isobel shuddered. She had deliberately avoided the thought of the birth, and remembered how Esther had stood up abruptly at the breakfast table and left. She had seen her sister hold her stomach as she reached the stairs. The thought that giving birth was a horrific business crossed her mind again.

Esther, though, was the image of calm. She had eased her feet up onto the bed and had lain back against the pillow. She watched Isobel, a slight smile at her lips.

'Why are you looking at me like that?' Isobel said.

'Because I can see how worried you are.'

'Of course I am. We're hundreds of miles away from people who might help us when the time comes, and you are only weeks away from giving birth.' Isobel's voice caught on a snag of panic. 'Jack was right to say that we had been foolhardy, taking a long trip at such a time.'

'There was a woman on the boat over.' Esther blinked up at the ceiling, the ball of her stomach rising and falling. 'We talked. She had a new baby with her—she was travelling out to meet her fiancé at the Cape of Good Hope.'

'She was unmarried?'

Esther snorted. 'That's your first question? Yes, she was unmarried, as it happened. As soon as the other passengers realised the fact, no one spoke to her. The first-class ones, at least. But I did. She was happy and so in love with the scrawny scrap of a child.'

'Did she tell you ...' Isobel sat down on the edge of the bed, her sister's boots pressed against her thigh. The touch was comforting. 'Did she tell you what to expect?'

'Yes.' Esther stared at the ceiling. 'She gave me a book. It was by a physician, a type of 'hints to mothers' about what would happen at the baby's birth.' She gave a small laugh. 'I ignored the recommendations for silk ropes with which to hold on to during the pushing, and did you know, the fellow—for of course it was written by a man—the fellow advised a woman did not scream during delivery! But aside from that, it was useful. I'm glad the passenger lent it to me to read. I couldn't keep it. She needed it back, perhaps to help her with the next baby. At least I have some idea now, about what lies ahead. You can't imagine our mother sitting me down and preparing me, can you?'

Isobel could not. Their mother had offered very little advice to her when she married Brendan, other than some grim-faced facts about what to expect in the marriage bed. 'Did Mother tell you anything at all?'

'She told me plenty of things, mostly about shame and honour, and reputation.' Esther's voice was thin and bitter. 'But nothing important. Nothing that counted—like how I could get this baby out of me without killing us both.'

Isobel caught her breath. The fear, so long unarticulated and trapped in her breast, had been said out loud, and said so easily and bluntly by the woman only weeks away from going through the ordeal. Esther could die.

But, it was not this knowledge that stopped the air in Isobel's throat. Her stomach clenched and her armpits clamped with moisture to admit it, but the chance that Esther might die in childbirth was not what Isobel feared most. Instead, she was most terrified that the *baby* could die. The baby that their mother had said she should persuade her sister to hand over, for Isobel to keep. It was a baby that she could not grow for herself; whether her body had failed, or Brendan's, was unimportant. The baby could be hers, if she found the words to convince Esther to hand the child over. The thought that the child might not live was terrifying.

Isobel felt ashamed. She glanced at Esther, crushed against the bed by the enormity of her belly, small and fragile under its weight. Esther was her little sister, the girl who drove her wild almost on a daily basis with her disregard for instructions to stay away from water, the child who refused to learn to bite back the retorts that enraged their mother. Night after night, Isobel would sneak bread and dripping up to her sister's room after Esther had been sent to bed without supper again, or would drape Esther's clothes around the kitchen fire, wet from the brook, hoping they would dry before morning and before their mother was up to see. Isobel remembered the smell of water, brackish and black, on the fabric, how squares of plaid lightened as they dried.

But now Esther possessed not one strip of plaid and Isobel had forced her to wait in the rain on Queen Street, so the judgmental hoi-polloi might not see her. And now Esther's belly was large with the child her sister hoped to plunder.

Isobel blinked back tears. The birth would be hard but, with luck and courage, both Esther and the baby would survive it. Isobel had some experience, after all, she tried to reassure herself. She had helped Hilda Riley with the woman on Sale Street, when the baby became stuck. The incoherent mother had lost so much blood that the floorboards became slippery underfoot, but Hilda had known what to do. The old woman's sure, able hands had pulled the child out in time, and she made short, thorough work of the red, liver-like stuff that came after. It had turned Isobel's stomach to look at it and she couldn't believe Hilda's muttered words that this bag of awfulness had kept the baby alive for the nine months it grew. Despite the horror, Isobel told herself, she had *been* there and done something. She could not allow terror to cloud her mind and blunt whatever help she could offer when the time came for Esther to deliver. The prize, for them all, was too great.

She turned purposefully back to her sister. 'We must not be afraid, Esther. It will be a frightening time when the baby comes, but I will be there.'

'Will you?' Esther's voice was soft and high and she seemed, at that moment, so young that Isobel reached out and touched her cheek.

'Of course I will. I would not leave you on your own.'

Esther

The change to her body had come quickly and unexpectedly and, despite Esther's calmness when speaking to Isobel about the imminent birth, she had been frightened. The days leading to their arrival in Picton had been long and horribly tedious. It had been impossible to read in the Cobbs that took them south to Wellington, for the rickety carriages lurched and shook with every dent in the road. So, instead, Esther kept her eyes closed and held on to the straps hanging from the Cobb roof, feeling the press of her sister beside her and the spike of mattress springs cutting through the thin cushions. The baby, though, seemed soothed by the rocking motion and stayed quiet throughout the journey. At night, when they lay down to rest in coaching houses or small hotels or, at Hastings, in a dry barn, the baby kicked up a tremendous fuss, rolling and jabbing with tiny feet, keeping Esther awake until the small hours.

When they eventually reached Picton, she was exhausted. Picton was pretty enough, with small wooden houses dotting the shoreline and, if she had had the energy, Esther would have liked to walk about its streets a little. The town had the air of transience, and seemed perfectly content with that. Travellers ebbed and flowed through its borders, and a healthy economy had sprung up, catering for those passing through. The guest house in which Jack found them rooms was the most comfortable they had stayed in so far, and Esther had slept deeply in the big double bed next to her sister.

But then, at breakfast, came the feeling of change at the bottom of her belly. Not a pain exactly, more that something had been shed. Sitting at the breakfast table, Esther had the strangest feeling that her body was opening up and the baby would slide out easily, amid the other guests and diners. She had hurried to the room she shared with Isobel and checked her clothes. The streak of mucus in her drawers had been frightening and she had removed them, putting them in her bag when Isobel appeared. There had been little blood, a little pain, and the sensation lingered that her body was leaking. More than it had before, and Esther grew fearful that a sudden movement might bring the child into the world early.

Earlier on their journey, before they reached Wellington, they had stopped at Greytown for horses to be changed. The Cobb had come to rest at the side of the road while the driver went into the station to see about water. The stop was little more than a muddy shack, and Jack had, for once, a seat inside the carriage rather than at the front. He was asleep, as was Isobel, and the jerking halt of the Cobb did not wake either of them. For half an hour or so, while the horses were untethered and the driver shouted and swore at those in the shack, Esther looked out at the farmland. A herd of cattle, no more than a dozen of them, grazed a few hundred yards away. They were stocky brown beasts and Esther wondered idly if the cheese made from their milk made its way to Waite's Dairy on Wellington Street, back in Auckland. She remembered Isobel encouraging her to eat cheese with every meal, to build up her strength and, as the cows chomped on dark green grass, Esther felt a rush of love for her sister. She turned to nudge her awake, but a sound from one of the animals stopped her.

One cow was smaller than the others and had collapsed, back legs in a bent heap. Something wet protruded from its rear. The cow brayed and strained; Esther realised it was giving birth.

She could not tear her eyes away. The noise the animal made was not loud enough to wake Isobel or Jack. Esther watched, taking in every gasp of the cow, and the slow, silent slide of the calf falling to earth.

The infant was delivered in a shiny mucus bag, around which a cloud of black flies immediately descended. It was surely her imagination, but Esther thought she could smell blood and the tang of wet earth. She saw the mother cow stumble to her feet, blood and matter weeping from her exposed rear, and the animal lumbered around to where the calf lay unmoving. She watched it nudge the bag, its child. But the small size of the calf and the disinterest of the other beasts in the herd told its own sad story.

There was no farmer in sight and nothing to be done. Esther could do nothing. She could hardly spring from the Cobb and hurry along the grass to the sightless, breathless calf herself. Animals could be born too early. Babies too. But the sight of the mother cow standing over her infant, and the scent of the birth—real or imagined—stayed in Esther's mind for the rest of the day.

In the bedroom at the Picton guest house, she allowed Isobel to finally ease her feet up onto the bed and cover her with a blanket. The fire from the night before had not gone out in the grate and the room was warm, but Esther knew how her sister needed to wrap her up like a child, so she acquiesced.

'Jack will let us know if he has found transport,' Isobel said, and she positioned herself in the armchair by the window. 'You rest.' She turned to look outside to the street below.

New Zealand had startled Esther. Leaving Auckland, she had assumed that towns on the way down to Wellington would be little more than a few streets strung together. Some were, and hours could pass between settlements. But New Zealand shouted at her through the windows of the carriage, asserting itself boldly and with vigour. The tired grey buildings she remembered from her childhood, of Derby and Nottingham, began to seem worn and ancient in comparison to the whitewashed energy New Zealand had to offer.

'You are impressed,' Jack said when they finally reached Wellington. They had taken rooms at a house near the harbour, which Esther insisted on paying for. They left their bags in their rooms and walked out to observe the boats sailing in and unloading passengers and goods. Isobel declined to join them. A bundle of newspapers had been left in the boarding house drawing room and she sat down to read them, her eyes moving rapidly over the personal notices, her face unreadable.

They were too far away from Auckland, or home, or anyone who mattered, to care if they were mistaken for a married or engaged couple when walking out together, so Esther took Jack's offered arm and followed her feet down to the harbour. They had arrived in Wellington in the early evening and the air had cooled. Esther was glad of her coat, even with the awkward panel she had sewed in the front to cover her belly. But Jack walked coatless, wearing his new soft cotton blue shirt. Uncut hair fell to the collar. Passers-by glanced at him, some more than once, particularly the women. A group of young girls walking three abreast moved to the side of the pavement to let them pass, and Esther heard their whispers and giggles as Jack tipped his hat to thank them.

At the harbour they found a small shop selling fried fish and Jack bought greasy yellow fish wrapped in newspaper. 'Try it,' he said, laughing as Esther eyed the contents dubiously. 'You've had fish before?'

'Of course,' Esther tutted and took the offered yellow flesh. 'Rachel Speedy gave Isobel fish all the time. Not like fish from home, though. Once my father caught a huge rainbow trout at Carsington Water in Derbyshire and baked it. My mother wouldn't touch it, but Isobel and I had some.'

'If you can fish, you'll never starve in New Zealand,' Jack said. 'There's a lake on my father's land. My brother and I used to fish and cook what we'd caught on the shore.'

Esther reached for another piece and chewed slowly. She hadn't felt hungry in days. The nausea brought on by the shudder of the coaches and Cobbs had been too much to bear. But the fish fried in batter was appetising, despite the grease. 'You don't talk much about your brother.'

'You don't talk much about your mother,' Jack said shortly.

Esther paused. They stood against the railing looking out over Wellington harbour, and at the mention of his brother Jack had turned his body, just slightly, so that she could not see his full face. He had cut her off. She felt wounded.

'I'm sorry. I shouldn't pry,' she said.

Jack sighed. He ate another piece of fish and turned back. 'I'm the one who's sorry. He died. That's all.'

'How terrible for you.'

'It was five years ago. He was fourteen.'

Esther did not speak. Jack held the fried fish in one hand; she reached over and took the other, grease from her fingers making the embrace slippery. Jack stared down. His own fingers closed around Esther's hand. His fingers were also wet. He rubbed his thumb slowly over Esther's knuckles.

A blast from a steamer moving out onto the water made them both jump, but their hands stayed linked. Esther felt Jack's eyes on her face. She gazed at the steamer throbbing out into Cook Strait. Jack's hand tightened around her own, and she finally turned her gaze to his face.

∽

The jump of the baby woke her. Esther came to groggily, incredulous that she had slept. Isobel, still sitting by the window in the Picton guesthouse, turned around.

'That was clever timing, Esther, to wake up now. I can see Jack coming back up the street. He's walking purposefully—does he walk like that all the time?'

'He'll have reserved us places on a coach,' Esther said. She swallowed, her tongue thick in her throat. She remained baffled that she had slept and had had the oddest dream, about a cow that had grown gills and swum in the dirty blue of Wellington harbour. She eased her legs around so they dangled off the bed and stood up. 'Let's go down to meet him. We can pay the bill as well.'

Jack had found them seats in a coach, as Esther predicted, and he hurried up to his room to fetch his belongings while Isobel settled up with the landlady. She held Esther's money in her purse, having offered to keep it safe on the journey down. So far there had been enough to see them south, and Jack paid for his own travel apart from when Esther had a fit of guilt and insisted on paying for his accommodation. The landlady looked on as Isobel counted out the coins to cover their stay, the stout lady's moustache quivering as Isobel snapped the purse shut.

'We should be careful of what we spend from now on,' Isobel murmured to Esther, returning to stand with her sister in the hallway as they waited for Jack.

'Are we almost out of money?' Esther asked, surprised. 'I thought there was more than enough.'

'There is.' Isobel glanced back at the landlady. 'But not enough to stay in places like this every night—not if you want to make purchases after you have seen your land.'

'Purchases?' Esther said faintly.

Isobel looked at her sister and shook her head. 'Have you considered, at all, what you might find when we get down to the Hatcher Valley? We have no idea if there's a dwelling place, or a house, or a shack. If you want to stay on this land, you need to think about how you will live.'

Esther hesitated. She had not spent any time thinking about living on the land, and Isobel's question caught her off guard. 'I don't know, Isobel. I haven't thought much beyond selling the land.'

'Even so, you would need to know how farmable the land is. Don't rely on the ownership paper—those land documents might have been drawn up by someone in Derby, or London, who had never even set foot in New Zealand, nor seen the land with their own eyes.'

She was right, Esther knew. The realisation made her dizzy. She stood, her eyes darting around the hall for something to focus on.

Isobel

Jack had not written to or telegraphed his father to prepare him for their arrival. After asking at the Picton guesthouse, Isobel did not raise the subject again but, at Christchurch, they had lunch at a small café while waiting for horses to take them on and sat at a table beside a group of men, who were loudly making plans for their onward journey. The men all wore dusty leather boots and sagging hats, and they smoked pipes over their roast mutton and boiled potatoes. Some tipped whisky into their coffee mugs when the waitress wasn't looking, and all the while they spoke of finding work on sheep runs in the area. When he mentioned the Enderby Run, Isobel saw Jack's face tighten at the name—that was his father's sheep farm. And then she knew Jack hadn't contacted his father.

They had arranged with a vendor to hire three horses for a week and then return them to Christchurch. Isobel and Esther found it an effort to mount the animals, Esther particularly so. The vendor watched in the stables, a stricken look upon his face as Esther's belly prevented her from swinging herself up into the saddle, before inspiration struck and he darted back into his office for a small foot stool. With Isobel's assistance, Esther settled into the saddle, her face scarlet and humiliated, her belly ponderous and huge.

They talked for part of the way as they rode toward the Enderby Run, shouting into the wind, pulling their collars up against the occasional chill. But the closer they drew to his father's land, the quieter Jack became. He no longer commented on the tabletop, brown landscape they passed through, or the sun-bleached sheep carcasses they stumbled over occasionally, remnants of the summer just past.

The proximity of the Enderby Run seemed to suck out Jack's interest and spark, and he rode the final ten miles up to the first marker pointing out the sheep run in silence.

They paused at the wooden stick, painted red at the tip. Another stood a few hundred yards ahead, and this one had a sign strung about it. *Enderby*.

'Is this the start of your father's farm?' Isobel asked. It was now midday and quite warm. She longed to rip away the fabric of her dress and loosen her stays.

Jack said nothing. His mouth thinned into an invisible line. They rode on to another marker, and stopped again.

'Jack, do you want to take another route to the Hatcher Valley and Esther's land?' Isobel pulled her horse alongside him. The beast was tired and needed to rest. Isobel patted the horse's neck gently.

'We can't avoid Enderby,' Jack said hollowly. 'There are some other landholders around here—the Sandersons have a run a few miles east, and there are some German families with smallholdings beyond them. But most of the land around here belongs to my father. We can't miss it. Not without adding hundreds of miles to the route.' He removed his hat and wiped his brow. 'If I travelled alone, I'd think about it. But not with women. Not with *her*.'

He nodded back to Esther some distance away, who sat resolutely on her horse, her jaw and eye fixed. It was no secret she hated riding, but the animal they had hired was peaceful and calm, and the ride hadn't been too hard on her. But they needed to stop and soon, and Isobel was relieved when she saw the resignation in Jack's face.

'We'll press on then. I don't know what has occurred between you and your father, Jack, but hopefully we need only to rest for a short while before striking out for Esther's land.' Isobel glanced back at her sister. 'And then I'd like to get back to Christchurch, if possible. Esther's baby might be closer to its arrival than she thinks.'

Jack's eyes widened and his nostrils flared, but under Isobel's warning gaze he was able to keep his panic in check. He simply nodded curtly, and they rode on.

They must have gone on for another ten miles before spotting the homestead, by which time Isobel's horse was wheezing and the poor beast's head was hanging low. They had carried water, but this was all gone. Isobel sat forward in her saddle and gave a small cry.

'Is that it, Jack? Is that your father's house?'

Jack's pained expression told her it was, and she turned excitedly to Esther. Her sister's face was pink and her eyes were almost closed against the glare of the sun. But Esther nodded to say she had seen it, and she followed Isobel through the brown tussock grass toward the house.

Jack lingered. He held the reins in a gloved hand, the horse breathing deeply beneath him. But as the women rode away from him, he sighed, nudged his feet into the animal's sides, and followed them.

The house was large and squat, just the one storey. It seemed to run away with itself; rooms looked to have been added to a central building at strange angles. Windows were inserted into walls in a haphazard way. The shape of the building was spidery and erratic and the paintwork white but dusty. The side facing north was orange and smeared with debris thrown by the hot winds. Chairs and a swing seat sat on the large porch and curtains hung low at every window. Broken grain barrels and rusting tools were littered about on the ground, crumbling under the sun. A couple of dogs had given up in the midday heat and lay, panting, near the front door.

A door opened as Isobel and Esther came near. A man came out to greet them. He was as smartly dressed as the farm was untidy, not at all like the men they had seen in Christchurch. He wore black flannels and a ruby waistcoat instead of rough working trousers and the typical stained blue shirt they had seen on many men looking for employment. He was diminutive and portly, his thick black hair oiled. Small glasses wobbled precariously on the end of his nose. He had a tick; one eye blinked erratically. In his hands he held a yellow cloth, which he turned over into ever decreasing folds.

'Help you, ladies?' he asked in an accent that Isobel recognised as still retaining faint undertones of the north east. Esther heard it too—the man sounded like Aunt Mabel from Grimsby.

Jack was some distance away, out of sight over the brow of a slight hill. Isobel slowly dismounted, knowing the man had not seen him. As she stepped down gingerly onto the dry earth, she looked more closely at the man. It was Jack's father all right, the look was unmistakable. The father shared the same crooked eyebrows, the same almond shape to his eyes. But his mouth was long and narrow, not boyish and full like Jack's. Untying the handkerchief from her neck, Isobel wondered if Jack's mother had passed this down to him instead.

'Bella, can you help?' Esther reached out for her sister's hand and carefully unfolded herself around the horse. She planted both feet on the ground, leaned her forehead against the animal's throbbing stomach, and sighed.

When she swung round to face Jack's father, he saw Esther's belly and gaped. The yellow cloth stilled in his hands.

'Sir, would it be possible to rest and water our horses here?' Isobel asked. 'We're heading for the Hatcher Valley, but our rides are exhausted.'

'As I expect you must also be,' the man said. He looked between the women uncertainly, and again at Esther's stomach. Then he remembered himself. 'Of course. I'll have one of my men take them to the barn.'

He stuck a couple of fingers in his mouth and let loose a piercing whistle. The panting dogs looked up and away again, and a young lad, probably no older than fifteen, appeared. He took the reins of the horses wordlessly, with barely a glance at old Mr Bellamy, and walked them away.

'Do you travel alone?' Jack's father asked. 'I apologise if I appear inquisitive, but it is highly unusual for women to travel to these parts alone. And, if you will forgive me'—he cleared his throat in Esther's direction—'in such an advanced state. Are you missionaries?'

'An advanced state! And us—missionaries!' At that Esther laughed, unable to help herself, and she clapped a hand over her mouth. Isobel heard the trill of hysteria to her sister's merriment, the rawness of the landscape in Esther's voice. She reached for her sister's hand and tried to soothe her. But all the while she wondered what she could say to the man waiting for an answer, how she could explain what they were doing there. Then Jack rode into view and the man gasped.

Isobel watched and the world funnelled away. The crunch of the grass beneath her feet and the bluster of northern winds faded to nothing. It seemed all living things on the farm turned their attention toward the point of connection between father and son. The heavy breath of the dogs melted away, the air was still.

Jack approached and his face was unreadable, which Isobel found shocking. Over the last few weeks she had grown used to telling the moods of this young man through the shape and contours of his face. She knew when he was tired, or worried, or when he was thinking of Esther. But now, as solitary cloud moved across the sky and cast a shadow over the group, she had no idea what her travelling companion was thinking as he neared his father. She stood back as his horse edged closer. Esther, too, hung back, her hands wrapped around her belly in their usual, protective hug.

Jack dismounted, still without speaking. He removed his hat. He stood up straight, back like a rod and looked down at his shorter, stunned father.

Jack's father, however, despite his shock, spoke first. 'It's you, is it?'

Jack cleared his throat. A bird took off from a bush somewhere, flapping noisily. Hush, Isobel wanted to cry. Hush!

'It's me,' Jack said after a moment. He put his hat back on and took a cloth from his trouser pocket, wiping his face. Then he stood, folding it over and over, mirroring the actions of his father earlier, when folding the yellow dust sheet.

'And you are together?' Jack's father asked, indicating to Isobel and Esther. Isobel opened her mouth to speak but Jack was there first.

'We are. These are my friends and travelling companions. Isobel Nelson and Esther Carter. Esther owns some land a day's ride from here, at the Hatcher Valley. We are going to inspect it.'

'I see.' Jack's father made a stiff bow. He eyed Jack again and Isobel saw a flash of anger in the old man's face. Her discomfort grew—that a father could be angry at seeing his son again, after all these years! But then she thought of her mother. Her mother would have been furious too.

'You are unexpected guests,' Jack's father said, 'but you are welcome. I wonder what you have talked about on your ride here—maybe this young man told you that the Enderby farm had some meaning to him beyond being a mere rest stop. Maybe he did not. I am Evan Bellamy.'

'They know you are my father,' Jack said quietly.

Evan Bellamy paused and there was that anger again—Isobel saw it in the line of his mouth. The yellow cloth was clenched in his fist. It took a moment to compose himself, but then the old man snapped his heels together curtly.

'We'll say no more. These young ladies must be weary. We have no servants here, save for the farmhands, but if you can find your way around a kitchen, madam, you are welcome to eat and drink as much as you need.' Evan extended his hand toward the house and nodded his head as Isobel murmured her thanks. He did not, she noticed, extend his invitation to his son. Instead he flicked Jack another glare, anger still there, and strolled away toward the house. Leading Esther, Isobel followed him inside. She glanced back over her shoulder at Jack, who had turned to his horse, lip folded under his teeth, stroking the animal's neck with shaking hands.

⁂

The kitchen was better equipped than Isobel expected, though chaotic. Evan Bellamy left them in the doorway to the kitchen and, saying something about tidying away a collection, disappeared into another part of the house.

'Did he say he had to get back to his collection of coins?' Esther said, sitting down wearily on a stool.

'I think so. He was most likely cleaning them when we arrived.' Isobel walked around a large table in the centre of the kitchen, upon which were piled pots and pans, and dishes that appeared big enough to serve a whole sheep. 'It would explain the cloth he was fiddling with.'

'Polishing his coins. What a pointless exercise.'

'He must find it entertaining,' Isobel answered, not really listening. The kitchen was vast—two sideboards stood together, and she opened their cupboards. 'Evan Bellamy might have enough saucepans and crockery to feed the whole valley, but the place is a mess. Look—roasting tins mixed in with wine glasses!'

'Not so loud, he might hear.' Esther pulled off her gloves and rubbed the back of her neck. 'Will Jack come inside, do you think?'

'I don't know. His father didn't invite him, only us.' Isobel stood up triumphantly, a small packet of biscuits in her hand. 'Found something. And there's cheese on that dish over there. And I'm sure I can find a kettle for tea.'

She found a huge copper kettle in a cupboard and managed to fire the stove. The iron range was cold. It did not seem that bread had been baked for some time, and it took a struggle with a box of matches to light it.

After a while, they heard a step in the hallway and, to their surprise, Jack stepped into the room. He had a hunched look about him. He pulled up a stool next to Esther and sat down.

Isobel and Esther exchanged a glance. Jack looked vulnerable, like an animal that had been beaten but had to return to its master. Isobel wanted to put her arms around him. There was dirt on the back of his neck and a small tear in the seam of his shirt. She could see white skin and finger-sized gaps between his ribs.

Esther, though, decided to approach the matter head on. She had been more forthright than ever in the past few weeks, Isobel noticed, as though the imminent birth of her baby had pushed aside the small amount of consideration she had for etiquette and reserve. Esther was, Isobel thought, about to go through an ordeal where artifice or politeness had no importance.

'I don't know what has occurred between you men,' Esther was saying, 'and it makes no difference to Isobel and me if you manage to make amends, but while we're in your father's house I think you should at least talk to him. You should thank him for his hospitality. You don't have to mean it.'

'We're leaving as soon as possible,' Jack muttered, picking at his nails.

'You said the horses needed to rest,' Isobel said. 'I'm sorry, Jack, but that will probably take much of the day, and we can't exactly set out for the Hatcher Valley in the dark.'

'Do you mean you want to spend the night here?' Jack sounded incredulous. He looked up now, eyes darting between the sisters wildly. 'That's out of the question, we simply cannot.'

'I want to press on as much as you do,' Esther said. She rubbed her belly ruefully. 'The quicker we see what my land is like and then head back to Christchurch, the better. We might even make it back to Auckland before my time comes.'

Isobel made a soft noise at the stove but said nothing. Jack's gaze settled on her and she gave the slightest shake of her head. *Impossible.*

'My father would never allow us to stay,' Jack said. 'And why should he? I haven't spoken to him in five years. He set me up in Auckland, purchasing those houses on George Street and making me landlord, and he knows nothing of my life since I left this house.'

'He set you up in business,' Esther said gently. A tired crease to her brow, and Isobel wondered if she was thinking of the baby's father, and of how he had pressed land ownership documents into her hands before she left for New Zealand. 'That's more generous than most. Doesn't it show that he wanted you to be successful?'

'He didn't do it to give me a future,' Jack said bitterly. He stood up quickly and the torn seam of his shirt gaped further. Isobel saw his belly, a scattering of black hair across his skin. She gripped the handle of the kettle, letting go in a hurry because of the heat.

When Jack spoke, he did so shakily. 'My father didn't want to give me a good start in Auckland. He sent me away. The houses on George Street were bought so I wouldn't ever come home again.'

Esther caught her breath, her tongue a tiny red peak between her teeth. 'Why would he do that?'

'My brother.' Jack paced, striding between the stove and the cabinets. Damp patches stained the back of his shirt. Isobel wanted to pull it from him and soak the garment in water. She forced herself to concentrate on the kettle, pouring water into a pot and adding pinches of tea she'd found in a drawer.

'What about your brother?' Esther asked.

'He died, remember?' Jack kept his voice low, but it was raw and harsh. 'My father blames me. He couldn't bear to look at me after Freddie died. Setting me up in Auckland was his solution.'

Esther seemed to flounder, as though she did not know what to say. She looked at Isobel helplessly, who now handed round cups of tea.

'How awful for you, Jack,' Isobel said quietly.

Jack paused in his pacing, tea cupped in one hand. He began to shake. Isobel saw the tea dance and slop over the side, burning his skin, and she hurriedly reached for the cup, taking it from him. Jack put his hands to his face, shoulders rounded into a silent sob.

Esther got up, alarmed, and between them the sisters managed to guide the man back to the stool and sit him down. There was little sound other than the settling hiss of the kettle. Isobel squatted down at Jack's side. Esther, unable to do the same, hesitated, and then dropped a hand onto his shivering shoulder. From a room along the hallway they heard the distracted hum and rustle of Evan Bellamy, seeing to his collection.

'The thing is,' Jack said, finally composing himself, 'it's true. My father is right—it was my fault.'

Esther

Jack could say nothing more, and as sunlight wound along the kitchen walls, Isobel announced she would have to speak to Evan Bellamy about their staying the night. The sisters had tried to ease more from Jack about what had happened to his brother, but the man had folded into himself. Glancing at Esther over Jack's head, Isobel got up and left the two together. She walked down the hallway to find Evan Bellamy.

'Do you think he'll let us stay?' Esther asked Jack after Isobel had left the room.

Jack had closed his eyes. Dirt from the ride across the plains streaked his face and there were black half-moons under his nails. 'I don't know. If it were me alone, asking for board, I should say he'd send me over to a hut on Chimney Pass, where the hands stay. Might be different with you here.'

'What happened, Jack?' Esther asked. It was a question that had burned in the half hour since he had said his brother's death was his fault, and she felt restless and on edge. The revelation had been too shocking; it filled her legs with hot acid, so that they moved constantly beneath her skirts. She wanted to run, but she could not, so she had to stay and ask.

Jack did not answer for a long while, and she thought she had offended him. The inability to stop asking questions was an aspect of Esther's personality that she had come to accept would never be blunted, would never be fully suppressed. She remembered lying in the master's bed at Gallerton Hall, legs moving up and down, up and down, until the question simply *had* to be asked: what was it like with her, with his wife? Did having children change her body, so the feel of her—to *that* part of him—was different? The master had lain rigidly when she asked and she thought for a second that she had offended him, that it was a mortifying question. But he had found the place that made her sigh and said his wife was *quite* different. When it was clear the baby was on its way, Esther cursed herself for asking such a question. She wondered how different her body would be after.

Then Jack spoke. 'He drowned.'

'Oh. I'm so sorry.'

'In the lake just a few hundred yards from here. The one we pump—my father pumps—the one that supplies the house.' Jack blinked slowly. 'We were fishing. Remember, when we took a walk along Wellington harbour and I told you my brother and I liked to fish together? Well, that's what we were doing.'

Esther waited.

'The water is cold here. Ice cold water, even in the heat of summer. There's nothing better than jumping in freezing water after a day in the saddle, chasing down foolish, missing sheep, or after an age sitting on the bank, waiting for a minnow or a salmon to bite.'

'He jumped in?'

'No.' Tears fell heavily now, too thick to hold back. 'I did. Freddie was never one for throwing himself into water, or anything for that matter. He was too cautious. He probably missed my mother too much. Pop always said his spirit had been blunted when she died, trying to give birth to my sister. No, I jumped, and played a trick on him. That's all it was—a terrible trick. I pretended I was in trouble. That my foot had caught on a branch or something. Freddie then waded in to help. Only then he started to flounder—maybe he was panicked in his hurry to get to me.'

Esther brought her hand to her mouth. 'Lord.'

Jack took a choking breath. 'I knew he'd gone by the time I'd dragged him back to the house. Laid him out in the big front room. Ma used to call it the drawing room, but that was only when visitors came to call, which was almost never. Freddie was blue. Pop and I laid down next to him, but we couldn't get him warm.'

Again Jack cried. He was some years past boyhood, but he cried like a child. His nose and eyes dripped and colour flared in his cheeks. When Esther went to wipe his face, she found his skin and shirt drenched. The man shuddered, barking sobs, and Esther ached to see his body jerk under the strength of them.

'Jack, Jack,' she murmured.

After a while the storm passed and Jack tipped his head back. Salt water ran down his temples and then all was quiet. Somewhere in the house a clock ticked and they could hear the ripple of voices as Isobel spoke to Evan Bellamy.

Their hands were entwined. Esther didn't know how it had happened, but her fingers were caught in Jack's grip and she felt the steady, pleasing pressure of his touch. She saw the abrupt cut of his sideburns and the creep of whiskers on his shaven face, hair that threaded down toward his throat. A pulse ticked in his neck and, with a certainty that brought heat and ache to her belly, she knew she wanted to press her tongue against it.

The kitchen was warm, so warm, even with all the windows thrown open. The fug seemed to nudge them together; when Esther looked up, Jack's eyes were open and he moved his free hand to touch her face. When he kissed her, it was soft and damp and she could taste the salt of his tears.

⁂

When Isobel returned to the kitchen, Esther was sure her sister would sense that something had happened. Her lips felt on fire from Jack's kiss, though he had been delicate, embracing her like he might a china doll. Her skin had lit up at his touch. She was sure her face was aflame.

After they kissed, Esther had leaned her head on the flesh of Jack's shoulder, feeling sharp bone beneath and smelling the hardness of his body. Jack's hand fell on her back and they sat together in the quiet of the kitchen.

If Isobel had noticed anything, she said nothing. She sat down next to them and plunged straight into a retelling of the conversation she'd had with Jack's father. Jack, whose face had returned to its normal colour and whose tears had been wiped away, listened in silence, his face as closed off as it had just been open and hungry.

'Your father will allow us to stay,' Isobel said. 'All of us, Jack. In fact, he insists that you sleep in the house if you are going to stay on his property—he says he will not allow you to sleep in a barn or out in the open.'

Jack snorted.

'There's a guest room Esther and I can share,' Isobel said. She opened her mouth to continue, but the words seemed to catch in her throat. 'But most of the other rooms in the house have been shut for many years. Mr Bellamy says he's run the place down a bit,' and here, Isobel cast a wry look about the cluttered kitchen, 'so Jack won't be able to sleep in his old room.'

'Where, then?'

A pause, a beat. Esther saw her sister's hands twitch. 'Your father says you can sleep in Freddie's room.' Isobel did not look at them.

'Oh, he is an old bastard,' Jack said bitterly.

'Jack, I don't know your father, of course,' Isobel said. 'But he did not speak with anger. Whatever anger he felt when we arrived has gone. He showed me his coin collection and we spoke about the farm, and then I asked if we could stay. When he said we could and he told me where we could sleep, I did not detect malice in him.'

Jack waved a hand, unbelieving. Isobel look at him helplessly, and then at Esther. 'What else can we do?' she said. 'This is his house. He had no warning we were due to arrive. Can we make the best of it? Esther, you can't ride any further today.'

Esther knew her sister was right, and the thought of heaving herself back onto the horse, as placid and mild a beast as it was, filled her with dread. If Jack insisted he could not sleep in his father's house and in his brother's old room, she would understand, and she was prepared to force her body to move again. But the very idea of sitting on a horse again today made her belly ball up and blood pound in her temples.

Jack was kicking at a broken tile on the kitchen floor, mutinous and angry. Esther saw a world pass through his face, memories like shadows on an open window. She waited, and eventually Jack nodded his agreement.

'Good,' Isobel said, relieved. 'I'll tell him. We can rest for the day and sleep and, at first light, we'll take the path to the Hatcher Valley.'

She left them again and Esther heard her soft voice in another room, speaking to Jack's father. 'Thank you for agreeing to stay, Jack,' she said.

Jack surprised her; he leaned over and cupped his hands either side of her belly. Esther felt the warmth of his touch through her dress. It was a shocking thing, to hold her in such a way, but joy lined the transgression. There was pleasure in his embrace.

She waited for him to speak, but Jack did not. Instead he lingered, hands cupping the child sleeping beneath a membrane of skin. Jack's touch unsettled her more than his kiss. She trembled, but when they heard Isobel's step in the corridor and Jack withdrew, she longed for the return of his hands immediately.

Isobel

Isobel came to realise that the kitchen in Evan Bellamy's farm-house was not unlike her mother's kitchen back in England. Both were cramped and filled with too much furniture. Sideboards and a large dresser jostled for space along one wall. The colonial stove scalded the air on the opposite side of the room. As she boiled water for fresh tea, she turned around to face Esther and Jack, her face full of purpose.

'We'll need a meal tonight, that's for certain, and we can't be expected to manage on whatever it is your father eats.' She motioned to the chaotic kitchen. 'How he's able to find his way around here to prepare a plate of something is beyond me. So I've decided. When we've finished here, Esther will go and rest and Jack will take a look at the farm. There's bound to be something that needs chopping or clearing away, and doing a few jobs outdoors will keep him away from Evan. In the meantime, I'm going to straighten this place up. It reminds me of home, though this place needs a good sweep and dust, and no doubt some of the pots and pans will need a soak. It's the least I can do to offer something for our board here overnight. So drink up.'

Esther's eyebrows shot up and Isobel could see her sister was amused at this determined air, but Esther said nothing. She looked close to exhaustion. As soon as she had drained her cup, Isobel helped her up and along the hallway to Evan Bellamy's guestroom. The room was similarly crowded as the kitchen, with odd bits of furniture that seemed to have been dumped, but the bed was made up and the sheets were clean. Isobel swung Esther's leg up onto the mattress and, after fetching their bags and placing them in the room, closed the door and returned to the kitchen.

Jack had disappeared when she got there. Through the open window, she saw him pick his way across the brown grass toward the barn, a forlorn shape with drooping shoulders. She was momentarily saddened for him, but brushed aside a desire to run out to him and throw her arms around his neck. Instead she reached for a large copper and heated up a pan of water. Steam rose from the pot and she squeezed her eyes shut, blinking away the image of Jack's white ribs poking through his torn shirt.

Although the kitchen was cluttered, it did not take long before Isobel was able to impose order on the room. She soaked crockery and cutlery that looked to never have been cleaned before, swept the floor, and found an old brush that she used to scrub the tiles. The dresser and sideboards were wiped down and dusted, and windows were cleaned. Isobel wound a handkerchief around her neck as she worked to protect her dress, but her back and armpits soon became clammy and she longed for a bath. The scent of her body as she toiled brought her mother back to her; she remembered Ma bent over a barrel of scalding hot water, swirling sheets around, wooden plank in hand, sweating over a scud of soap suds. Her mother's sweat was privately spilled—taking in washing was a way to make money, but it was done secretly. Mother made an arrangement with a few women in town—she collected their sheets late in the evening when no neighbour was around to observe, and returned them two days later, again at night. The washing barrel and paddle was removed to an outhouse, and eventually there was money and Ma was able to pay for a girl to do the washing for her.

There was a small pantry to the side of the kitchen, which appeared to have been used as a storeroom for animal feed. Isobel swept it out and cleaned the floor and, without stopping to consider, boiled up another fresh pan of water. She shaved soap curls onto the surface, finding an old bar in a cupboard, and carried the pan into the smaller room. She fetched her bag from the guest room, taking care not to wake Esther, who was sound asleep. Then, returning to the kitchen and the side room, she shut herself in and quickly took off her dress.

Isobel hesitated for a second and then stripped away her stay and underwear. She stood, quite naked, in the kitchen of Evan Bellamy's farmhouse and stepped into the pan of water.

The water was hot and delicious. She couldn't remember the last time she had taken a bath. There had been no places to wash such as this the whole trail down. The pan was not big enough for her to sit down in, but she cupped water and dripped it over her body, wiping away sweat and dust and grime.

It was a glorious thing to be clean again and Isobel felt the shudder and grit of the journey from Auckland melt away. She soaped the back of her neck, the skin under her breasts, the flesh between her toes. Finally, when there was no dirt left on her body and a film of muck lay on top of the water, shed like a lizard's skin, she stepped out of the copper pan and pulled on a clean dress.

Then she wanted to sleep. She tipped the dirty water away at the back door, feeling the growing warmth as the afternoon ticked on, and then padded softly up the hallway to the guestroom. Esther did not stir as her sister got in beside her and, within seconds, Isobel was asleep.

∽

It was obvious that Evan Bellamy did not host many visitors, for Isobel's suggestion that they sit down to dinner that evening was received bewilderingly. The man appeared shocked at the idea, incredulity spreading across his face like a wine stain as Isobel relayed her efforts in the kitchen and how she would cook a meal of mutton, potatoes, and onions.

'Do you think we need to dress for dinner?' Esther asked. She was sitting on an ancient swing seat on the porch. Isobel had brought her a glass of freshly pumped water and she ground her teeth against the cold.

'No. Mr Bellamy won't care if we do and, besides, I have nothing left to change into.' Isobel grabbed a handful of her skirt, with its many patches and thin hem. 'This is the last of my clean clothes. When we make it back up to Christchurch, I will need to send my clothes out to be washed.'

Esther was content that she would not be required to change and sighed. She gazed out at the dogs lying in the fading light, but her eyes were drawn repeatedly to the barn, where Jack might be. Her longing for him was undisguised, searing in its urgency. Isobel watched her, her insides twisted in a way she could not quite understand.

'I had better prepare the meal,' Isobel said eventually. 'I promised our host a feed and he offered to clear the dining room for us. I can't renege on my side of the bargain.'

They sat down together at eight o'clock. The sun moved around the house and cast long shadows onto the plains, and then night fell swiftly, shocking Isobel with its completeness. She found some lamps and lit them, finishing her cooking in semi-gloom.

For a moment, as she carried the plates into the dining room, she thought that Jack would not attend. He had been out of sight all afternoon, appearing in the kitchen only ten minutes before they were due to eat. He had listened to Isobel's dinner plans with a fixed, distant expression and Isobel feared he was angry at her; she quailed, wondering if she had gone too far and was unfairly forcing father and son together. Yet Jack stepped into the dining room just as she was setting his plate down on the table. He was clean shaven and wore a fresh blue shirt.

'Should I carry some lamps through for you?' he asked quietly. 'I never thought there was enough light in the dining room.'

He set off down the hallway to the kitchen to fetch them, and when he returned, Evan Bellamy had joined them, Esther on his arm. Jack paused and Isobel saw the tightness in his jaw mirrored in the older man's grimace. Then Evan nodded silently and the group sat down. Esther sat next to Mr Bellamy, Isobel opposite her with Jack to her left.

'It is not necessary to say grace,' Evan said, though no one had asked. He glanced at them all, ducking his eyes away when they fell on his son. 'I stopped praying some years ago.'

Jack speared a potato, fork scraping across the china. The residual warmth of the day bulged in the room.

'Do you attend a church out here, Mr Bellamy?' Isobel asked. She was casting about for conversation and tried not to catch Esther's eye, knowing her sister would smirk.

Evan Bellamy swallowed a slice of mutton and shook his head. 'No place of worship for miles. The boys' mother used to hold bible readings, years ago. Few of the cockies would attend.'

'The what?' Esther asked.

Evan snorted and chewed on another piece of meat. 'Cockatoos. It's what we call the small farmers round about here. Some of them might not have impressed a magistrate back home, if you catch my meaning. Still, Jack's mother thought we should welcome them all to the big house, so she held bible readings in the parlour or, if the weather was fine, out on the back paddock.'

Jack coughed and took a glass of water. The tension in the room thickened and Isobel blinked out her frustration. Maybe this meal had not been such a good idea.

Outside a dog barked and someone spoke sharply. Isobel tried again. 'Do you have many men working for you?'

'Half a dozen. The hands live on Chimney Pass. Easier for them to round up the flock and a couple of lads stay in a whare beyond the paddock.'

'I see.' Isobel looked down at her plate helplessly. She felt lost as to what more she could say, though the urge to soothe and make the evening pleasant was strong. Jack's father spoke roughly, edges of words adding flint to the room. She had no knowledge of farming and sheep and the heat of nor-westers funnelling across the grass. She also realised Esther knew nothing either, despite owning land.

Evan Bellamy's thoughts had a similar turn, for he addressed Esther beside him. 'Tell me, how is it that you have acquired land at the Hatcher Valley?'

Esther put down her knife and fork and wiped her mouth on a napkin. She leaned back to speak and Isobel saw her hands slip behind her, kneading her lower back. 'It was a gift. A complicated story. I'm not sure what I will do with it, but I have a strong desire to look it over.'

'Well, it is fertile land, I know that much,' Evan said. 'I don't mind telling you, miss, but I've been puzzling over your ownership of such land all afternoon.'

'Why so?'

'Well, I'm sure Jack remembers the Olivers of Peach Point, not forty miles from here.' For the first time, Evan looked pointedly at his son. After a pause, during which Isobel felt blood bubble under her skin, Jack nodded.

'The Olivers gridironed the land all around Hatcher Valley.' Evan had finished his meat and absently dipped his finger into the juices, smeared over his plate.

'What do you mean, gridironed?' Esther asked.

Evan grinned ruefully. 'If you plan on making a go of it, young lady, these are words you will come to know.'

'Gridiron means to buy strips of land around a larger piece, but doing it in such a way that the central piece can't properly be used,' Jack said.

'But why would anyone do that?' Isobel asked.

'To force a sale. It's a stealth-like way of forcing a neighbour to give up their land, especially if you've land-spotted and cut off access to water.' Evan saw his visitors did not understand. 'Land-spotted is what we say when resources have been blocked.'

'But I own this land,' Esther said quietly. Her fingers pressed the flesh on her back, over and over. 'Whether the land was gridironed or not, I still own it.'

'You do.' Evan nodded. 'Which tells me the person who gifted it to you had no idea what the land was worth or the competition over it. The Olivers have been in these parts for years. Some say the first Oliver came over on the First Fleet. If they find out you're here to see the land you own, they'll offer you a fine price or make it hard for you to farm.'

'Well,' Esther said, and Isobel saw the old stubbornness slip over her sister like a caul. 'I'll not be made to decide one way or another.'

Evan seemed to appreciate this, for he laughed heartily and stood up. 'There's a bottle of port in this room somewhere. I say we make a night of it.'

Evan Bellamy was evidently not much of a drinker, for the bottle was dusty and near full. He rummaged around in a cupboard for a moment and found four tumblers, all mismatched, and poured a healthy slug of port in each glass. He ignored Esther's protestations.

'Get that into you,' he said, not unkindly. 'Jack's mother used to sink a shot of port nightly when she carried him and his brother. And the girl.' Evan looked again at his son. The corners of the old man's eyes were as red as the liquid in their glasses.

Isobel took a sip. Since gulping back Brendan's hidden brandy before they left Auckland, she had not touched alcohol. Her tongue recoiled in anticipation, her mouth remembering the sharp, burning taste of the grog. But the port was smooth and gentle. She took a deeper drink.

Jack had barely eaten and glared at the glass offered to him by his father. He studiously avoided Evan's gaze. Then he exhaled noisily. 'I don't want a drink.'

'Yes, you do,' Evan insisted. He waved the glass closer to Jack's face, and for a moment Isobel thought he would throw it over his son. He did not though, and eventually Jack took it.

'Good,' Evan said, satisfied. The old man's twitch had worsened and now his left eye was almost closed. 'You were very partial to port when you were a youngster, I remember.'

Jack paused with the tumbler at his lips. 'I don't believe so.'

'Oh, you don't believe so?' Evan scoffed, though again his tone was not cruel. He sat down again and raised his own glass in Isobel's direction. 'I was up most of the night with this young fellow on his fifteenth birthday. He'd decided to have a little taste of everything in my drinks cabinet. The port seemed his particular favourite. Don't you remember? Freddie and I took turns to walk you round the house until you threw up.'

There was that name again. Evan said the name of his other, forever-absent son easily and with pride, as though the boy were overseas and not lying in the earth. Isobel saw Jack wince.

Then Jack emptied his glass in one swift movement and thudded the tumbler back onto the table. 'Happy now, old man?'

Esther made a sighing sound.

'Well done,' Evan said. He tilted his glass. 'I once bet Freddie a sovereign that you wouldn't touch it again. Obviously I was wrong.'

Jack thumped his fist down. Cutlery jumped on plates and gravy splashed over the sides, staining the tablecloth. Isobel edged her chair back and saw alarm on her sister's face.

'You will insist upon it, will you?' Jack snarled. 'Freddie, Freddie, Freddie! Do you think I am afraid to say his name too?'

'Jack, no, that is not what …' Evan started, looking over the top of Jack's head as though trying to pick out a face in the evening gloom.

Lost, Isobel thought. *The old man is lost. He's saying the name of his dead son just to bring him back.* She laid a hand softly on Jack's wrist, but he shrugged her off.

'I say his name every day,' Jack barked. His voice rasped from him as though from a torn throat, and Isobel saw the strain, the bulge of veins in his neck. 'Every day. Does he hear it? I don't know—I was never comforted by the gospels like Ma was. But he deserves his name to be said, at least, and you won't shame me by throwing it in my face here.'

'Jack.' Evan bowed his head to his plate and Isobel was shocked to see a wash of tears fall amid mutton and potatoes unfinished. She got up to move, cursing this moment and the very idea of forcing father and son to eat together.

But Esther comforted Evan before she did. She turned awkwardly in her chair, vast belly pressing against the table as she patted Evan's shaking shoulder.

A dog barked again outside. A bird called out, yack-yacking its disinterest in the woes and troubles in the broken dining room.

'I wish'—Evan lifted his grey head, tell-tale wisps of white escaping from beneath his black pelt—'that I'd said his name to you more when you were here, boy. He could have healed us both and stopped me blaming you for something that was not your fault.'

The air caught in Isobel's mouth. She saw shadow and fire cross Jack's face and he became as still as a rock. And Isobel felt within a great sorrow, piercing like hunger. So this is what parental forgiveness looks like, she thought. What a messy, tear-stained thing, but how beautiful. She finally remembered to breathe and swallowed down bitter, jealous bile. She wanted to reach out and grab Jack's face. *Own your father's forgiveness, man! Some of us will wait forever to receive it.* And she wanted to kiss and kiss and kiss him.

It took a moment to realise that Esther had started to weep too, and Evan clumsily reached around and drew the woman to him. The movement broke the spell in the room; Jack suddenly threw back his chair and, with a glower that might have seared a less tear-soaked man, stormed from the house.

Esther

She couldn't see him from the house so she had to step out into the night, away from the solidity of the farmhouse walls and into a cold that was shocking and intense. Esther crossed her arms over her chest, shivering in the Canterbury evening. The place was burning warm by day—it would be burning hot in the summer—and glacial the moment the sun sank beneath brown burr.

Then she saw him. Jack was sitting on a small bank of earth some distance away. He was hunched over, and Esther saw he had been crying by the time she eventually lumbered over.

Jack sprang up to take her hand as she approached and helped to ease her down. He smiled ruefully. 'This ground won't be comfortable.'

Esther shrugged. 'It's preferable to watching Isobel race around, trying to find coffee for your father.'

Jack picked up a dry piece of grass and threw it away. 'I'm sorry,' he said.

'There's nothing to be sorry about. I understand your anger.'

'Do you?'

Esther mirrored Jack's tight smile. 'My mother didn't—doesn't—like the person I am. She has never offered me her forgiveness and nor have I asked for it. I would be angry, like you, if she had imposed it on me.'

Jack was silent. Out on the plans a bird cooed. Esther squinted into the velvet darkness. Where would a bird roost? she wondered. There were no trees around the homestead, only rolling, unremitting grassland.

She felt Jack's arm creep around her and she leaned against him, breathing in the heat of his anger on his skin.

'I've been sitting out here, asking myself what would have happened if we'd not come this way,' Jack said quietly. 'If you hadn't wanted to see your land and we'd not had to stop at my father's house, would I have spent the next five years thinking he blamed me for Freddie's death? He hasn't written to me the whole time I've been in Auckland. And what if he doesn't really mean what he said tonight? What if the emotion of being together again, so unexpectedly, made those words burst out without thought? He might be sitting in that dining room, your sister forcing coffee down his throat, still hating me.'

Esther turned and pressed her lips against Jack's arm. 'But Jack, so what if he does hate you?'

Jack gasped and looked down at his companion. Her red hair curled over his shirt.

'You said earlier today that what happened to your brother was your fault,' Esther said. 'But it doesn't sound like it was. You played a trick on him—that's what siblings do. I used to lie in the brook near to our house, fully clothed, knowing Isobel would be furious. I did it anyway. I wanted to live in water when I was younger. I was a strange child.'

Jack moved, about to speak, but Esther continued.

'One day, I could hear her calling for me. Our mother was out for the afternoon, secretly working—she could never be open about these things, even though we had no money after Father borrowed too much and then died—and Isobel was terrified Mother would blame her again for my wet clothes. She wanted me to come back with her to the kitchen and sit in my undergarments while she dried my dress over the fire.' Esther laughed softly, mouth still pressed against Jack's arm. 'I pretended I had drowned in the brook. I kept my eyes open and staring, as though I'd really gone. When Isobel found me, I didn't think she'd stop screaming.'

'That's a wicked trick,' Jack breathed.

Esther nodded. 'It was. But I was a child and it's what siblings do. It's no different to the game you played with Freddie. You must believe that. I mean, you must really take that belief deep into your bones, so that it doesn't matter what your father thinks.'

'But he's my father and he thinks I killed his son.'

'You didn't. The lake did. Or Freddie's boots did, because they were too heavy. Or a fallen tree did, because it lurked under the surface and Freddie was caught in its branches.' Esther sat back and placed her right palm on Jack's cheek. 'Arm yourself with the belief you did nothing wrong. Be pleased that your father realises that now, but do not let him, or the thoughts of anyone else, define you.'

Jack snorted. 'You sound like a suffragist!'

'No, that's Isobel.' Esther grinned. 'Well, it's one part of her, anyway. I hope she unleashes it.'

They sat together a while longer, Esther nestled comfortably in the crook of Jack's arm. So far, her back was holding up and not protesting at the hard ground upon which they sat. Her big, warm belly stretched over her thighs and she was glad of it.

The blacksmith's boy, the master at Gallerton Hall. Jack. More than enough men for most women, more than many knew in a whole lifetime, and she was only twenty-one. She was sure, in the eyes of some women, she would be considered a Jezebel. She had heard her mother call the thatcher's wife back home a dollymop, and she wondered how her mother would describe her youngest daughter. It hardly mattered. She knew it didn't matter to Jack either, who had embraced her with another man's child in her belly. For that she felt a strange, crushing feeling in her chest, and she sighed and nestled against him.

'Will you be able to ride out to your land tomorrow?' Jack asked.

'Yes. I think so, anyway. I want to. Is it far?'

'Few hours' ride.'

'What will it be like?'

Jack pursed his lips. 'Pa says it's good pasture land, and there's water. Too much for the Olivers to gridiron, whatever Pa says. It's the kind of land prospectors snap up and lease out. Perfect for a home-stead. It is quite a gift.'

Esther stiffened. 'The man who gave me the deeds probably didn't realise it was valuable. Or he knew exactly what it was worth and hoped it would keep me out here.'

Jack hesitated. 'Will you keep the land, then? Stay out here?'

Her back finally started to pinch and Esther leaned away, arching her shoulders. 'Tomorrow will tell. We'll see what the place is really like.'

∽

Jack's father was waiting at the door when they eventually returned to the house. Jack paused and hung back, letting Esther go on ahead. She nodded to Evan Bellamy and, as she passed him to enter the house, she touched the older man's arm briefly. He looked at her and the glitter of a sad smile passed over his face.

She heard gruff talk behind her, but couldn't hear what was said. There was the chink of a bottle. And then Evan spoke clear-ly—'Come, we'll drink this and talk. It's about time'—and she pad-ded softly down the corridor to the spare room. She heard Jack's step behind her and for a moment she thought he had spurned his father's suggestion. But the door to the dining room closed softly and she knew the two men had gone inside.

Esther stepped into the bedroom with a sigh and Isobel, in the middle of turning down the sheets, looked up. 'He persuaded Jack to sit with him, then?'

Esther sat down heavily. 'Sounds like it. Oh, I am weary.'

'It's been a long and trying day.' Isobel kneeled on the floor in front of Esther and began to untie her boot laces. 'Get these off and I'll help you into your nightdress.'

But Esther yawned and waved her hand. 'I am too tired to even undress. I think I'll sleep in my clothes. It's cold enough, anyway.'

Isobel sat back on her haunches. Esther saw strands of hair

falling from Isobel's bun and creases around her eyes—her sister was exhausted too.

Isobel bit her lip. 'Esther, it would best if you could get as much rest as possible.'

'I intend to.'

'No, I mean … do you think you really should try to ride out to the Hatcher Valley tomorrow? After what happened in Picton with the—you know …' It was clear Isobel didn't really understand what had happened to her sister's body in the guest house, but she gamely ploughed on. 'The baby might be closer than you think.'

'I told you. Women can have a show a few weeks before the birth. There's plenty of time yet.' Esther yawned again. 'We'll get back up to Christchurch, at the very least.'

Isobel frowned and pulled at Esther's laces distractedly. 'I would be of no help to you if something happened out on the plains.'

Esther squinted down at her sister, eyes stinging with fatigue, but suddenly realising why Isobel was troubled. 'Is that what worries you, Bella? That this baby might want to make a grand entrance and you would have to help it into the world?' She leaned forward and caught Isobel's hands in her own. 'I'm not in the least bit worried. If you can, try to be reassured. I know my own body. This baby isn't moving quite yet.'

But she could see Isobel wasn't convinced and, when they eventually settled down and lay under the blankets together, Isobel lay tense and still beside her.

∽

They were woken the following morning by the sound of crashing and shouting from down the hallway. Esther sat up, groggy with sleep, hips aching from the pressure of her belly. She had not moved all night, though had been aware of Isobel shuffling up close behind her, shivering in the bitter Canterbury night. Esther had been relieved she had kept her dress on—she would have frozen in her nightdress—and, after working out the noises came from a person lumbering around in the kitchen, she lay back down again and drew Isobel to her.

Isobel's hair tickled her cheek, but the sisters lay quietly. Isobel threw her arm over Esther's chest and gripped her arm tightly. They lay for a while, embracing, and then the baby moved. Esther felt her belly distend and stretch, and Isobel giggled.

'It kicked me!'

'He's saying hello to his Aunt Bella.'

'He?'

Esther shrugged. 'Or she. It's just an expression.'

'You have no inkling either way?'

'None at all.'

Isobel placed her hand cautiously on Esther's stomach. She gasped as the baby stretched again. This time the kick was so forceful they both saw the bedclothes move.

'What do you prefer?' Isobel asked. 'A boy or a girl?'

Esther hesitated, quietly stunned by the question. She had no idea. 'I hadn't even thought about it.'

Isobel propped herself up on her elbow and frowned down at her sister. 'Have you even thought of names?'

Esther threw back the covers. Panic rose in her chest like a flame; names, a boy or girl … she had contemplated none of those things. She had measured the child in terms of what it was not, not what it would be. It was not a monthly stain in her underwear, nor an uncomfortable bloating from too much bread at suppertime. It was not a heat caused by a heavy quilt. It was not a way to heal the endless wound between Esther and her mother. She had not considered the child to be real, pink, squalling, and in need of a name.

Had she done enough sewing? Had she packed enough clothes for the child, should it arrive while they were away from Auckland?

'Do you think that's Jack or his father making that noise?' she asked. She knew Isobel wouldn't appreciate her changing the subject and would be worried, but she couldn't stop herself. She could not run, not like before. So she fell back into the old patterns of deflecting, diverting. 'When I first woke, I feared they were fighting. Oh, I hope it's Jack and that he has put the kettle on the stove.'

Isobel sighed and rolled out of bed. She was cross and agitated, as Esther suspected she might be. She muttered something as she stamped about the room, pulling on her dress. Esther heard the snap and twitch of Isobel's brush as she pulled it through her hair hurriedly. And then Isobel marched from the room, without a glance at her sister. Esther heard her storm down the hallway to the kitchen.

Esther exhaled noisily and slowly stood up. There was a long mirror shoved against the far wall and she waddled over toward it. She turned to the side and viewed herself in profile. Her face had thinned and tendons stood out on her neck. It was as though all her flesh had decided to migrate and gather at her belly, which stuck out unapologetically. Esther pressed her hands down on it. It was solid and still, as though there was no baby inside, only rocks. Her back began to sing so she shifted position and, hearing the kettle whistle, shuffled off to the kitchen.

Jack and his father were both sitting at the kitchen table and Isobel was handing them cups of tea when Esther walked into the room. The place had been transformed, no doubt Isobel's doing. Pots were stacked neatly on shelves, drawers were put back into dressers. The floor had been swept and the table, the centre of much of the kitchen's clutter when they first arrived at Evan's farm, was clear and neat. Evan Bellamy squinted up at Esther when she appeared at his elbow and sheepishly waved his hand around the room.

'Your sister has done a grand job,' he said. The sour mash of his breath was overwhelming and Esther fought to keep her hand by her side, rather than over her nose. 'I lost my way around this place a few years ago. Never was great at keeping house.'

The old man's eyes were pink-ringed and bloodshot and his son, peering gloomily into a cup on the chair beside him, looked much the same.

Esther sat down opposite and accepted tea from her sister. Isobel passed it to her wordlessly.

'You must forgive us,' Evan hiccupped. Again, another powerful wave of foul breath. 'We saw the bottom of one bottle and then the bottom of another. A bottom each!'

Esther watched, incredulous, as the man began to giggle and slap his side. He nudged his son and Jack barely lifted his head, throwing up his hand in agreement.

Isobel sat down. 'They are still drunk!' she hissed to Esther. Esther saw her sister raise a cup to her lips and a momentary, far-away look glaze her eyes. Esther knew she was thinking of Brendan.

The comparison did not seem fair, though, with the two men swaying gently in their inebriation. Evan continued to snigger to himself and Jack appeared to be in danger of falling asleep. They wore their drunkenness like a heavy coat, welcoming the weight of it. She did not see Brendan's mean, filthy actions in their familial, boozy haze.

But there was the issue of riding out to see her land. Jack had promised they would leave that morning. He'd edged close to her last night, the heat of his chest pressed against her arm. She'd wanted to pull his shirt up and place her hands on his skin. She itched to find out if his chest was smooth or if there was hair, as thick as the pelt on his head.

'Jack, when do you think you'll be ready to leave?' she asked cautiously. She tried to keep her voice level and free of emotion, though her stomach felt laced with frustration.

Jack blinked and the blue of his eyes seemed bright in the sunshine. He coughed twice and rubbed his hand over his face. 'I haven't forgotten, don't worry. Well, maybe I forgot at three o'clock this morning, but I remember now.'

Evan laughed hysterically at that and slapped his son on the back. Then he leaned against Jack's arm and closed his eyes.

Isobel watched him with a transfixed expression and Esther suddenly realised that her sister might never have seen a drunk like Evan. That is, a soft, comical drunk, empty of malice and disconnected from his fists. Of course, Brendan must have been so different when he'd had a drink, Esther thought sadly. Oh, how she longed to leave and get out onto the plains!

'So, Jack …' She leaned over the table, as far as her vast belly would allow. 'When will you be ready?'

Jack cleared his throat. 'There's something I need to do first.'

At that, Evan's eyes snapped open. He sat up. 'Are you sure?'

Esther watched the look pass between father and son and her brow creased. Isobel spoke for her.

'What is it?' she asked. 'If we are to travel, we should do it soon. The heat is too much by midday.'

'It won't take long.' Jack got up, stumbling from his seat. His tea slopped over and he righted it awkwardly.

'Wait, son.' Evan gripped his arm. The drink appeared to have left him suddenly, and his old face looked stricken. 'It's all very well to talk about doing this when we've both seen the bottom of a bottle of port, but it's a different matter when morning comes. Don't do it. You know how cold it will be.'

And then Esther understood. At some point in the sodden, port-stained night, when Evan and Jack purged themselves of blame and hate and all the black things men take into their hearts, someone had mentioned the lake. The lake beyond the farm from which it pumped its water, the lake in which Freddie had drowned. Jack was going to swim in it.

'How long has it been since you went in?' she asked softly. She felt Isobel's head swivel from Jack to her and knew her sister didn't understand.

Jack paused and breathed deeply. 'Not since that night.'

'It is a mad idea,' Evan insisted. 'I don't want to lose another son. You've had too much to drink to swim safely.'

And then Esther felt Isobel stiffen and knew she had realised. 'Oh,' Isobel said. 'You are going out to the water.'

Jack nodded. 'I am.'

At this his father threw up his hands and made a strangled noise, like a beast. His torture bent him forward over the table. Isobel got up swiftly and went to his side. She put an arm around his shoulders.

Esther hadn't moved her gaze from Jack's face. She inclined her head slowly—*I see you.* She thought of the sailor who had fallen from the *Lady Jasmine*, all those months ago. He'd toppled into still, calm water, brine as thick as milk, washing over his head. His panic hadn't been so great. He'd been pulled back onboard—Esther had been shocked to discover he couldn't swim; most sailors can't, someone said—and the man was told he'd been baptised. She'd envied him his new life. If it wouldn't be shocking beyond measure, she would have jumped in herself. The sea washed out the grime of life.

She would go out and watch Jack. It was apparent that Evan could not, for he was now sobbing and making no move to follow Jack as his son edged toward the door. Esther pressed her palms on the table and heaved herself up. She would go and see that the plunge was done and that Jack came to the surface again.

But as she stood, backache flared again, this time sharp enough to catch her breath. The pain was unlike a pain she had experienced before. She knew she could not sit on the ground to watch Jack swim in the place where his brother drowned.

The pain passed, and luckily Isobel hadn't noticed, too engrossed in patting Evan's back and muttering awkward words of reassurance. 'I will wait for you to return,' Esther said, trying to keep the wobble from her voice as her back began to scream again. 'I will gather a few things in my room so we can leave as soon as you … as soon as you're ready.'

Jack gave her a curt nod and disappeared. With that, Esther edged gingerly to the door and back to the bedroom.

Isobel

It took a few moments for Isobel to realise that Evan, no longer hiccupping with sobs, had actually fallen asleep. The old man snorted and flinched, just once, and then his breath came low and regular. Isobel steadied her hand, done with her rhythmic patting in her attempt to comfort him. When she looked up to see what Esther made of it all, she realised her sister was no longer in the room. Jack had also left.

Isobel stood up, carefully extracting the cup of tea from Evan's hand before it slopped onto the table. She hesitated and then gently pushed Evan forward until his head rested on the table surface. He spluttered and his arms came up, as though he were lying in bed, on his belly. And then he began to snore.

'What an odyssey we are on,' Isobel muttered and left the kitchen. She made for the room she had shared with Esther, but the bedroom door was closed. She heard Esther moving behind it and knocked.

'I'm getting changed, Bella,' Esther said, her voice faint. Isobel imagined her pulling a dress over her head, forcing it down over her distended belly. 'I'll be along shortly.'

'All right,' Isobel called back. 'I think I'll go outside. It's already too warm.'

It wasn't too warm and the lie came so unexpectedly that Isobel stood for a moment with her hand on the door, tongue pushed against her teeth as though she had tasted something sour. Her heart thumped skittishly in her chest.

She wanted to watch Jack. She wondered if Esther would sense her intention and what she would make of it, if her sister might feel an acid pang of jealousy. Isobel had watched them the night before; how Esther had leaned against Jack's arm out on the burnt grass, how his head ducked down from time to time to kiss the top of her head, dipping into the thick red sea of Esther's hair.

The discomfort Isobel had felt when watching them silently from the porch was a twisted snake in her guts. She hated herself a little. She would not have looked at Jack, not once, if he'd stood against Brendan in those early days, when Brendan was decked out in his decent suit and his face was not yet scrubbed raw with drink. He had been a fine looking man, a man Isobel was proud to take the arm of when they were courting. But he was different now and Jack was a handsome man, still.

He stood facing the water when she approached. Some distance from the house, the lake was shockingly, painfully blue, white whorls and circles appearing on its surface as a timid breeze skipped across it. Isobel shivered, sensing that the water would leave ice on the skin of anyone foolish enough to swim in it.

Jack stood with his hands on his hips. His white shirt was loose around his waist, braces hanging down the sides of brown work trousers. Isobel came to stand beside him and saw his grimace, how his eyes squinted ahead, how his mouth was a squashed line of concentration. He turned to face her and wiped damp hair from his eyes.

'Are you here to talk me out of it too?'

'I'm not.' Isobel glanced at the lake again, lying treacherously a few feet away. 'But I hope you are prepared for how bitterly cold the water will be.'

'I am prepared.' Jack bent down and began to undo his boots. In the distance a bird called, shrieking out a warning, and a group of sheep, little more than white dots, scurried as one away from the sound.

Boots undone, Jack reached up and, with one swooping motion, pulled his shirt over his head. He bunched it in his hands, barechested, sweating in the arid air.

Isobel kept her eyes studiously on the ground, but the shape
of the man next to her seemed to bloom in her peripheral vision.
Pale skin—apart from neck and forearms—a scatter of black hair,
a bird-cage of ribs. She drew her arms across her front, lacing them
together, as though she were afraid her hands would flutter out and
touch him. He stood a few inches taller than her; she sensed him
edge closer and throw shadow across her body.

'Do you understand why I need to do this?' Jack asked. He wound
the white shirt around his hands, and finally Isobel turned to look
at him. 'I think Esther knows my need to swim in this place again.'

So even as Isobel allowed herself to fleetingly look upon his body,
he thought of her sister. The dip of Jack's throat, the hollow that
throbbed with his heart, the spike of his collar bone through skin
that seemed tired and aged and yet energised—Esther could have
these things if she wanted, and Isobel felt turned inside out.

'Why don't you tell me why you want to swim in the lake?' she
said eventually. 'Your father is dead against it—tell me why you need
to do it.'

'Freddie,' Jack said simply. He pushed at his eyes with the heel of
his hand. 'Just Freddie.'

'Of course.' Isobel thought of Esther's story about her crossing,
and how a sailor had fallen into the sea. She also remembered the
tale of the old man who died and had been left in the water by his
family. 'Be careful, Jack. Oh, please, be careful.'

She had never swum in the sea at Auckland or the Public Baths.
She had never seen a man in a swimming outfit, but somehow
expected that Jack would wear one. What Jack did next shocked her.
He moved away and, without a further word, stripped off his trou-
sers. He wore no underwear and Isobel's hand came to her mouth as
Jack walked, quite naked, to the water.

It was impossible to look away, despite the rising panic in her
chest. Isobel could hear her mother sucking on her teeth, outraged
at the indecency and appalled that Isobel was so close to it—but she
could not look away. Instead, as Jack waded into the lake, gasping as

icy water flowed over his skin, Isobel began to feel something close to joy. She felt a band of cold creep up her own thighs, she felt the hair on her head stand on end as Jack plunged his face into the water. She felt immersed in the moment, just as Jack was, and when he dived under the surface and reappeared, she threw back her head and laughed.

Jack turned to face her, treading water. He wore a puzzled, stricken look, and she knew he was mystified by her reaction. He raised a hand and waved to her.

Was he inviting her in? Suddenly Isobel wanted nothing more than to be in the water with him. She wanted to feel the ice raddle her skin, she wanted to lift her hands in front of her face and see her fingernails turn blue. She wanted to feel water seep through every pore of her clothing, washing out her insides, filling her mouth with its glacial cleanness. She thought of Elizabeth Ellis, now Elizabeth Peter, and how her friend had gulped down cup after cup of tea after that terrible discovery at the house at Onehunga, and how Isobel had feared her friend would flood her insides with all that liquid. Such a ludicrous thought! And now Isobel wanted to be flooded, to be filled, and all her fear to be washed out.

Then she thought of her mother and the woman's brutal, clear outrage were she to take off her clothes in front of a man to whom she was not married. And, despite everything, she thought of Brendan and what he would say if she undressed in front of another man.

But then she found her feet crunching across grass until her boots were drenched on the shoreline. The cold hit her toes mercilessly but Jack's growing enthusiasm for the water was infectious. She saw him rub at his face and that he was crying, and again felt her body surge toward him.

'I want to come in, Jack,' Isobel called out. Even as she said it, her fingers pulled at the buttons of her dress.

She saw his surprise and then his fear. And, at the edges, curiosity. 'Are you sure?'

No, I'm not sure, of course I'm not! I can see my mother's face and I know what Brendan's anger would be like. 'I am. But I can't swim.'

'Well.' He swam a little closer to a point where he could stand. Lines of black hair slid down his chest; he moved nearer the shore until the water lapped just over his hips. The thought of seeing all of him was almost too much and nearly drove Isobel back up the slope away from the water. She called out.

'Will you help me?'

'I will.' He bobbed down again. His interest had waned and she could see he had returned to think of his brother. 'Just watch your footing.'

She did not remove her cotton slip, but she undid every single, small button of her tired old dress, and pulled the clothes away. 'You can stay here, Mother,' she muttered, dropping her dress to the ground. 'And you too,' she said to Brendan, kicking off her boots, careful of Rachel's knife hidden away. She had never stood outside in just her undergarments before. Never, not once had she unbuttoned her dress and allowed the sun to beat down on her bare arms and legs.

She didn't look behind her. If she'd glanced back at the homestead, with dogs asleep on the ground and windows blinking solemnly in the morning sun, her courage might have failed her. She did not turn to see if Esther had finished dressing and come outside, or if Evan had woken and was standing, appalled, on his veranda. Instead she took a gasping step into the water and, before her screaming body could drag her back to the shore, Isobel waded in until water covered her shoulders.

It was a cold she had never experienced. She ground a shriek between her teeth and screwed up her face. Just out of reach, Jack laughed and she knew she must have looked a sight. Icy fingers tore down her arms and the water felt absurdly sharp, like a knife.

She had made a foolish mistake. She was not of these lands, she could not navigate the brutal wildness New Zealand offered. She was a fragile flower, a usurper, out of place in a field of spear grass. Where was her dress? Panic seized her and the scream, so far held back by gritted teeth, threatened to burst out.

But then there was an arm around her waist. Jack pulled her in. The water suddenly seemed to become warm—she knew it was simply that her body had become numb—but Isobel was grateful for the change anyway. Jack held her close to him and she opened her eyes. Her hands reached up to his wet, bare chest.

'Take a deep breath,' he said. 'Don't let the water overwhelm you. There, that's it. Stand up straight and widen your stance. Like this.'

He moved and water lapped up to Isobel's throat, but she did as he said. Her feet found rock underneath. When she stood, the water came to just below her breasts, her soaked undergarments clinging to her skin. Jack glanced at her and away. Her breasts floated on the water. The cold had whitened Jack's skin; she could not tell if he blushed.

Although Isobel had now found her footing and felt more stable than before, she did not want him to let go of her waist. When Jack moved his hand away, she grabbed his wrist. Her fingers grazed other skin, under the water, possibly his thigh. She blinked.

'I can't swim, remember? Please, I want to hold your hand.'

He nodded without speaking and they stood for a while together, water settling around them. A gentle breeze slipped around their freezing bodies and Isobel felt her skin rise up, and her breasts ache with cold. Her teeth began to chatter.

Jack eyed her. 'Do you want to wade back to shore?'

Too cold now to reply, Isobel nodded.

'There's just one more thing you should do,' Jack said. He untangled his fingers carefully and held up his hand reassuringly. 'Watch.'

With a swift motion he bobbed down until he had disappeared completely, his head submerged. Then he resurfaced again, panting. 'Try that.' And he began to laugh again.

Isobel didn't want to. The momentary warmth of numbed, shocked skin had passed and she now wanted to be back in the sun, hugging the fabric of her dress to her. But Jack's gaze and the hoot of his laughter felt like encouragement. If I am going to find peace and cleansing in this lake, I should do what he does, she thought.

So, holding her breath, Isobel plunged under the water. She was under just for a second, but a million splinters scraped her skin; she felt as though a giant had grabbed two handfuls of her hair and was trying to pull it out by the roots. When she resurfaced, she could not see. She began to splutter and cry, and panic.

And then strong arms were around her and she was being held. Her body was pressed against the form of a man, his body unapologetically naked. Her breasts were squashed against his chest and their hips were mashed together. She felt a soft sway of flesh collide against her thighs.

Jack held her firmly. His thick, wild hair stood up in clumps. She saw patches of stubble, grown overnight.

'Calm, I've got you,' he said in her ear.

'Jack.' Isobel's slip billowed in the water around her. She knew that, with one easy movement, she could wrap her thighs around his waist and he would feel no weight at all.

So that was what she did. She jumped and brought her thighs around his waist. He gasped and his hands came down automatically to cup her skin and hold her. They stood swaying and, as Jack stared down into Isobel's face and made no move to push her away, she locked her ankles together behind his back.

The quiet flesh between his legs that had moved with the water now became something else, something solid and urgent, and Isobel arched as she felt it press against her buttock. She moved until Jack's skin was beneath her, at the vital point, and his mouth was parted. She saw the red tip of his tongue and moved to kiss him.

But as suddenly as he embraced her, Jack released her. He backed away, his hand still on her arm to make sure she was safe, but his body was reclaimed as his own and his face was a mask of horror.

'I thought—I thought you had lost your footing. I didn't want you to panic,' he said. The fact he felt an explanation was necessary shamed Isobel. She folded her arms across her breasts, now painfully aware that the pink of her skin was visible through white cotton.

Jack turned to the side, away from her. She knew he was hiding his body and that it mortified him. Lord, she felt mortified too.

'It's quite all right, Jack,' she said, though it was a great effort to speak. Oh, I want to be a hundred miles away from this place! she thought. 'But we must get out now. I cannot bear it any longer.'

He didn't ask what she could not bear but, at a distance that was as respectful as possible, Jack followed Isobel out of the lake and back onto shore.

The welcome of the sun on her body made Isobel feel faint and she could not pull on her dress for several moments. So she sat on the ground in her wet underclothes, her back to Jack as he pulled on his own shirt and trousers. She closed her eyes as warmth finally edged back into her bones.

Then she felt movement beside her and opened her eyes to see Jack striding by, eyes fixed on his father's house. He walked toward it purposefully and did not turn round to look at her.

Esther

Esther had wanted to watch Jack swim, but the comfort of the bed pulled her in. She lay on her back, counting out the moments between pangs that scraped and snapped at her insides. The ache was worse than ever and had started to build up to a crescendo. But it had eventually settled and Esther, grateful and exhausted, had rested.

She understood instinctively why Jack wanted to immerse himself in flinchingly cold water. She thought of the brook back home and how it was often the only thing to soothe her rage or the injustice she often felt toward her mother.

Jack sought forgiveness from Freddie in the lake. Esther did not think he would seek to make amends, not by trying to drown himself or something mad like that. Instead she sensed Jack wanted to leave his hurt and grief there, and give himself the permission to start his life again. Maybe a life with her.

Oh, she wanted him to want her. She wanted to swim in his gentleness, his cool, unsullied goodness.

She heard Jack return after his swim and, for a moment, wondered if he would walk to her room and see her. If his acceptance of a new life would start straight away and that he would pull her into an embrace. But Jack didn't appear in her doorway. Instead she heard a door slam noisily.

Esther intended on getting up and going to him, whatever his mood, whatever the state of his dress. She even hoped he would be changing and she would see his bare skin for the first time. But, instead, she rolled onto her side and fell asleep.

She awoke to find Isobel brushing her hair at the dresser. Esther squinted as sunlight streamed through the window. Wind blustered around the farmhouse, but the room was baking hot.

'Have you been swimming?' Esther saw Isobel's hair was damp.

Isobel gave a short laugh and craned even closer to the mirror. 'I've washed my hair, is all. The sweat of the day was too much. Feeling better?'

Esther yawned. 'I am. A touch of backache, but it's gone now. Oh, I want to see my land more than anything right now.'

Isobel put the last hairpin in place and stood up. 'We'll go, shall we?'

Esther swung her legs over the side of the bed with a grunt and slowly stood up. 'Is Jack ready?'

Isobel turned quickly back to the mirror and began to fuss with her hair again. 'I'm not sure. Will you check?'

Jack and his father were sharing a pot of coffee on the veranda. Both looked up and grinned when Esther appeared and Jack stood. He came to her side and touched her on the shoulder. She frowned at him, at his skittishness.

'Headache gone?' she asked. She looked closely at his face for traces of anger, remembering the slammed door. But there was no fury in his face and Jack bounced a little as he spoke.

'All gone.' He startled her by sliding a hand around her waist. 'The horses are rested and ready. If we leave now, we can be at the Hatcher Valley in a couple of hours.'

Esther nodded and gently pulled Jack's hand away from her side, puzzled by his mood. It seemed as though life fizzed beneath his skin, as if swimming in the lake had awoken him.

Then Isobel arrived and Jack stepped away, his face oddly creased. He hurried a farewell to Evan and Esther found herself bustled toward the stables. Jack put a stool beside her horse and Isobel, without a word to Jack, helped to heave Esther into place. Esther barely had time to grip the reins and stash the water bottle thrust into her hands, and they were off.

The horse kicked up dust, and dry, burnt grass stretched out in front of them, flat as a plate, for as far as they could see. Esther's eyes swam, blurring the edges between sky and earth. Blue, brown, blue, brown.

Evan Bellamy had given them a pack of sliced mutton and they stopped after an hour or so at an area of grass that was oddly green. Esther looked at the thick blades quizzically and Jack, helping her down from the horse, shrugged.

'The snow can bank in strange peaks and troughs,' he said. 'Water seeps far underground in places. Maybe there's water beneath our feet, enough to feed the grass.'

The thought was intriguing and Esther felt her heart lift. New Zealand continued to startle her, with its ability to give new life, and she turned to smile at Isobel. But her sister was looking away, studying something in the sky, avoiding her gaze.

Jack gave the horses water and the riders drank deeply also. Then Jack pointed into the distance.

'That's it. The Hatcher Valley.'

Esther stopped chewing, the mutton suddenly tough and heavy in her mouth. 'That's my land?'

'Yep. Good grazing land too, like Pop said.'

Esther turned to look at Isobel, her heart banging in her throat. 'We're nearly there! I can't believe it. After such a journey.'

Isobel nodded slowly. 'What is it like, Jack?'

'You'll see soon enough.' Jack threw the last piece of his meat into the grass. 'Come on.'

The horses were not happy at being ridden again so soon. There was some resistance, and Esther had to wait a while before her normally peaceful mare was calm enough for Jack to help her up. But before she knew it, she was urging the beast on, forgetting her dislike of riding, only thinking of the land.

It took another hour to reach the Hatcher Valley and, when they pulled the horses to a stop, Esther looked up at the Southern Alps rising solemnly in the distance. The peaks were crowned with snow and she was sure she could hear the trill of running water nearby. The grass was another shade of brown, darker and richer than the burnished area they'd ridden through. White dots moved about in the far distance—sheep grazing languidly. The air was sweet and warm. Esther felt her heart swell. She accepted Jack's outstretched hand and dismounted from her horse again.

'He had no idea what he gave you,' Jack muttered as she stood beside him. 'Did he even make any enquiries about the kind of land it is?'

Isobel had walked into the distance and crouched down to look at a flower in the grass. She could not hear them. Esther linked her fingers through Jack's, pulling his hand behind her so the embrace was hidden. She did not want to think about the master at Gallerton Hall, not out here, with Jack. 'You're right, he had no idea. He didn't care.'

'Do you care?' Jack kicked a piece of rolled turf, avoiding her eye but allowing his fingers to stay entwined with hers. 'I mean, were you hurt that he sent you to the other side of the world?'

Esther held her breath. Jack's jaw was tight and she saw damp hair at the back of his neck. He had skin she wanted to touch, to lick; but more than that, right now, she wanted him to be silent. She didn't want his questions.

'It seems a long time ago,' she said, knowing this was not really an answer at all.

'Only a few months ago.' He cleared his throat and looked pointedly at Esther's stomach. 'Who was he?'

She wondered if the fact he had brought her to her land made him feel he had the right to ask. Or if it was that he had given up his life in Auckland—for a short time, at least—to come on this adventure with her. Jack stared at her and he would not be placated easily. Over his shoulder she could see Isobel, still looking at flowers.

'I will tell you,' Esther answered deliberately. 'But this will be the only time we'll speak of it. Do you understand? I will give you this because you have taken me to my land. And, oh Jack, you have given me hope too!'

She pulled their laced hands from behind her back, resting them on the top of her belly. She felt the round points of Jack's knuckles. His skin was rough, but warm.

'He was a man I worked for. The master of a large house.' She laughed ruefully. 'It sounds like a plot in one of those penny dreadfuls my mother used to buy. She didn't know I knew about her secret store—Isobel and I were only allowed to read the earnest books in my father's library. That's what Mother thought, anyway.'

'I never went in much for reading,' Jack said shortly. 'Barely enough time to wash after a day out rounding up the clip.'

'Did your mother read?'

'All the time. Sometimes she lent a book or two to the cockies who came for bible readings.'

Esther smiled. 'She might not have appreciated the kind of books I read, after sneaking them from my mother's room.'

'Did he take advantage of you?' Jack breathed noisily through his nose, mouth a tight line. She could see the effort it had taken to ask her such a question. The round of his shoulders seemed prepared for a blow, as though her answer might cause him physical pain.

She took a moment to think. Grass rolled away from her like a brown carpet, patched with green where spring started to come through. Her land was huge and magnificent; it enveloped the memory of her mother's house on the border, swallowing remembered hedgerows and farmland, reducing the significance of home in one easy stretch of brown tussock. Water churned nearby, replenished by bitter cold water sliding down from blue mountains. There could be life and living here, if they stayed the course. Dirty, but honest.

She had to be honest with Jack too. 'No, he did not. I wanted it as much as he did. I'm sorry if that shocks you.'

It did, a little, and she saw that in the way Jack's eyes grew round as sovereigns. But he didn't move away. Nor did he drop her hand.

'But he was married. When it started, I worked for him. My father had lost a fortune, you see. Quite a painter, but useless in business. Then my mother inherited wealth and all seemed right again.' Esther laughed bitterly. 'His wife found out about us, and he gave me this land to make the problem go away.'

Jack listened silently and then, just when Esther thought he really was appalled beneath the calm veneer, he brought her fingers to his lips and kissed them gently. 'And here you are,' he said. His voice was dusty, but it was a sweet, sweet sound.

'Here I am,' and Esther allowed herself to be pulled close.

∽

Isobel had spent some time walking along the banks of a stream, long enough for Esther to become troubled and wonder if something was wrong. When she returned to Esther and Jack, she said nothing about the pair holding hands. Esther saw how Isobel looked studiously away and wondered if her sister was embarrassed. But she felt so lightheaded, as though her insides were filled with air—because Jack was holding her—that Esther couldn't let go of his hand.

Then they noticed the figure in the distance, riding a horse. Isobel pointed. 'Look.'

They watched as the horse drew nearer. The horse was being rode at a fair canter, dust thrown up by the hooves. Jack dropped Esther's hand and they all covered their mouths as the stranger drew close.

'Apologies. Pardon the dirt,' the stranger said, and it was then they realised the rider was a woman. She had a neckerchief pulled up over her face, up to her nose, but the voice was unmistakable. Esther stared as the woman yanked hard on the reins and controlled the huge, snorting beast. 'You'll be Evan Bellamy's son.'

This was not a question, and Jack tipped his head, startled. Then he laughed. 'It's been a long time, Mrs Oliver.'

'It has.' The woman pulled the neckerchief away and leaned down to shake Jack's proffered hand. She had tanned, weather-beaten skin and dark blonde hair pulled back into a knot. Her blouse was roughly made from blue flannel—Esther could see uneven stitching under the woman's arms and she knew Isobel would have spotted it too. Her skirt was filthy and may once have been cream, but was now dyed brown and spotted with age and weather. But the riding boots gripping the stirrups were tough and well-made and the woman wore a pale blue cameo at her throat.

'And what brings you back here, after that trouble with your father?' The horse jerked and the woman cuffed it sharply, smacking obedience into the side of the animal's head. She narrowed her eyes at Esther and Isobel. 'And then I want to know who these people are.'

Jack grinned and Esther was startled to see how comfortable he was with the strange woman's questions. 'How are your sons, Mrs Oliver?'

The woman sniffed and drew a hand across her nose. Esther's curiosity doubled. She remembered Evan Bellamy's words from the night before, about the Olivers being a wealthy family in the area, and likely keen to buy her land. She could not fit the image of the coarse, blunt-speaking woman who wiped her wet nose on her arm with the thought of money. But there was the cameo at her throat …

'Jonas went to Dunedin and seems intent on drinking it dry,' the woman said. 'The twins are much the same. They've been running the place since their father passed on.'

Jack bowed his head. 'I am sorry to hear Mr Oliver died.' He turned to Isobel and Esther. 'Mrs Oliver's younger sons—twin boys—were my great friends when we were growing up.'

'They still speak of you, despite that business with your brother.' The woman held out her hand to Jack, flicking her fingers in a gesture that indicated she wanted assistance down from her horse. Esther watched as Jack went to help her, his face calm at the mention of Freddie. So much had changed in just a few hours.

Mrs Oliver dismounted easily and stood squarely in front of Esther. 'Jack, what are you doing here with a woman who has a belly that size?' Mrs Oliver pointed at Esther's stomach. 'Is she your wife? Seems foolish to bring her out here so close to her time.'

Isobel twitched her shoulders and Esther knew she was offended. Esther was shocked too, taken aback by the blunt nature of the woman's questions. She shivered, a little thrill climbing up her spine.

'This is my sister, Esther Carter,' Isobel said. 'I'm Isobel Nelson. And no, Esther is not Jack's wife. He is our guide and friend. Esther has come to see her land.'

'Her land?' Mrs Oliver immediately lost interest in Esther's round belly. 'This is your land?'

Esther nodded. She could not yet find words to speak to this forceful, unexpected, alluring woman.

Mrs Oliver turned to Jack, as if seeking confirmation. Jack held out his palms and smiled. 'Esther has come to see what she can make of it.'

'Now, this is a very strange state of affairs,' Mrs Oliver said. Her hand strayed to the blue brooch at her throat. 'My husband and I made enquiries over the years about this place, and we were told by a scoundrel at an over-furnished office in Christchurch that it belonged to a prospector in England, and there was no hope of his selling it.' She turned back to Esther. 'How did it come into your possession?'

Isobel opened her mouth to speak, but Esther finally felt words flood into her mouth and spoke first. 'That's not something I wish to discuss with strangers. Suffice to say, I want to see if the land is habitable.'

She sensed the woman would respect forceful speaking and she was right.

Mrs Oliver snorted. 'Oh, it's habitable enough! Have you told her, Jack, what fine grazing land this is?'

'I have.'

Mrs Oliver leaned over and grabbed the reins of her horse, which appeared in danger of wandering off. 'My husband and I set up our homestead thirty years ago. The early years were a struggle, no doubt about that—we lost whole flocks in snowstorms or floods, and once footrot wiped out our entire profits for the year. But we hung in and the only regret we have is not buying this bit of land right at the start.'

She passed the reins to Jack without looking at him and came to stand in front of Esther, feet squarely, proprietarily apart. 'Last year we made a profit large enough to buy four properties on Colombo Street, right in the heart of Christchurch. I could make you an offer, right now, for this land. One that could not be beaten.'

'You want to buy Esther's land?' Isobel asked. She drew close to her sister, her voice thick with suspicion.

Mrs Oliver nodded, just once, her head bobbing forward in a thrusting, forceful motion. 'I would need to see the deeds, of course, and a trip up to Christchurch to make it legal would be required. I'd meet you halfway on the fees. But yes, I want this land—always have. I could give you way more than a prospector in some expensive bank with leather chairs.'

Esther gazed at the woman, fascinated and repelled. What must it be like to have money and the freedom to spend it on what you want? She looked with new longing at Mrs Oliver's dirty, flapping skirt and the blue blouse under which the woman was, obviously, corset-less. The constricting fabric of her own dress and the memory of the absurd coat she wore in Auckland with its extra, concealing panel made her feel bitter. Mrs Oliver wore her freedom and wealth easily.

'I don't know,' she said eventually. 'I had to see the place—simply had to. Maybe you don't understand but, as dangerous as it is with the baby almost here, I needed to stand on the grass I owned and hear the stream for myself. And see where the mountains are and where there is shade.'

Mrs Oliver nodded sagely. Her eyes sparked with understanding. 'It's a hard kind of living out here. Ask Jack. He was born to it, but the years grind life from you. I could offer you money that would give you a future without the worry and strain of managing a farm. Don't forget, it's not just farming—you'd have to build a house too. I could give you enough money for you to buy one of those new, pretty little houses I see on the rare visits I make to town.'

She sniffed and her disdain was unmistakable. Esther could see how little the settler woman thought of gentrified life in the city.

Then Esther thought of the women on George Street, and mugs

of tea in the shared courtyard, and helping, open hands when plates and purses were empty. The thought of a neat townhouse full of trinkets and no friends did not appeal to her either.

'I need to think about this,' she said. 'Would you have a card or a way I could contact you later?'

Mrs Oliver snorted. 'A card? What possible use would I have for calling cards out here, with neighbours half a day's riding away? If you want to take me up on your offer, Jack knows where to find me.'

With that, the bronze-faced woman with thick, powerful shoulders nodded a farewell to Jack and took the reins for her horse. She bent her knees, readying herself to mount her horse again and, just as she swung her leg over the saddle, Esther felt a circle of pain squeeze and crush her belly. She let out a cry; it was stronger and unlike any pain she had felt before. Isobel grabbed her arm and looked into her face anxiously.

Mrs Oliver leaned forward and pointed down at them all. 'You'd best get that girl home. Baby's on its way.'

Isobel

The night was long and washed through with waves of fear. There were many times on the ride back to Evan Bellamy's farm that Isobel thought they would not make it and she would have to deliver Esther's baby in the grass. Jack, his face a sick, pale mask, urged the horses on, asking more of them than they might ordinarily give. Esther moaned in her saddle and gripped the reins so tightly that they left clefts in her skin. Sometimes she screamed and Isobel had to gulp back tears. She could do nothing to help her.

Somehow the baby stayed in Esther's belly until they reached the homestead. When Jack came to help Esther down from her horse, they saw the saddle was wet and smeared. Isobel pulled Esther's arm around her neck and led her inside while Jack took the horse and saddle to be washed down, his mouth tight and afraid.

Immediately alert as to what was happening, Evan hurried himself into the kitchen and Isobel heard him muttering about hot water. She didn't know if that was the right thing to do. She couldn't remember what Hilda Riley had done when they'd helped the woman on Sale Street give birth. She couldn't think what to say, how to calm Esther, who was now terrified.

There was a moment when Isobel stood in the doorway of their bedroom, wringing her hands, while Esther squealed into a rolled sheet—and she caught a glimpse of her own reflection in the mirror. White, shocked face, hair wild, eyes red-ringed. Isobel looked as frightened as Esther, and the realisation was the shake Isobel needed. Esther was about to have a baby and risk her life to do so. Isobel had to control herself and help her.

'Come on, you'll feel better if you undress,' Isobel said and, between bands of pain, Esther was able to remove her clothes with Isobel's assistance. Isobel had never seen Esther's unclothed belly before and the swell of it alarmed her. Purple veins webbed across pale skin, appearing delicate enough to tear. She saw Esther's bellybutton, pushed out and distorted, and felt sick. But she helped Esther into a nightdress and swung her sister's legs onto the bed, piling cushions behind Esther's back.

'Tell me what to do, Esther. You've read the books. I can't remember anything from the time I helped the woman on Sale Street.'

'I have to wait. The pain comes and goes,' Esther jabbered, twisting the bedsheets in her fists. Then she screamed again and Isobel caught her as she reared up.

A knock on the door and Jack edged in to the room, a saucepan of hot water steaming in his hands. Instinctively, Isobel reached over and pulled a sheet over Esther's body.

'I'm sorry,' Jack mumbled. He placed the saucepan of water on the carpet and studiously kept his eyes down. 'Pop said to be careful of the cord, when the time comes.'

'The cord?' Isobel said.

Unbelievably, between pants, Esther laughed. 'The cord between the baby and me. You'll see it, Isobel.'

'And he said …' Jack stood up, looking at the wall. 'He said make sure you get everything after the birth. There will be a sac that comes with it. Get it all or there could be an infection. It's what killed my mother.'

Isobel listened, incredulous, a rivulet of anger growing in her chest that there was so *much* to this, so much to this nightmare— and she knew nothing.

Jack began to back toward the door and Esther called out. 'Stay!'

'Esther.' Isobel saw her sister clutch at the sheets again, another wave of pain bearing down. 'He'll be just outside, he can fetch whatever you need.'

'I want you to stay!' Esther's face was a crease of pain and she hitched in her breath again, ready to scream.

Jack shook his head frantically, but Esther yelled again.

'Perhaps for a little while, Jack,' Isobel said. 'To calm her.'

He swallowed, his Adam's apple surging up and down in his throat. But then Esther reached out for him. There was nowhere for him to go, so he simply held her and allowed her to hold him.

∽

It seemed many hours before the baby began to make its way into the world. The room had darkened and Isobel could see lamps elsewhere on the homestead, lighting up outhouses and the barn. Jack had helped her wash Esther's body, neither speaking as Esther's nightdress gathered up around her waist. At one point Jack left the room to find clean bedsheets and Esther panicked, calling for him until he stumbled back into the room with laden arms. He sat on the floor with Esther leaning against him while Isobel stripped and remade the bed, and then they helped her back into position.

Then, in that long night, it was time. Esther made a deep noise in her throat, different to the screams and cries, and Isobel saw her sister's shoulders hunch in.

'We need my father,' Jack said, getting rapidly to his feet, face stricken. 'He helped my mother.'

They were too far into the night and had seen too much for Isobel to object for decorum's sake and, within seconds, Evan Bellamy had scurried into the room, so quickly that Isobel wondered if he had been waiting outside. He saw Esther's coiled position and understood how close she was.

Esther screamed again, and again, and again, and Jack had backed against the wall, his hand over his mouth. And then the strangest thing happened. A purple bag appeared on the bed between Esther's legs, and Evan's hands moved quickly over it. Isobel saw a ribbed, slippery rope wrapped around the bag, which Evan pulled away, and the thing lay silently on the sheet.

'She's here, you've done it!' Evan shouted and then Isobel saw that the purple bag was actually a baby, that there were limbs and eyes, and a squashed face. But it was quiet. There was no cry.

Esther, crying now, reached down. 'A girl? Is she dead?'

'Wait.' Evan gently reached into the baby's mouth with his fingers and wiped a clot of something away. There was a long, hideous second where there was still no sound, and Isobel felt her stomach roll away—after all Esther had been through, for the baby to die!—and then the tiny chest expanded and the sweetest, shrillest cry filled the room.

Evan Bellamy sat back and sighed and, with a towel handed to him by Jack, the small, old, marvellous man wrapped the infant up and handed her to her mother.

She had red, red hair and a furious face, and glared around at the group as if she simply could not understand why they had brought her there.

There was more from Esther's body, and she cried again when the sac was delivered, bloodied and shining. Isobel stared down at it, horrified and fascinated, and waited as Evan studied it carefully. He nodded, satisfied.

'That's all of it. But, Esther, if you feel hot or pain in your belly again, you must say immediately.'

'I will.' But Esther was not really listening. Instead she was staring down into the face of her child, wearing a delighted, serene expression that Isobel had never seen before. And it tore at her throat. She saw the way her sister's arm curved under the baby, the easy way Esther stroked the infant's cheek and nose. She thought of their mother's letter and the glimmer of hope it had given her that she—Isobel—might finally become a mother.

Tears caught in her mouth and Esther looked up.

'Oh, Isobel, isn't she beautiful?'

Isobel nodded, unable to speak.

'We should leave mother to her baby for a while,' Evan said. He had stood up and gathered the bloodied sac up in a sheet. 'Come, Jack. We're not needed now. Let Isobel settle her sister.'

Jack nodded quickly, his hand on the door handle. Isobel thought that Esther might object and want him to stay, but her sister's gaze had fallen back to her daughter and she looked at nothing else. While the men left the room and Isobel busied herself by putting fresh sheets on the bed, Esther edged to the side but did not look up.

Isobel could not bear it. The soft noises that Esther made as she put the child to her breast for the first time, and tiny cries and snuffling; they were like shrieks to Isobel's ears. She stood at the side of Esther's bed and carefully ran her palm over the top of the baby's head, then left the room.

⁣℘

She found Jack and Evan on the veranda. The night air was frigid and brutal against her skin, but she welcomed it after the claustrophobic heat of the hours before. Her breath came in short bursts and the muscles in her legs trembled. Evan, sitting on the cracked swing seat, looked over and reached for her hand.

'Come.' He eased her gently beside him. Jack stood apart, looking out over the plains, and Isobel saw how his back was drenched in sweat. He wore no jacket. His shirt stuck to him.

'You should feel proud of yourself, dear.' Evan patted Isobel's hand. 'You brought your sister's child into the world and kept Esther alive.'

Isobel looked down at the old man's hand, his skin still tanned and smooth, and wondered again at what they would have done without him. Their journey would have been so much harder. 'I had no clue what I was doing,' she admitted. 'You were the one, at the end. You made sure the baby and Esther made it.'

Evan bent his head low. 'Jack's mother had a child when Jack was about ten and Freddie was five.' He was talking down into his chest and Isobel could see how the disclosure hurt him, but also that the night had given him licence to speak. 'The baby came earlier than it should. A girl, as well. Do you remember, Jack?'

Jack murmured something, but didn't turn round.

'It couldn't live.' Evan sighed. 'And my wife wasn't able to deliver all of the afterbirth. She lasted a week.'

'She died as well?'

'She did.'

Isobel felt his body shudder. 'I'm sorry. That's why you wanted to check Esther.'

'It is. And Jack had the cord wrapped around his neck when he was born, and we nearly lost him.' Evan spoke to his son. 'Dangerous business to get and keep you, lad. Having a baby is a gamble.'

Jack still did not turn around. Evan stared at his back for a while and then shrugged.

'I'm going to sleep now,' he said. 'It seemed as though this night would never end and now it has, my old bones need to rest. I suggest you both do the same. Look in on Esther, but make sure you sleep.'

Isobel glanced over her shoulder to the window of her sister's room, a pale light burning on the sill. The homestead was still and quiet, no hint of the screams and fear that had torn the air only a short time before. She couldn't imagine sleeping, however. A solitary dog snored near where the horses were stabled.

As Evan left, he clapped a hand to Jack's shoulder and it looked for a moment as though the men would embrace. But then they simply nodded and Evan went on his way, back inside. They heard a door close softly in the farmhouse and silence fell between them again.

Now they were alone, Isobel realised they hadn't properly spoken since the incident in the lake. Esther had been between them on the ride out to the Hatcher Valley, and there had been no time in the theatre of the birth. Isobel hesitated on the swing seat, swaying back and forth into the unspoken blackness between them.

Jack spoke first. 'Do you think she looks like him?'

'Who?'

Jack coughed. 'The baby. Does she look like her father?'

Isobel shifted in her seat, unsettled. 'I can't remember.'

'You knew him?'

'I had met him, yes. It was a long time ago.'

Jack began to pace. 'I imagine that Esther sees him in the child. Why wouldn't she? Despite all that red hair just like Esther's … when she looks at the baby, she sees him.'

Isobel watched his restless movements, trying to follow the thread of his thoughts. 'I think Esther is just relieved the baby is here, alive. And that she's made it through as well.'

'Pop saw Freddie in me,' Jack said shortly. 'That's why he sent me away, as well as blaming me. He saw Freddie when he looked at my face. Esther sees the man when she looks at her child.'

Agitation rolled from him, and Isobel remembered how he had resisted Esther's clawing hands during the worst of the evening, how it jarred with the tenderness he had shown her up to that point.

'I can't believe she's here,' Jack muttered, and Isobel could not be sure whom he meant. 'I'm going to the lake.'

Was he inviting her to join him? The plains stretched out around them like a sea. Jack walked to the wooden edge of the veranda and rocked, feet hanging down into the grass. From within the building came a small mewl. The baby, crying. Isobel wondered if he would change his mind and go back inside.

Instead he spoke over his shoulder. 'It will be as cold as it was before.' And then he stepped off into the grass and was quickly lost from view.

Isobel did not follow him immediately. The baby's cries grew and she stood up, feeling the pull of her sister. But then the child settled and was quiet. A bird called out from somewhere in the dark.

Her clothes stuck to her. Her dress was damp with perspiration and the strain of the evening. Esther's body had stained her sleeves. The lake, with its cool water, would welcome her. She could pile her clothes in a neat heap at the water's edge. She followed Jack into the darkness.

The sound of splashing water guided her, though she stumbled a few times. When she reached the water, Jack was already swimming. He was a black shadow in the water and the farm, with the one light in Esther's window, seemed far away.

She hesitated on the shoreline, like she had done before. Was it only yesterday when they swam in the water? Isobel could scarcely believe it. She wanted to be clean, but held back, smelling the cold of the lake, its bracing, raw scent. She thought of Esther and thought of Jack, and her heart shivered in her ribcage.

Jack called out. 'Your dress is covered in blood. Take it off.'

His voice was different. It was low and gravelly, as though he had drunk too much coffee too quickly.

Esther would be feeding her child or would be asleep. Isobel strained to hear them, but there was no sound except for the gentle lap of Jack moving in the water.

'Take it off.'

The sky pressed down upon them. Isobel felt her ears fill, as though she was already underwater. The world seemed to narrow to a single point; to a man, swimming in the lake.

It was the simplest thing in the world to undress completely. She piled her cloths in a heap. Rachel's knife, kept secreted away in her boot, was placed on top. Icy wind rolled across the plains and stabbed her, pushing her forward toward the water. She held her hands across her breasts and, as she waded in, Jack came to greet her.

Before, he had been shocked at the closeness of their flesh, but now he was curious. He pulled Isobel further into the lake until water came up to their necks, and Isobel grew afraid that she would lose her footing. She was afraid of the rushing flood around her and the way it moved her. She had never learned to swim, not even when Esther had badgered her when they were children. She shifted her weight, trying to find her balance. But Jack had her, one hand cupped beneath her buttocks, the other in the small of her back.

And then he lifted her up and the thought crossed her mind that he was slimmer than Brendan. Her thighs locked easily about his waist. She moved to make room and then the part of Jack that he had kept from her was suddenly in the right place, and he made a noise like sighing. There was no splashing, only rocking, and then Isobel no longer cared that she was out of her depth or that only a few hundred metres away her sister and newborn niece lay quietly together.

Esther

It took a few days for Esther to settle on a name for the child, but finally she did and, when she said it out loud for the first time, it seemed perfect. The baby was on Isobel's knee when she announced it; the three of them were alone. Esther had pushed the infant into Isobel's arms, brushing aside her sister's protests. Isobel did not seem to want to handle the baby, and Esther wondered if her sister was scared of the child's fragility.

Not that the baby was fragile when she was emptying her breasts. Esther's chest was cracked and sore from constant feeding, so much so that Isobel tore up an old towel and dunked the strips in cold water. Esther lay back against her pillows or sat in the armchair that Jack had dragged in from the kitchen, icy wet pieces of towel over her nipples, her outraged and hungry daughter screaming on her knee.

Catherine. Esther said the name as Isobel held the child and wondered why on earth she had not thought of it before. Cathy, for short, if the girl liked it. The name of the girl in the book Esther had stolen from her father's study. Isobel had gasped when she had said it.

'Don't you like it?' Esther asked, puzzled.

Isobel bit her lip and shook her head. She seemed to wince down at her niece. 'It's just that it's Kate's name. The woman in Christchurch organising the petition for women's votes. It seems perfect.'

Esther had forgotten about the push for suffrage back in Auckland, and the writing of names on a ream of paper. In fact, she felt like she had forgotten everything, save for the heat of her room in the day and the few precious hours when she could sleep between feeds. Auckland seemed at the other end of the world.

'I didn't think about voting, or a petition, or anything to do with your work in Auckland,' she said. 'I only thought about Father's book. I took it from his library without asking Mother. Imagine, Isobel, what she would make of Cathy.' Suddenly the desire to laugh was too much to bear and Esther began to snort. 'At least she doesn't have Mother's awful teeth.'

At the mention of their mother, Isobel shifted in her seat and her smile was thin. 'Not yet, anyway. Here, take her. She wants you.'

'She's fine, Isobel.' But Esther took her daughter back on her knee and watched, mirth giving way to confusion as Isobel abruptly left the room.

Isobel's sudden distance mystified her, but the child soon sucked up Esther's attention again. It was impossible to focus on much else for long. The child was a wonder and Esther could not stop looking at her. From the moment Evan Bellamy placed the swaddled, angry bundle in her arms, her astonishment at the infant grew. How was it possible for her eyes to be so blue and her skin so white? The pearl of the child's nails made her bring them to her mouth and kiss them; the way Cathy's legs kicked when she was hungry was astonishing.

She could not believe she had grown such a thing in her belly. Her disbelief, though, was shadowed by a darker feeling; the creep of memory about the other child—the one before Cathy—the one she had stopped before her belly grew big. Sometimes guilt and grief crushed her and she wept.

When she wasn't feeding or crying, Esther was leaking. Her body continued to forget its borders and she had to change her clothes several times a day. Isobel washed the underclothes without comment. But after a couple of weeks or so, the bleeding and aching stopped, and Esther looked outside the window and saw the Canterbury sun. She nursed the baby on the veranda and let her body heal.

She had not seen Jack for days so, when he walked around the barn into her line of sight, Esther's heart sprang into her ribs. She was holding Catherine against her shoulder and the child snorted softly into her ear. She waved to Jack.

He walked over slowly and she saw he wore a dirty white shirt that was torn at the neck, and he carried a rake in his hand. He nodded curtly as he approached, glancing at the baby and glancing away.

Esther puzzled at him. She had missed him these past days but, when she asked Isobel where he was and why he didn't come to see her, Isobel had replied he was probably giving her time to bond with the child. It was an unsatisfying answer and, watching the man kick at dust and refuse to meet her gaze, Esther's bewilderment grew. First Isobel and now Jack.

'Where have you been?' she asked simply.

'I had to take our horses back to Christchurch. We'd only paid to have them for a week. And then I bought one outright, to bring me back here. Fences on the east border needed fixing too, and that was a couple of day's ride,' Jack said quietly. 'How are you?'

'Tired.' Esther patted the baby on her shoulder. 'She wants to feed around the clock. But we're getting by. Do you want to see her?'

She eased Catherine down onto her lap, the baby's mouth a pursed, satisfied line. Jack hung back, and Esther sat forward on the swing seat, holding Catherine closer.

Jack rubbed the back of his head. 'She looks different.'

'Fatter, you mean.' Esther teased an affectionate finger down her daughter's cheek.

'I have to go, Esther.' Jack stepped back. 'I said I'd help repair the water pump. Pa said it's leaking.'

'Jack, wait.' Esther edged the baby into the crook of her elbow and held out her hand. After a long moment, Jack took it. She reeled him into the seat beside her. 'I haven't been able to say thank you. For the night she was born.'

'You don't need to,' Jack mumbled.

'No, I do. Thank you for being there. I can't remember everything that happened, but if it wasn't for you, and Isobel, and your father— well, she might not be here.' Esther looked down at her child. 'I might not be here.'

'It's fine, Esther. Really.'

The reluctance in his voice was a knife. A ball of tears swelled into her mouth and Esther swallowed hard, exasperated at how emotional she was these days. 'Would you like to hold her?'

'No.'

'No?' Esther was shocked. 'Why? Jack, what's wrong? Was the birth so awful? I'm sorry, I can't …'

'Does she look like him?'

'Who?'

'Her father.' A muscle pulsed in Jack's jaw.

'I … I don't know.' And Esther wasn't being evasive. She couldn't remember what the master of Gallerton Hall looked like. She had thought about him as Catherine's birth approached, wondering if he would be marking time for when his child would arrive somewhere in the world, but always when she thought of him, Esther's memories were fuzzy and grey. A cloud came down over the man's face so she couldn't see it as a whole. A memory of a smile, yes, a patch of skin on his temple that she used to like to press her tongue against— but she could not define him in her mind as a whole being. He was as unreal and distant as Jack was present, hot, and angry.

It was obvious he was angry. She could not quite understand why. 'I don't know,' she said again. 'I really can't remember.'

Jack gave a short, ugly laugh and made to stand up.

Esther touched his wrist quickly, and the light pressure of her fingers kept him momentarily in place. 'Please, Jack. I'm not pretending, or hiding anything. It's just that he seems as though he's from a lifetime ago. I haven't seen him since he told me to leave and sent me out here.'

'But you've thought of him.' Jack would not look at her.

'I did, in the early days.' Esther remembered the moments in Isobel's tiny cottage on George Street, when her legs and belly still held the sway of the boat. She had pined for the man, her turbulent body flooded with strange longing and feeling. 'But then I forgot him. It's true—once I started to help Isobel with her sewing and saw so much of the city, the thought of what might have been back home melted away.'

Immediately she saw she had chosen the wrong words, for Jack pushed aside her hand and stood up. 'What might have been?' he scowled. 'So if you were back home, you might have been with him?'

'No.' The baby began to cry and Esther put her back over her shoulder. She wondered if the child would feel the race of her heart and the way her body hitched for breath. 'I don't mean that either. Oh, Jack, what does it matter if she looks like him!'

'It matters to me.' Jack gripped the rake, looking as though he wanted to be anywhere but next to Esther. 'And if you can't work out why it matters, you're not as clever as I thought you were.'

He strode away, without a single glance back. Esther patted her daughter, comforting her, trying to calm herself.

⁊

Evan Bellamy had said that morning that, somewhere in the sprawling pile of his house, he might have some old clothes once belonging to Jack and Freddie and, soon after Jack walked away from Esther, he arrived on the veranda with his arms laden. He stood in front of Esther and beamed.

'See! I knew I had them somewhere. Don't know why I kept them—it's not like they were all made by Jack's mother, so it wasn't for any sentimental reason. Will you be able to use them and make clothes for the baby?'

The kindly old man was so excited by his rediscovery that he did not notice Esther's distress at first. When he did, he put the pile of clothes down on the wooden deck and sat down.

'My wife said these early days after the birth of a child were the most emotional,' he said. 'She would sob one moment and laugh like a kea the next.'

Esther held Catherine in place while wiping her eyes with the heel of her hand. 'My stomach feels like it's a bouncing ball on a string.'

Evan pursed his lips sympathetically and held out his hands for the baby. He settled back onto the swing seat with her, sighing contentedly. 'The key to feeling yourself again is plenty of rest.'

Esther grunted. 'She has other ideas. She feeds constantly.'

'She's not feeding now,' Evan said simply. 'I can sit here in the sun and hold this child, and you can close your eyes for a couple of hours. Your sister is baking in the kitchen.' He patted his waist. 'I haven't eaten so well in years! The rest of the house is silent. Warm and stuffy, but quiet.'

He was right and Esther knew she should take the opportunity to rest. Catherine woke regularly through the night for a feed and a change and, although Isobel had helped to clean and swaddle, only Esther could fill her baby's belly. She was exhausted. But she lingered on the swing seat.

'Go!' Evan gave her a gentle push. 'She'll be fine with me. I think you know how I love to hold her.'

She didn't go. Instead Esther looked down at her hands and spoke softly. 'Why is Jack angry with me?'

She sensed Evan frowning down at the baby and again felt sorrow that they had turned the old man's world upside down. In less than a week, his son had returned, bringing with him two strangers, quickly joined by a third, squalling house guest.

'I'm sorry, we have imposed enough on you,' she said. 'Forget I asked. I will go for a sleep, as you suggested.'

He reached out and caught her hand as she stood, and Esther paused.

'Of all the things I did after Freddie died, blaming Jack is the thing I feel most shame for.' Evan sniffed. 'I didn't hide my anger toward him. Nor did I try to give us both time to come to terms with what we had lost. He didn't have to tell me that he'd played a trick on Freddie in the lake, but he confessed, and I treated him cruelly because of it. I couldn't bear to look at him—all I saw was Freddie, or what Freddie should have looked like when he was older. I told Jack that as well.'

Esther could hear the heaviness of Evan's breath and the old man's body sagged further back into the swing seat.

'Jack asked me if the baby looked like her father,' she said.

Evan looked at her from the side of his eye. 'Does she?'

Esther smiled ruefully. 'I can tell you the same thing I told Jack. I honestly can't remember.'

'You have no portrait or miniature of him?'

'We parted unexpectedly.'

'I see.' Evan smoothed a curl of hair from Catherine's brow. 'I'm sure you'll find, in certain places in this country—just as back home—a fatherless child will cause the judgmental to raise their eyebrows and draw assumptions. You won't find that attitude down here, though. Maybe some circles in Christchurch care for such type of matters, but out on the plains, the sheep and the weather and whether you can get through a winter with your flock intact are the types of things we value.'

'So why did Jack ask?'

Unexpectedly, Evan laughed. He turned to look at Esther and his face was split by a wide, fond grin.

'It's not obvious? He loves you. And he's trying to work out if he can love and be a father to your child.'

Isobel

Isobel had baked three loaves already and was sweeping the kitchen floor when Esther appeared in the doorway. The kitchen was stiflingly hot and her clothes clung to her, but she resisted the urge to leave. No one wanted to enter the kitchen while it was warm outside and the stove was lit, so Isobel felt safe. She was alone to knead out her thoughts into the dough, away from Esther and Jack, and the crying, feeding, gurning baby.

Isobel winced when Esther walked into the room. She had her back turned to the door, but knew it was Esther from her sigh. Isobel turned around and saw that Esther's face was pink and her eyes were bright. Isobel could not tell if she had been crying or laughing.

'Are you feeling well, Esther?' she asked, leaning the broom against the storeroom door. 'Do you want some water?'

'You're such a good nurse.' Esther stepped forward and grasped her sister's hands. 'Evan told me I needed to rest, but I can't—my head is in too much of a spin!'

'What is it?' Isobel gently untangled her fingers from her sister's clasp, her brow a frown.

'It's Jack.' Esther walked toward the kitchen window, which looked out onto the farmyard and plains beyond. The window was an orange block, burnt grass stretching as far as the eye could see. 'I couldn't understand why he was so angry with me. He asked me if the baby looked like her father and wouldn't accept that I couldn't remember. I really can't, you know.'

Isobel said nothing. Jack had asked her the same thing, out on the veranda, the night they had … She closed her eyes briefly. Jack stood in her mind's eye, a rippling half-image, threatening to overwhelm her.

'I talked to Evan,' Esther muttered. 'He helped me see what is obvious.'

'What?' Though Isobel knew, and her heart bled at the words she knew Esther would say.

'Jack wants to be with me.' Esther turned back to face Isobel and her cheeks were aflame. 'Isn't that astonishing? He wants to look after Cathy and I. Both of us.'

'Evan told you that?'

'He did.'

'And do you want to be with him?' The muscles in Isobel's neck were beginning to ache. She remembered how she had gripped Jack so tightly in the water, and how every tiny particle of her skin seemed to stand on end as they lay on the shoreline together, bodies locked, freezing air pressing down on them.

'I do.' Esther suddenly spun around on the spot, her skirts flying. 'I have to talk to him, of course.'

Isobel swallowed. Jack had not spoken to her for days, not once, not since that night. He had not joined them at mealtimes, but had spent all of his day outside, working on the homestead. Once, he came into the kitchen when he thought she was not there and left abruptly when Isobel walked out of the pantry. She had looked for him out on the plains, seeking out his shape the way she had once sought a glimpse of her neighbour's babies, back on George Street. Food was tasteless in her mouth. She wanted only to speak to Jack, to feel his arms around her waist again.

'Aren't you happy for me?' Esther asked. She frowned at Isobel. 'Why do you say nothing?'

'Of course I'm happy for you,' Isobel said. She reached for the broom again, to have something to do. 'Don't be so dramatic, Esther.'

Esther snorted. 'There's something wrong. You have been distant ever since Cathy was born. What is it?'

Isobel had made her way to the pantry doorway and she stood

between the two spaces, casting her eyes from side to side. She wanted Esther to go away, she wanted her sister to take her happiness and her chance at love and go and jump in the lake. But Esther would not go and she grabbed the broom from Isobel's hands.

'Esther!'

'Talk to me! Tell me what is wrong!'

Jack, the lake. The baby. Their mother's letter. Where could she begin? And now Esther was angry and shouting.

'Have you thought about the child in all of this?' Isobel finally asked.

'Of course. Weren't you listening to what I said? Evan thinks …'

'Yes, you told me what Evan thinks. But what if Catherine *does* grow up to look more like her father than she looks like you? What if Jack finds it impossible to love her?'

Esther's brow creased. 'He won't. How could he not love her?'

Isobel sighed impatiently. 'You're bound to say that, being her mother. But what if you decide to create a family, the three of you, and then Jack finds it too hard? He might leave you. He might leave Catherine.'

'I can't believe you are saying this, Isobel!' Esther was appalled. 'He wouldn't do that.'

'You've not changed at all, have you?' Isobel took a step back into the kitchen. 'You got yourself into this mess by following your desires, not your responsibilities, and we've all picked up the pieces. You made us come down here when you should have been preparing for the birth of your child. We've invaded a kind old man's home and turned it upside down. All to satisfy your needs.'

'That's not true!'

'And now you will risk your child's happiness and security on a gamble.' Rarely had Isobel spoken in such a way and her throat was raw from the strain of it. 'You can't have it all.'

'What's wrong with wanting to give my child a father?' Esther spat.

'You should have thought of that before.'

They were both staggered at the words and the rage that erupted from nowhere. Isobel felt the kitchen close in on her, the air even hotter. Esther was shaking her head, her eyes wet with confusion and fury. She backed away to the kitchen door, ready to leave.

'There is an alternative,' Isobel said abruptly.

'What do you mean? An alternative to what?'

Don't say it, don't say it—but Isobel could remember every single word of her mother's secret letter and it spilled from her like wine from a toppled glass. 'You could give Cathy to me.'

Esther froze. 'What?'

'If you want to see if you and Jack can make a go of it, give me the child. I will give her a secure home. I could take her back to Auckland—not to Brendan, of course, but we could find a place where we could live together and I could raise her. You could give Jack everything of yourself and know that your daughter was being cared for properly.'

Esther's eyes were wide and she shook her head. 'Why on earth would I give you my daughter?' And then, pity. 'Oh, Isobel, I know how much you wanted a baby. She will be like a daughter to you, you'll see.'

The slight tilt to Esther's head and the soft tone that crept into her voice was almost more than Isobel could bear. She didn't want the leftovers of her sister's heart.

'You could even go back home,' she spat. 'Back to that man or Mother, like it never happened.'

'It?' Esther shook her head. '*Cathy*, not it. She isn't a thing to throw away.'

'Not even if you could go back to the way your life was? Hell, you could take Jack back home with you. Mother might like this one.'

'Where is this coming from, Isobel?' Esther tried to catch her sister's hand. 'I've never heard you speak in this way.'

Isobel wrenched her fingers away. The room seemed to sway and she was not sure if it was the heat or anger. Her tongue rattled in her mouth and she could not stop. 'It was Mother's idea.'

'Mother's idea?'

'She wrote a letter. To you, not to me—she would have known I wouldn't take much persuading. She wants you to give the baby to me.'

'I didn't receive a letter.' Esther was confused. 'She hasn't written to me the whole time since I came out here. You know that.'

Isobel gripped the handle of the brush tightly. 'It was in your trunk.'

'My trunk? The one I brought over with me on the boat?' Esther threw up her hands. 'You've had this idea for months!'

Then Isobel felt ashamed and her face burned. 'Not for months, no. It seemed too incredible an idea at first. But Mother is right—I could give you a choice. You have the whole world at your feet—you're luckier than many women I know. Luckier than I. You could sell the deeds to your land and go home a rich woman. Or live here a rich woman. You could start again, without any shame.'

'Shame!' Esther shouted, and tears sprang into her eyes. 'I'm not ashamed to have a child and no husband. I cannot believe you have thought about this for so long. I cannot believe you took a letter that belonged to me.' She stopped and pressed her hand to her chest. 'Did you think about taking my daughter those times in Auckland, when you made me wait out on Queen Street while you delivered the mending?'

'Of course not.' But Isobel remembered the little thread of thoughts when she parted from Esther on the side of Queen Street. Public display, shame—it might weaken Esther's resolve and force her to give up her child. Isobel looked away.

'Isobel, I will never give you my child,' Esther said. She backed out of the room, shaking her head venomously. 'Not ever.'

Isobel heard her sister walk back onto the veranda, Esther's boots thumping noisily on the wooden slats. The kitchen window was open and, as Isobel sank onto a chair and laid her head on the kitchen table, she heard Esther take her baby back from Evan Bellamy, and heard the old man yawn. A few moments later, Evan wandered back into the house and somewhere a door closed, presumably the door to his room where he would take a nap.

The wooden table was warm but Isobel did not lift her head. Instead she pressed the flat of her palms down upon its surface, squeezing her eyes shut. She had been an angry fool. Of course Esther would not give up her child. She would keep the baby and love it, and keep Jack too.

The pain she felt when thinking of Jack was almost as acute as the image of Catherine lying asleep in Esther's arms. She had thought of him and the baby, and barely anything else for the last week. When she pushed up the sleeves of her dress to knead dough, she thought of Jack's tanned skin and how smooth the inside of his elbows were to touch and kiss. When she peeled her damp dress away from her back and let it settle again on her skin, she thought of his wet chest, pressed against her shoulder blades, as they lay together on the shore of the lake. Yet he wouldn't talk to her and could not look at her in the eye.

Then she heard his voice. Isobel lifted her head. Jack was back on the veranda. She couldn't make out what he was saying, but then the swing seat creaked and she knew he had sat down next to Esther.

Isobel stood up slowly, careful not to scrape her chair on the stone floor. She padded over to the window where the voices were clearer, drifting into the room on a hot, tangy breeze.

'Perhaps it can be done in Christchurch, if you've a mind.' Jack's voice, low and furrowed, as though he were embarrassed. 'But I don't want you to think I want you for your money. I don't want any of it. Sure, we could find a lawyer and write something out.'

Isobel strained to hear, but could not make out Esther's response. Then Jack laughed, the sound making Isobel sink to the ground.

'You will? The baby too? That makes me happy.'

Esther

She found Isobel packing. After the baby's birth, Isobel cleared a small room further along the hallway and slept in there, and it was there that Esther found her, folding up her possessions and putting them into her bag.

Esther stood with her arms crossed, leaning against the door-frame. She had left Catherine with Jack, out on the veranda where the day was heating up. He had wanted to hold her. She had let him.

'You're leaving,' Esther said.

Isobel did not look up. 'It's for the best.'

'Where are you going?'

'Back to Auckland.' Isobel busied herself over a small table, gathering together a hairbrush and mirror.

'To Brendan?'

'No. Rachel will let me stay with her for a while, I'm sure. I'll ask Brendan for a divorce.'

Esther's eyebrows shot up to her hairline, but she bit back a response. Isobel squashed the hairbrush and mirror down into her bag.

'I don't care what he throws at me in retaliation,' Isobel said. 'He can claim I abandoned him, or I was a terrible wife. He can make it all my fault. Just as long as I don't have to stay married to that man a moment longer.'

'Good for you,' Esther said eventually. She struggled to contain the urge to run across the room to her sister, to fling her arms about her. They had never argued the way they had in the kitchen, and Esther's chest felt bruised. She didn't want her to leave. But instead she said, 'You can't ride all the way back to Christchurch on your own.'

Isobel snapped the fastening on her bag shut. 'Evan's man will be back from Christchurch today. He's staying here tonight and resting his horse and then Evan is sending him back to town. He has a collection of new coins to collect from the post office. It seems Evan collects Roman coins as well as coins from all manner of places.'

'I'm not interested in his coins,' Esther said faintly.

Isobel shrugged. 'I'm not either. But I'll ride with Evan's man and I'll make my way back to Auckland. Lots of women travel alone around this country these days.'

She stood up, and when she looked at Esther, her sister was shocked at the dispassion and coolness written across her face. She looks as though she has already left, Esther thought, and it was true; Isobel held herself in a different way. Her bones seemed sharper.

'You're really leaving then?' Esther asked.

'Yes.'

'But—I don't want you to leave.' Esther extended her palms, but then brought her hands back to her side when her sister made no move to catch her fingers. 'Don't leave like this.'

And then Isobel smiled slightly. She stepped toward her sister and brushed a strand of hair behind Esther's ear. 'Wearing you hair up really becomes you. Did I ever tell you that?'

'Isobel.' Tears now.

'Hush.' Isobel's hand traced the curve of her sister's cheek. 'Leaving is the right thing to do and you know that. Make a life here, for yourself. Make it with Jack and Cathy. You don't need me over your shoulder—you'll constantly think that I'm judging you and comparing how you are raising your child to the way I would do it. I wouldn't judge, you know, but I could never convince you otherwise.'

'I need you here,' Esther choked.

'You don't. And I can't be here. You must understand that it would be too hard for me.'

Esther shifted her feet, as though the ground beneath her had shifted and was unstable. She did not know this kind of Isobel, with her simple strength and angular body. It unnerved her and, when she saw there was no persuading, made her cry harder.

Isobel patted her back, and for a while they stood together in the quiet room. Esther lay her head on Isobel's shoulder and shut her eyes, breathing in her sister's hot, busy scent.

Then there were noises outside. An unfamiliar voice and then Evan Bellamy shouting out a hello. Isobel released Esther and walked into the hallway.

'Evan's man,' she called out. 'He's returned.'

Which brings Isobel's departure ever closer, Esther thought, but she wiped her eyes on the sleeve of her dress and followed her sister into the rough courtyard.

Evan was helping his man down from the horse and the two were deep in conversation. The rider's face was sun-bronzed and he wore a dirty red neckerchief, which, after dismounting and handing over a bag of papers to Evan, he used to wipe his sweaty brow.

'Christchurch is a whirlwind,' Esther heard him say. 'Busier than hell. Got your banking done, sir, and then stayed in my rooms. Couldn't get near the Botanic Gardens. Plus people were taking to the streets. Place was thronged with folk.'

'What's happening up there?' Evan asked, curious.

The man nodded to the sheaf of newspapers he'd handed over to Evan. 'Petition went through. Women got the vote, didn't they?'

Esther gasped and turned to look at Isobel. Her sister stood rigidly, mouth slightly open, eyes like rain droplets. And then she clapped her hand to her mouth and squealed.

'It's in the paper,' the man said. He frowned at Isobel's reaction, gaze snapping between the two women. Then his brow cleared. 'Ah, suffragist.'

'And proud of it,' Isobel said shakily. She beamed at Esther. 'Oh, I must get back to Auckland!'

Evan laughed and slapped his man's horse. 'Give this beast and my man a day or two and we'll get you on your way. You've waited years for this—another day won't hurt you.'

Isobel smiled wider—too wide—and for a second, Esther felt alarm. But then Isobel nodded her head and reached for the horse's reins. 'I'll take him over to the barn and remove his saddle.'

Evan Bellamy's man tipped his head toward her. 'Much obliged.'

They watched Isobel walk away, Esther seeing again how at ease her sister had become with horses.

'And you'll be hungry, McBride,' Evan said after a moment, to his man. 'There's bread and cheese inside.'

The man whistled. 'Sounds tip top. That and a smoko will see me right. Reckon we could feed that fella as well?'

He pointed toward a man leading a horse around the side of the house toward them. The group squinted into the sunlight. Esther could not make him out, other than a shadow and a sheen of water around the horse's bit.

'Met him in Christchurch,' McBride was saying. 'He said he was looking for the Hatcher Valley. Has business down there. Figured I couldn't let him get lost along the way, for he didn't look too comfortable on a horse or reading a map.'

'Is that so?' Evan held his hand above his eye and Esther looked again. The man approached. She could make out green corduroy trousers and dusty brown boots. A long and ill-fitting blue shirt. The man wore a wide-brimmed hat pulled down over his face.

Then he was but a few feet away and she saw his face. She gasped and her insides lurched. The man removed his hat and grinned at her. It was Brendan.

It took until she saw Jack before Esther was able to speak. Until she saw Jack step outside, carrying her daughter in her arms, her mouth and jaw was locked. It was as though a giant had reached out and grabbed her face and held her lips together. It was the strangest, most frightening thing—as a girl she had bitten back retorts to her mother and sometimes pinched her lips together, clamping her fingers over her face. But now, standing beside a bemused Evan

Bellamy, who could tell something was amiss, Esther was unable to speak. Or shriek, or holler for Brendan to go away.

She could only raise her hand and point, her finger shaking. Then, when Jack approached and saw the stranger's face under his softly sagging hat, she heard his gasp of recognition and Esther's tongue came loose.

'How did you find us, you heathen?' she spat.

McBride made a shocked sound and backed away. Evan snapped his head back and forth between Esther and Brendan, Brendan and his son.

'I reckon I'll go now,' McBride mumbled, and the man stumbled away, a stricken look upon his face. No doubt he knows he's blundered, bringing him here, Esther thought savagely, watching the man trip on his way inside.

'Do you know this man, Esther?' Evan asked. He frowned.

'Unfortunately I do.'

'Is he—' Evan pointed at the sleeping baby. 'Forgive me, but your reaction, it makes me wonder ...'

'Not ever,' Esther snapped. 'How did you track us?'

'Well, that's not a pretty welcome.' Brendan removed his hat, twirling it in his hands. The tips of his ears were burnt red, matching the explosion of veins across his face. He smelled dirty and unwashed.

'You deserve nothing better.' Now the stone had rolled away from her tongue, Esther found her words easily. 'She won't come back with you.'

'Mr Nelson, it's clear you aren't welcome here,' Jack said quietly.

Evan watched. He clasped his hands in front of his body, which Esther found unsettling. The old man is afraid, she thought.

'Is that my niece?' Brendan stepped closer to the baby in Jack's arms. 'Congratulations, Esther. I did think of you often, during these past weeks. I thought your time must be close. How did it go?'

'As if I would share such details with you!' Esther said coldly. 'Get away from here. Get away from my child.'

'Now, be reasonable.' Brendan grinned flintily. Esther saw he had lost a tooth. She wondered if someone had punched it out in a bar. 'I'm going nowhere until I have seen my wife.'

'Ah, you're Isobel's husband,' Evan said placidly, suddenly comprehending.

Brendan turned around to nod at the old man, and Esther saw how he thought he had spotted a weak link in the group. A man he could manipulate. All the hateful thoughts she had gathered about Brendan since that night in the cottage on George Street, when he hurt her sister so terribly, washed over her and Esther's hands twitched.

Brendan went on. 'I am. Brendan Nelson. I've come to speak to my wife. Did she tell you she abandoned me?'

'She escaped, you brute,' Esther shouted. 'You know what you did.'

She heard someone hitch in their breath and was not sure who made the sound. Evan shook his head.

'I don't want to know anymore,' the old man said. 'Sir, take the water you need and then leave. You are not welcome here.'

Brendan laughed sourly. 'You don't understand. I'm not leaving without Isobel.' He put his hand on his waistband, moving aside the blue shirt so they could see the handle of something, likely a knife. He traced a finger down the side, caressing the torn fabric wrapped around the handle. Esther felt sick.

Jack moved slowly. 'Pop, take the baby and go inside.'

Evan, eyes wide and startled, held out his hands and drew Catherine close. 'Don't do anything foolish, anyone. Please.'

Brendan spat casually into the dirt. 'I just want to talk to my wife. I've been civil. It's the least she owes me after I've travelled all this way to find her.'

'Pop.' Jack looked over his shoulder to the shade of the house. 'Please.'

Evan bobbed his head hurriedly and strode purposefully away. He held Catherine over his shoulder; Esther saw the fuzz of her daughter's red hair and two sleepy eyes peek over the old man's collar.

Shakily, she turned back to Brendan. 'How did you find us?'

Brendan had removed the long-bladed knife from his waist-band and was looking at it intently. His face was heavier than Esther remembered it. A fetid smell rose from his body, darker and more wretched than anything Esther had smelled in a pub or hotel bar. The meanness he had been able to keep mostly in check while living with Isobel had come loose and unfettered.

'Rachel told me,' Brendan said after a moment, and he grinned at Esther. She squeezed her eyes shut for a second, thinking of Isobel's sweet friend. What had he done to her?

Brendan seemed to read her thoughts. 'Don't worry. She was quite well when I left her. It took a while, but eventually she saw it was only right that she told an abandoned husband where he could find his wife.'

'Mr Nelson, I don't know the circumstances behind Isobel leaving you,' Jack said, 'but your appearing here unexpectedly, carrying a knife—there's no way she will return with you.'

'And no way that we would let her,' Esther shot at him.

Brendan shrugged. 'I've made no threat. I simply want to talk to her. I want to know why she disappeared without a single word. I also want her to know what it was like for me after she'd left.'

Esther snorted. 'Were you asked to leave another job?'

'It was embarrassing. I asked her friends, who professed to know nothing, of course.' Brendan glared at Esther, his eyes watery and unfocused. 'What was a man to do?'

'Let me guess.' She knew she should hold back, and that while Brendan cut a dishevelled figure, he also held his knife comfortably. But Esther could not stop. She heard Isobel's soft cries, her pleading and the betraying spring of the bed on George Street. Oh, she wanted to kill him. 'You turned to the bottle to numb the pain.'

Then a hand shot out—it was Jack—and he grabbed at Brendan's arm, trying to knock the knife into the dirt. He had moved carefully, closer to the stinking man, gambling that Brendan had not noticed. But he had. He tore his arm from Jack's fingers and, almost casually, slashed the air. Jack shouted out and fell to the ground, clutching his shoulder.

'Jack!' Esther dropped to her knees beside him. She touched him and Jack hissed, curling up. Blood seeped through his fingers and within seconds the arm of his shirt was wet.

'You should have listened to your father,' Brendan said, wiping the tip of the knife on his trousers. 'Now, where is my wife?'

Esther kicked out, aiming for the man's shins, but Brendan easily moved out of the way, laughing.

'You always were the little firebrand, weren't you? That's was your downfall—act first, think later. Little Esther, I will gut you as easily as a fish. It doesn't matter that we shared meals at your mother's kitchen table. I never was good enough for her, was I?'

'Go away!' Esther raged and kicked again, and this time Brendan booted her back, hard. Her thigh sang.

Jack hollered and made to stand up and Brendan kicked him as well. He pulled his foot back, ready to aim again, and then a look of shock flooded his face. He made to turn around and then his body became rigid.

His features were a crease of pure confusion and then he fell on the ground, inches away from Esther, who squealed and shuffled away. She could not see what had happened. The sun blazed down. And then she heard sobs, ones she recognised, and her heart felt torn.

It was Isobel. In her hand she held a knife of her own, the blade of which was red. Her knuckles were white around the handle. She made a gulping sound, half-eaten cries bursting through tight lips.

Then she swung again. Brendan's exposed, sliced neck was cut again. Isobel had forced the blade into her husband, and Brendan was quite, quite dead.

Isobel

I sobel had been daydreaming in the barn. The news from Evan's man, about the vote—the vote! She could hardly believe it. She thought of her friend, Elizabeth Peter, and the street map that she laid out in the room behind the church, back in Auckland—how Elizabeth had organised the temperance women to march up and down and through the streets, cajoling women to add their names to the petition. *Elizabeth must be delirious with joy*, Isobel thought, and the muscles in her legs flinched, as though her body ached to be back in the north.

And what would Rachel make of it? Sweet, iron-tongued Rachel, who had shown her how to feed herself that time on the beach, and slipped a knife into her hand when they left. Isobel bent down to touch the knife, the one she kept in her boot. She would return it when she made it back to Auckland.

She had just pumped fresh water for the horse when she heard raised voices. She cocked her head, her hand still on the animal's flank, listening. She could feel the horse's pulse, pounding away urgently.

Esther was shouting. Isobel felt a momentary panic—had Jack told her what had happened that night at the lake? The urge to throw a saddle back onto the horse and take off on the plains was almost overwhelming. But something in the tone of Esther's yell told Isobel her sister didn't know about the betrayal with Jack. Isobel edged around the side of the barn and squinted over at the group.

A stranger was standing with Esther, Jack, and Evan. Evan's man had disappeared—he must have brought the stranger to the farm.

The interloper stood with one hand on his hip and the other laced in his back pocket. He wore dirty green trousers and, as he moved his shirt aside, Isobel saw the glint of a knife in his waistband.

Her heart blocked her throat, the skin on her back prickled with alarm. She watched as the man brought the knife to his face and studied it, and then her stomach made a shuddering flip. It was Brendan.

How? Isobel breathed, pressing her body against the barn door. How did he find me? She put a hand over her mouth, afraid she might scream, but the spit in her mouth had dried up and her breath felt too ragged, too out of control to have the momentum enough to shout out.

She watched Evan Bellamy take Esther's baby and scurry away, and she wondered if he would spot her. But the old man didn't see; his eyes were fixed on the house and on the infant in his arms.

Brendan had changed in the weeks since she had left Auckland. She could see, even from this distance, how his belly had thickened. Auckland had gifted him a paunch in the early days, almost as soon as he stepped off the boat. Beer from the bars and hotels gathered like milk in an udder under his belt. The gift of the New World, one that slapped against Isobel's own stomach in the years they were still marital. Now his belly was even bigger. Isobel wondered if he apologised for it when dropping his trousers in front of a girl from Sale Street.

He hadn't apologised to her. She hadn't given him the opportunity, having left the day after that dreadful night, but there was nothing he could say or do that would make the thing he did go away. He could not make it right and Isobel knew, deep in the private crease of her heart, that he would not even try. The assault on the sweetness that once existed between them was almost as much a trauma as the act itself.

She did not feel love or longing when she looked upon him. She felt nothing, only desperation that he would leave.

But then Jack yelled and she saw him fall to the ground. Esther dropped to her knees and Brendan stood over them both. The knife was a shard of light. Isobel saw a man she no longer knew move above her sister and Jack, and her knife, hidden in her boot, was in her hands.

She ran toward them. Her feet were quick and light and the man didn't hear her. The man—Brendan. He didn't see her approach, and when she stabbed him in his fat, jowly neck, she was amazed that there was so much blood and that Rachel's short, stubby knife could gut a man as efficiently as a pipi.

The ground rushed up to meet her and she collapsed, falling beside Brendan. The knife was cast to the side. For a second Isobel's head brushed his and she had a wild thought that it was just like it used to be, when they shared a bed. Her fingers reached out to touch his hair, but then Esther was upon her, coughing tears, clutching her face.

'Isobel, Isobel.' Esther pulled her sister onto her lap, her thin arms as ferociously strong as Isobel remembered them to be. Isobel was pressed against her sister's breast and rocked back and forth. Esther's arms held her tightly, as though holding her baby, and Isobel was crushed. Out of the corner of her eye she could see Jack. He had taken off his shirt and was pressing it to a wound on his shoulder.

Esther finally released her and crawled back to Jack, cupping her hands around his shoulder. He winced and hissed, but then slowly hauled himself to his feet. He glared down at Brendan, lying quietly on the ground. He brought his boot back and kicked the man sharply on the side of his head. Isobel felt his gore rise as her husband's head bounced to the side and lay still.

Esther rocked on her haunches and then got up, reaching out to pull her sister up. They stood together at Brendan's feet.

'You killed him,' Esther said tonelessly. 'Good.'

'I thought he was going to hurt you.'

'He might have done.' Jack blinked, the pain of his shoulder wound bringing sweat to his lips. 'Ah, no. Pop.'

Evan Bellamy was slowly making his way back across the courtyard, the baby nowhere to be seen. His face widened with shock as he drew closer to the group and the silent, prone man on the ground.

'Where is Catherine?' Esther asked.

'Asleep, in her crib.' Evan's old knees popped as he crouched down to look at Brendan. 'Someone tell me what happened.'

'I did this,' Isobel said, but her words were quickly swallowed by Esther's hurried response.

'No, I did it. I killed him.' The corner of Esther's mouth curled up in a sneer. 'I don't regret it.'

'We all had a hand in it,' Jack said, wincing, and his father stood up, concerned.

'Let me see, son.' Evan peeled back the bundled shirt soaking blood from Jack's wound. He gave a low whistle. 'You will need stitches. But, Lord! A dead man on my property!'

'Evan, it's all my fault.' Isobel pressed her hands over her face, her insides a riot of feeling. She was a murderer. She was protecting her sister. She had killed the man she had promised to love and obey, but he had hurt her terribly. What on earth were they going to do?

It was as though Esther had read her thoughts, for she sniffed and brushed hair from her face. Determined, ready. 'Evan, we need to dispose of him. We can't summon a policeman. It wasn't murder, it was self-defence.'

Evan nudged Brendan's discarded knife with the tip of his boot. 'I believe he came here to kill someone, yes. You, I think.' He eyed Isobel, his mouth a rueful line. He was contemplating, deciding which way to go. 'You would be able to convince a magistrate that he was a danger, I should think. If you all swear to it.'

'A magistrate wouldn't take the word of an unmarried mother,' Esther said, her voice pleading. 'Nor the word of a woman who abandoned her husband—because that's how they will portray us, you know that. No, we can't risk it.'

Evan sighed. 'Jack?'

Jack's bleeding had stopped and he held his arm across his body. 'He would have killed me if he could, Pop. And he hurt Esther.'

'That's not all.' Esther looked at Isobel, her face stricken. 'He forced Rachel to tell him where you were.'

Isobel's stomach fluttered to the back of her throat, for she knew what that meant. Sweet, strange, strong Rachel—she would not have given such information up easily. Tears fell, then, down Isobel's cheeks. 'He must have hurt her.'

'Or worse, Isobel,' Esther said quietly. 'He said she was well when he left her, but Brendan is a liar.'

'I could try to find out,' Jack said. 'I can make enquiries. I have to return to Auckland, anyway. If ...' He glanced at Esther, colour brightening his face. Isobel could see how thoughts of her sister made the man catch his breath, even at this time. She felt terribly sad. 'If we are to stay here, I will need to appoint a deputy to collect rent. Or sell the properties. I can find out what he did to Rachel without revealing that he came down here.'

'No one would miss him anyway.' Isobel was very sure of this. Brendan had made no friends in New Zealand. He did not talk to the women or menfolk sitting out in the courtyard on George Street, nor had he become acquainted with those he worked with. He rarely worked in a place long enough to make friends. No one would wonder where he'd gone, should he disappear. What a waste of a life, Isobel thought. What a waste of Rachel's life, if he's hurt her.

Esther's hand slipped into hers and squeezed her fingers. There was blood on Esther's breast, from where she had hugged Isobel to her, and red smeared shockingly over her throat. Brendan's blood was so garish and out of place on Esther's body that Isobel could not stop looking at it. But Esther had not noticed.

'This changes everything,' Esther said. She gripped Isobel's hand even tighter. 'Don't you see? You can't go back to Auckland now. Not even to see Elizabeth Peter and celebrate the vote, not even to look for Rachel. Too many questions will be asked of you. You have to stay here with us.'

'Here?'

'The Hatcher Valley. We—I—it's decided.' Esther smiled around at the little group, an incongruous, absurdly hopeful thing to do when a dead man lay at her feet. 'I'm going to take it on. We're going to live there, and farm.'

Evan gasped. 'Do you mean with Jack?'

'We'll be married, Pop.' Jack's face grew purple. He avoided Isobel's eye.

'But that's wonderful.' Evan wrapped his fingers together under his chin and swayed. Isobel saw that the poor man looked stunned and almost as though he might faint. She grew regretful again for all they had brought to his doorstep.

But Jack. And Esther. Esther and Jack. Married. That night by the lake would never happen again and would never be spoken of. The man who had touched her skin would not touch her again. They would circle each other instead, like birds in the sky. Wary, silent, respectful.

The sun blazed behind her and Isobel felt its heat pressing down on her shoulders, bowing her head, beating her with its strength. She felt defeated, and yet, Brendan at her feet, she felt free; and torn inside with longing for a man who had wanted her for one night only, but then loved her sister. The child, too … the child inside the house, resting in sweet innocence. Oh, this land had given her the right to vote and elect, and a kind of life that was free but she was frightened.

Was this how Esther had felt, all those years they lived with their mother? It was impossible to tell, for Esther beamed unashamedly now, clasping Jack's hand so that they formed a chain. Isobel, Esther, Jack.

'You have to live with us,' Esther was saying. 'That's simply how it has to be. You can help me with Catherine and, when we can, we'll build you your own little house.'

'What …' Isobel faltered. 'What about Mother?'

Esther laughed bitterly. 'Oh, I'll write to her. I'll let her know there has been a change of plan. That can wait. We need to deal with *him* first.'

She kicked out at the body lying in the dirt. Jack glanced around, checking none of the farmhands were nearby to see.

'We'll have to bury him. Quickly,' he said.

Evan nodded. He was in on this now, the news about Esther and Jack staying on the Hatcher Valley seeming to settle things for him. 'Hide him in the barn for now. We can bury him tonight.'

Without a further word, father and son leaned down and grabbed an arm each, dragging Brendan away from the place where he fell. Jack winced and grunted as he did so, but Esther and Isobel stood and watched as they hauled the dead man away. Isobel's mouth felt watery and loose, and she thought she should say something, or touch her husband for one last time. But she let Jack and Evan do their work and allowed Esther to draw her close.

'Will it be all right?' she asked, peering into Esther's content, comfortable face. 'Will this work?'

'Hiding Brendan's body or farming the Hatcher Valley?'

'All of it.'

'Of course it will.' Esther dropped her hands to Isobel's shoulders and gave her sister a little shake. 'All this time and you haven't figured it out. It will be all right because we will make it so. We'll make a home here and we'll be a family, and we'll never tell anyone about what happened today.'

'Can we keep it secret? Really?' Oh, Isobel wanted it to be true, but her heart was cleaved. Three men were heading toward the barn; two of them were her past and future, and she was being asked to give up both. There were too many secrets, overlapping each other.

Esther was forceful, though, and caught on a wave of hope. 'Live for now, let go of all those silly ways that have bound you, Isobel. New Zealand can give you the space to breathe. I really believe that!'

The sisters turned, their backs to the barn where a dead man was being hidden, and looked out over the unremitting plains and the blue-tinged Southern Alps in the distance. The sky was clear and still, save for the cry of a kea, and the grass was brown and burnt. The land rolled in front of them, waiting to be shaped or to resist.

Isobel could make out the lake, into which she had walked, naked, shed of clothes and inhibitions. It glittered like ice and she shivered, remembering.

And then Esther and Isobel linked arms, entwined, eyes turned to the Hatcher Valley where something, maybe a life, waited for them.

Notes

The following articles and websites have been very useful in the research of this book:

The New Zealand Electronic Text Collection
http://nzetc.victoria.ac.nz

Te Ara—*The Encyclopedia of New Zealand*
https://teara.govt.nz/en

Thomas Bull, *Hints to Mothers, For the Management of Health During the Period of Pregnancy, and in the Lying-in Room: with an Exposure of Popular Errors in Connection with those Subjects and Hints Upon Nursing, for info about Victorian approaches to childbirth*, 1865.
https://archive.org/stream/b28088360/b28088360_djvu.txt

Paul Husbands, 'Poverty in Freeman's Bay 1886–1913', *New Zealand Journal of History* (vol. 28, issue 1), 1994.

Charlotte MacDonald and Frances Porter (eds), *My Hand Will Write What My Heart Dictates: The Unsettled Lives of Women in Nineteenth-Century New Zealand As Revealed to Sisters, Family and Friends*, Bridget Williams Books 1996.

There is a wonderful, searchable map of Auckland online, dating from 1908. This gives an evocative idea of the Auckland street layout over a hundred years ago:

http://www.aucklandcity.govt.nz/dbtw-wpd/CityArchives/
1908Map/browse1908map.htm

About the Author

Rebecca Burns is an award-winning writer of short stories, over thirty of which have been published online or in print. Her short story collections—*Catching the Barramundi* and *The Settling Earth*—were both longlisted for the prestigious Edge Hill Short Story Award, the UK's only prize for short story collections. *The Bishop's Girl*, her first novel, was published in September 2016. *Artefacts and Other Stories*, her third collection of short stories, was published in September 2017. *Beyond the Bay* is her fifth published work.

She was nominated for a Pushcart Prize in 2011, winner of the Fowey Festival of Words and Music Short Story Competition in 2013 (and runner-up in 2014), won the Black Pear Press short story competition in 2014, was shortlisted for the Green Lady Press Short Story Competition in 2015, and was either short or longlisted for the Evesham Festival Short Story Competition, Chipping Norton Competition and the Sunderland Short Story Award in 2016.

She has been profiled as part of the University of Leicester's 'Grassroutes Project'—a project that showcases the 50 best transcultural writers in the county.